"I'm not hidin **might be," M**~~eredith challenged him.~~

"I've just had a demonstration of Edward Atheling's presence."

"Another one?" Jackson said, one of his thick black eyebrows lifting skeptically. "What was it this time?"

"Something much more interesting than a warning." She went on to tell him about the ghostly face in the mirror.

He nodded slowly. "All right, let's not argue about it. Let's suppose this vision was more than imagination. How can you be sure it was the ghost of Edward Atheling?"

"I can't be certain, of course. Except for one undeniable thing."

"Which is?"

"What I haven't told you yet. That face in the mirror, Jackson, was a dead ringer for you."

Dear Harlequin Intrigue Reader,

To mark a month of fall festivals, screeching goblins and hot apple cider, Harlequin Intrigue has a provocative October lineup guaranteed to spice things up!

Debra Webb launches her brand-new spin-off series, COLBY AGENCY: INTERNAL AFFAIRS, with *Situation: Out of Control*. This first installment sets the stage for the most crucial mission of all…smoking out a mole in their midst. The adrenaline keeps flowing in *Rules of Engagement* by acclaimed author Gayle Wilson, who continues her PHOENIX BROTHERHOOD series with a gripping murder mystery that hurls an unlikely couple into a vortex of danger.

Also this month, a strictly business arrangement turns into a lethal attraction, in *Cowboy Accomplice* by B.J. Daniels—book #2 in her Western series, McCALLS' MONTANA. And just in time for Halloween, October's haunting ECLIPSE selection, *The Legacy of Croft Castle* by Jean Barrett, promises to put you in that spooky frame of mind.

There are more thrills to come when Kara Lennox unveils the next story in her CODE OF THE COBRA series, with *Bounty Hunter Redemption*, which pits an alpha male lawman against a sexy parole officer when mayhem strikes. And, finally this month, watch for the action-packed political thriller *Shadow Soldier* by talented newcomer Dana Marton. This debut book spotlights an antiterrorist operative who embarks on a high-stakes mission to dismantle a diabolical ticking time bomb.

Enjoy!

Denise O'Sullivan
Senior Editor
Harlequin Intrigue

THE LEGACY OF
CROFT CASTLE
JEAN BARRETT

HARLEQUIN®

TORONTO • NEW YORK • LONDON
AMSTERDAM • PARIS • SYDNEY • HAMBURG
STOCKHOLM • ATHENS • TOKYO • MILAN • MADRID
PRAGUE • WARSAW • BUDAPEST • AUCKLAND

ISBN 0-373-22804-X

THE LEGACY OF CROFT CASTLE

Copyright © 2004 by Jean Barrett

This edition published by arrangement with Harlequin Books S.A.

® and TM are trademarks of the publisher. Trademarks indicated with
® are registered in the United States Patent and Trademark Office, the
Canadian Trade Marks Office and in other countries.

www.eHarlequin.com

Printed in U.S.A.

ABOUT THE AUTHOR

If setting has anything to do with it, Jean Barrett claims she has no reason not to be inspired. She and her husband live on Wisconsin's scenic Door Peninsula in an antique-filled country cottage overlooking Lake Michigan. A teacher for many years, she left the classroom to write full-time. She is the author of a number of romance novels.

Write to Jean at P.O. Box 623, Sister Bay, WI 54234. SASE appreciated.

Books by Jean Barrett

HARLEQUIN INTRIGUE
308—THE SHELTER OF HER ARMS
351—WHITE WEDDING
384—MAN OF THE MIDNIGHT SUN
475—FUGITIVE FATHER
528—MY LOVER'S SECRET
605—THE HUNT FOR HAWKE'S DAUGHTER*
652—PRIVATE INVESTIGATIONS*
692—OFFICIAL ESCORT*
728—COWBOY PI*
770—SUDDEN RECALL*
804—THE LEGACY OF CROFT CASTLE*

*The Hawke Family Detective Agency

CLASSIFIEDS

CAST OF CHARACTERS

Meredith Allen—She isn't sure which is more dangerous, the evil at Croft Castle or the man who threatens her heart.

Jackson Hawke—Unlike his rival investigator, Meredith, he doesn't believe in ghosts, but can he believe in the possibility of love?

Guy, Lord Danely—His life and business are at serious risk from a mysterious enemy.

Judith, Lady Danely—She is deeply worried about her husband, but how far does her love go?

Imogen—Is Croft Castle's cook as loyal as she is eccentric?

Rob Curzon—Is the young man more than just the pilot of the launch that serves Croft Island?

Archie Wallace—Who is the mysterious American photographer, and why is he following Meredith and Jackson?

Colin Sheppard—The genial landlord of the local inn knows everyone on the island—perhaps even the real killer.

Detective Chief Inspector Ramsay—He has his eye on Meredith and Jackson and is determined not to have them interfere with his investigation.

Simon Boynton—The professor has uncovered an astonishing secret—but would he kill his own daughter to protect it?

To the members of my writers' group,
the Greater Green Bay Area of WisRWA.
Each and every one of you is very special to me,
both for your support and your friendship.

Prologue

Had their home become a place of evil?

It was certainly not a pleasant question to ask yourself. But Lady Danely found herself doing just that as she huddled in the chair, her gaze on the pair of stone gargoyles that supported the hood of the sitting room's fireplace. She had never liked them. They had always struck her as chilling in their grotesqueness. At this moment the gargoyles seemed particularly malevolent.

She supposed her sudden shudder of foreboding was understandable, considering all that had been happening in the ancient castle. The trouble was, it was getting worse. Much worse. And now—

Lady Danely cast her anxious gaze in the direction of the closed door to the bedroom. What was taking them so long? She couldn't bear much more of this waiting.

Orders or no orders, she was on her feet and prepared to invade the bedroom when the door opened and the youthful figure of Dr. Finch emerged, medical bag in hand.

"He's getting dressed."

"Is he—"

"He's all right, Judith."

"Thank God."

"*This* time," Dr. Finch added severely, his warning implying that the next time Guy had an attack it could be something far more serious. "That angina of his is a problem. He's under far too much stress with it."

He *knows* about our troubles here, Lady Danely thought. It wasn't surprising. Dr. Finch's sister would have told him all about them. He had been visiting his sister when Guy suffered his attack. Judith had blessed both his presence on the island and his prompt arrival at the castle.

What Dr. Finch didn't know, unless Guy had confided it during his examination, and Lady Danely doubted her proud husband would have done so, was the awful scene that had triggered his attack.

Judith could still hear them—the thumps and thuds in one of the guest rooms overhead, the crash of overturned furniture, the shatter of glass. All of it had been followed by the terrified shriek of Mrs. Forbes-Walsh fleeing from her room. Guy had rushed toward the stairs and paid the penalty for his alarm with a seizure.

The horror had been the latest in the series of ghostly happenings that seemed determined to destroy them. She and Guy couldn't go on like this, Judith thought. Not now when this force, whatever it was, threatened her husband's life.

"I told Guy," Dr. Finch said, "that he's to ring up my surgery and make an appointment at the earliest opportunity. I want to do a complete workup on him. If there are any other incidents before then, you have old Dr. Merrick here on the island. Retired or not, the man is still capable in an emergency."

Judith thanked him and he departed. Her husband, Lord Danely, appeared from the bedroom, tucking the folds of his shirt into his trousers.

"You ought to be resting."

"Sorry to give you a scare like that, old girl, but the spasms have completely passed. I'm fine now."

He *wasn't* fine, and Judith knew that. Although they were both in their early fifties, she was still a slim, handsome woman with an unlined face beneath a cap of silver hair. But no matter what Guy pretended, the last few weeks had aged him. She could see it in the slump of his shoulders. Could swear that the ginger hair on his head, already on the scant side, had thinned even more and that the grooves on either side of his carefully trimmed mustache had deepened.

"Was that the phone I heard while Finch was checking me over?"

Judith had hoped he wouldn't have been aware of its ring from the other side of the closed bedroom door. She hated having to share more bad news with him. On the other hand, if there was any hope of relieving the stress that was endangering his health, he needed to understand that something must be done.

"It was another cancellation, I'm afraid. Of course she had some excuse about an illness in the family. None of them want to admit the actual reason for canceling their reservations. They're all scared."

I'm beginning to think that I am, too. But Judith didn't relate her thought to Guy. He would be deeply troubled by such an admission. Instead, she went to him, placing an earnest hand on his arm.

"Darling, this is getting serious. It's May already. We should be fully booked. Instead of which, with Mrs. Forbes-Walsh refusing to spend another night in the castle, we're empty."

"It's all a lot of mischief. Whoever is responsible for it will get bored soon and quit."

Whatever his certainty, Judith didn't miss the bleak note in his voice. It was just short of desperation. There was so much at stake for them.

"Guy, I think we have to face at least the possibility that Croft Castle *is* haunted, and that we need professional help. There must be some specialist who—"

"A ghost hunter?" He snorted in disgust. "All a lot of rubbish."

Judith had lived in this country for over twenty years, and

she had yet to understand its people. They were supposed to be proud of the ghosts that haunted their stately homes. Yet here was her own husband—thoroughly British—refusing to consider, in the face of growing evidence, that they might be suffering from an evil intent on destroying them. While she, his practical, American-born wife, was ironically prepared to believe just that.

It was Guy's family pride, of course. He feared that the rumors might turn into widespread publicity if they were to call in any investigator, that Croft Castle would become a target for jests.

"No, love," he said, "if it comes to the worst, we'll let the police handle it."

Judith gazed at him in helpless despair. There had to be some way to convince him of the urgency of their situation. That he was risking not just their future, but his very life if they didn't—

Her head turned as the door to their private apartment burst open. The tall, rawboned figure of Croft Castle's cook rushed into the sitting room. Her hands and arms were covered with flour to her elbows, a smudge of it on one ruddy cheek. The stuff drifted down on the Persian rug.

Oh, dear, thought Judith, I suppose she's left a trail all the way from the kitchen. "What is it, Imogen?"

"Turn on the telly!" the cook commanded with the brusqueness she never failed to use, whether it be with maid or employer. Except this time, Judith detected a genuine excitement in her tone. "The Derek Manners program up in London! Not that he has any."

"Imogen, why—"

"Miss it if you don't look lively! And this is one you don't want to miss! Said as much to myself when I caught it on the set in the kitchen. Right. I'll just get on with it then, shall I?"

Not expecting an answer, the cook retreated, pulling the door shut behind her. It wasn't like Imogen to be mysterious, thought Judith, reaching for the remote. After all that had been happening, she was almost afraid to turn on the set. But she did.

The screen came to life on the close-up of a young woman's face. Judith stared at the image in shocked recognition.

Chapter One

London in May.

Shouldn't it have boasted soft temperatures? Meredith asked herself. A mood-lifting, blue sky? The window boxes along Buckingham Palace Road exploding with the color of spring blooms?

Apparently not, since the day was anything but kind. A chill wind blew off the Thames, the dismal gray sky dripped rain, and the only color she could see from her cab window was the vivid red of a double-decker bus.

The bus, Meredith noted, was stalled like her cab on the rain-slick street choked with traffic. The sidewalks, too, were packed with humanity, late shoppers heading in the direction of the nearest underground, commuters hurrying toward Victoria Station to catch their trains. Most of them with bobbing umbrellas.

Watching the dreary scene, she wondered if the weather in the West Country was any sweeter. And then instantly reminded herself she wasn't here in England for *that*. It was a mistake to even consider it, whatever her mixed feelings in that direction. She had lectures to deliver next week to the British Society for Psychical Research. She should be spending her time until then familiarizing herself with British findings on her subject.

At the moment, however, all Meredith longed for was to reach her hotel, sink into a hot bath, and try to forget that miserable interview. Why had she ever agreed to participate in the program? Hadn't her past encounters with that man back in the States taught her anything?

He was responsible for her low mood, she decided. She wouldn't have permitted herself to think about Devonshire if—

Ah, they were moving again.

Within minutes, the cab pulled up in front of her small hotel. She felt better already. Even the neon lights along the street, casting shimmering reflections on the wet pavement, seemed warm and friendly to her as she stepped from the cab. Until disaster overtook her once more.

She would have managed to escape into the hotel if it hadn't been for the currency. Would have been in the lift and on her way to her room, if dealing with the unfamiliar British money while paying for her taxi fare hadn't delayed her. As it was, she was still out on the street, trying to work out a tip for her driver, when another of the small, snub-nosed black cabs pulled up to the curb.

"Yo, Meredith!"

Her heart slid in the direction of her stomach as the deep-voiced, rangy figure emerged from the cab, hailing her with one of his cocky, two-fingered salutes. Oh, no! Not Jackson Hawke again!

Pressing several pound coins into the cabbie's hand, knowing it was probably too much and not caring, Meredith was prepared to flee into the hotel. But Jackson's long-legged, energetic stride cut her off.

"You sure don't make it easy to catch up with you, do you? Care to tell me why you rushed away from the TV station like that?"

Like it or not, she found herself gazing up into his cobalt blue eyes. The kind of bold blue eyes that captured a woman's immediate attention. She met his complaint with one of her own.

"Why are you following me? And how did you know where I went?"

"Doorman at the station. Remember, he got you a cab and gave the driver the name of your hotel for you."

"What do you want?"

"To ask you to go to dinner with me."

Meredith was incredulous. "You're asking me out on a date?"

"I guess you could call it that."

"Let me get this straight. You have the nerve, the actual nerve, to want to go out with me after that little performance of yours in front of a viewing audience of—well, who knows how many thousands, maybe even millions, might have been tuned in."

"What peformance would that be?"

Meredith couldn't believe the man. Couldn't believe his colossal ego. "The one in which you did your damnedest to discredit both me and my profession. You made me sound like a fraudulent medium who goes around exorcising spirits instead of a respected psychologist."

"Well, hell, you said yourself you believe in ghosts."

"What I said," she corrected him sharply, "is I believe in the *possibility* of them. That I've experienced phenomena that indicate certain past events and emotions can leave behind imprints in the atmosphere, a kind of energy that gets stuck in time."

"Yeah, but—"

"And that my work is not to communicate with ghosts but to help clients who are suffering from unexplained disturbances. All of which apparently failed to register with you since you were so busy shamelessly plugging your new agency here. The American P.I. who's arrived in England to debunk all those things that go bump in the night! That was your brash claim to the interviewer, wasn't it?"

"So we have opposite positions on the subject of ghosts. I just happen to believe people don't hang around after they're dead. What's wrong with that? It's nothing personal."

"Oh, of course not. Just like it wasn't personal back in the States when I was trying to work with that client disturbed by an encounter with what he was convinced was an ignis fatuus. And his wife went to you, and you told her the possibility it was a spectral light was all a lot of—in your word—bull, and if you had the case, you'd prove it was nothing more than marsh gas. *Marsh gas* in the Mojave Desert!"

"Listen, there had to be some logical explanation for—"

"And then there was that other sensitive situation, when I was dealing with a subject experiencing retrocognition, and you turned up claiming it was all an act. I suppose that wasn't personal, either."

"No, it was just business. I was called in on that one because it was a matter of an inheritance, and the wife—"

"Yes, another wife. You seem to have a way with wives."

"Just the ones who agree with me when it comes to ghosts."

"Since you don't believe in them, why are you haunting me? It was bad enough back home, but now you turn up in England, of all places. Just how did I get so lucky?"

"You could find out by coming to dinner with me."

Why did he have to be so tall? Meredith was getting a crick in her neck looking up at him. She was also getting very suspicious. "What's this all about? You're hiding something."

"Sweetheart, you're not giving me a chance here to hide anything. All I'm trying to do is explain how there's something I need to discuss with you, and I thought that over dinner we could—"

"What *something*?" she demanded.

"A phone call that came into the station after the program. Some couple who'd seen the interview and were trying to reach us, and if you hadn't run off— Anyway, they have a problem, a big problem, and they want to hire us."

"*Both* of us?"

"Seems she believes in the possibility of a ghost, and he doesn't. A castle, no less. Can you beat it? Well, it is England, and they did sound desperate."

"In case you've forgotten, we happen to be rivals."

"Doesn't mean we couldn't work together. Hey, if it's because you think I was pulling something sneaky about this dinner date, I want you to know I was going to ask you out anyway." He leaned toward her intimately, an outrageous grin on that wide mouth. "You know, two Americans abroad. I figured we—"

"Are not going out to dinner together, so just forget it."

"Afraid I might try to demonstrate just how well you and I could work together?"

It was a challenge issued in a husky voice that was too suggestive by a man who was too sure of himself. And far too potent as he loomed over her with that tantalizing grin still on his mouth. Meredith backed away from him.

"I'm not in England to accept cases. I don't have the time."

"Sure you do. A whole week of it before those lectures of yours. See, I was listening."

"Just why is this job so important to you?"

"It's important to this couple, and the way they see it, we come as a package or not at all. I guess they want a balanced investigation of this moldering old pile of theirs. Could be interesting, huh?"

"In other words, if one of us can't help them, then maybe the other can."

"Something like that."

She didn't trust him. There was something funny about the whole thing. Jackson seemed eager enough to have her join him on the case. Almost too eager, as if it was vital to him. But reading people, as she had learned to do in her profession, she could also detect a reluctance. He wanted her, and yet he didn't want her. It was odd.

"I see," she said cautiously. "And, if during the course of this little contest, you manage to prove I'm wrong about the existence of ghosts and that you're right…well, that would kind of make your reputation, wouldn't it? Sorry, it isn't going to happen."

"You haven't heard the particulars of the case."

"Not interested."

She started to turn away, and he stopped her. "Just what *would* it take to interest you?"

The man was unbelievable. Immune to any version of no. She gazed up at him, wishing he didn't have a jaw so square and a mouth so sensual. She snatched at the first thing that came to mind. "A summons from beyond the grave," she said dryly, "and since you don't believe in those, I guess I'm safe."

Stay away from me, Jackson Hawke. This, in effect, was what she was telling him when she left him there on the sidewalk and hurried into the hotel before he could stop her again. As she waited in the lobby for one of the two lifts, she checked herself in a gold-framed mirror on the wall between the lifts. Her appearance had suffered from the damp weather. She had one of those heads of hair that resisted all discipline when the humidity was high. Her hair, the color of golden wheat, curled in little wisps around her face. And with her fair coloring and small, even features, the result was like a halo on a porcelain doll. An angelic image that wasn't at all who she was.

Seized by a sudden realization, Meredith's green eyes in the mirror flashed an angry fire back at her.

My God, what are you doing?

But it was only too clear exactly what she had been doing. Consciously or subconsciously—and it didn't matter which—she had been fretting over how she must have looked to Jackson Hawke as they'd stood out there in the drizzle.

What did it matter what she had looked like? And why did the man have to be so infuriatingly sexy with hair as black as midnight and that lean, long-limbed body of his? All right, so she found Jackson Hawke attractive. Was even susceptible to those wicked blue eyes in that strong, good-looking face. But she sure didn't like what was behind those eyes. Nor anything else about him.

Work together on a case? In a pig's—

The lift had arrived. Meredith scooted into it with relief, willing herself to forget Jackson Hawke, to think of nothing but that hot bath waiting for her in her room. But she never got to the tub.

The phone was ringing when she unlocked her door. Answering it, she identified herself with a breathless "Meredith Allen."

There was a brief pause, and then a voice with a note of pleading in it said hesitantly, "Meredith, it's me."

It wasn't the summons she had so flippantly specified in order to get rid of Jackson Hawke. But it was as good as one, because it had all the impact of a call from beyond the grave

Chapter Two

He wasn't here.

Did that mean he was just very late, Meredith wondered, or that he wasn't coming at all? That maybe, just maybe, he'd decided not to take the case, after all? And wouldn't that be welcome news.

She found herself longing for the possibility. This whole thing was going to be complicated enough without having an overbearing Jackson Hawke at her side. But if he didn't turn up, if she was able to get down on her knees and give thanks to all the gods for delivering her from him...

Lovely prospect, and her own fault for not knowing. At her insistence, they'd had no contact since London. She had come down to Cornwall by train. What his own travel plans were she hadn't learned. Nor was the laconic young man in charge of the launch able to enlighten her.

"Dunno, now, do I? Two for the island on my afternoon run. That's all I know."

He and the driver of a lorry with provisions for the island went back to shifting cartons into the launch. Meredith waited impatiently on the quay while the gulls circled and mewed overhead.

She was relieved when the launch was finally loaded. But its pilot, who had a gold hoop in one ear and a scrap of a goatee on his chin, and the lorry driver, who apparently was in no hurry to depart, stood around discussing a football match.

"Look," Meredith interrupted them, "it's obvious he isn't coming. Could we just go?"

"In a tic."

But a "tic" turned out to be another ten minutes before the pilot, whose name she had learned by then was Rob, finally parted from the driver with an offhand, "Ta, Billy," and prepared to cast off his lines.

Meredith started to climb down into the launch. And never made it. She was stopped by the furious blasting of a horn. Swinging around on the quay, she watched in dismay as an open sports car tore down the steep street of Treferro, came within inches of overturning a call box, and skidded to a halt on the quayside.

Its driver, with a last toot on her horn to make certain the launch wouldn't depart, emerged from the two-seater, revealing herself as a leggy, luscious brunette. She could easily be a model for lingerie, Meredith thought. The erotic variety.

Meredith's last hope vanished as the brunette's passenger unfolded his length from the other side of the car. She ought to have known he wouldn't fail to appear. And wasn't it just like him to arrive with a fanfare?

Cozy, too, with his ride. Meredith watched him lean over and thank the brunette with a kiss on the side of her mouth. Then, bag in hand, he started toward the launch.

Don't let him do it, Meredith prayed. Don't let him pull another of those snappy, military-style salutations of his.

But that hope also expired when his free hand came up to his brow in a two-fingered salute that was accompanied by his perpetually familiar, "Yo, Meredith."

"I see you caught a lift," she observed as Jackson Hawke joined her.

"Yeah, and I'm a little late. We didn't get much sleep last night."

"Busy, huh?" Meredith nodded in the direction of the brunette, who had climbed back into her red sports car and, with a little wave in Jackson's direction, went roaring up the street again.

"The three of us were pretty occupied," he admitted.

Meredith pointedly arched one eyebrow. "*Two* of them? No wonder the time got away from you. You must be exhausted."

"Uh-huh. And you can stop thinking all those naughty thoughts. Kimberly and her husband are friends from America. They've taken a cottage along the coast here. I stayed the night with them, most of which we spent catching up on each other's lives. Listen, I don't know if you've noticed, but that guy in the boat over there looks anxious to get underway. I don't think we should keep him waiting like this."

Smacking him would probably not be a good way to begin this investigation, Meredith thought.

She managed to resist the temptation, even when he complained about the lack of room as they started to settle themselves in the launch.

"What is all this stuff?"

"Provisions for the island, I was told."

She wasn't happy about the limited space, either. The only clear spot was one half of a bench seat, which she would have to share with both Jackson and their luggage.

"Looks like our only choice is to get intimate."

And he did, squeezing in beside her on the seat. She hadn't counted on being packed so tightly against his solid length. Or experiencing his body searing her own. The sensation made her want to squirm away from him. Had there been any room for squirming, that is, which there was not.

It could have been worse, though. He could have taken advantage of the situation if he'd been in any state to attempt it. As it was, the launch barely pulled away from the quay before he had the baseball cap he was wearing tilted down over his eyes, his long legs stretched out in front of him and crossed at the ankle and his arms folded over his ribs. She could tell from the way his chin was lowered that he was asleep even before they left the harbor. Evidence of his long night with the brunette. All right, the brunette *and* her husband.

The trouble was, Meredith kept casting her gaze in his direction. Noticing things she would have been better off not noticing. Like his well-molded, muscular legs in those snug jeans. The breadth of his chest and the narrowness of his hips. Admit it. The man oozed pheromones from every pore.

None of her observations would have been so bad if, while turned toward him for one of the glimpses she was sneaking, she hadn't found herself staring into a cobalt blue eye peering out at her from under the brim of the cap. The worst had happened. He had caught her checking him out.

Meredith grabbed at the first excuse that came to mind. "Do you always dress like one of the dark demons you don't believe in?"

Well, it was true. Yesterday in London he'd worn black slacks and a matching black blazer over an equally black turtleneck. Today he was in black jeans and a black sweater. Even his baseball cap was black. While black definitely suited him, lending a tough, almost dangerous quality to his dynamic sexiness, the total absence of any color in his wardrobe *was* a little eccentric.

He sat up, shoving the baseball cap to the back of his head. "It's not a fashion statement, Meredith. It's a question of safety."

"You mean like blending in with the shadows when you're chasing bad guys down dark alleys?"

"No, I mean like not risking funny looks if my ties don't match my socks. But if I stick with black, I can't go wrong."

"I still don't see—" She broke off in sudden understanding, issuing a contrite little, "Oh."

"Right. I'm color-blind. Well, deficient when it comes to clearly distinguishing reds from greens, anyway."

"And I was being insensitive. Sorry. But, uh—"

"What?"

"Aside from the problem of clothes, don't you find it a handicap with your work?"

"Hasn't been so far."

Meredith didn't ask, but she seemed to remember reading somewhere that the condition was inherited. She recalled hearing, too, that Jackson's cousins back in the States were also private investigators, with their own agencies in various parts of the country. She wondered if any of them were color-blind.

"Of course," he said, "if you and I were to stick close during this case, you could let me know what color the slime is oozing under the doors. If it turns out to be red, I'd know it was an angry ghost, and if it's green, it would have to be the result of bad plumbing."

He deserved no answer, and Meredith gave him none.

"No, I didn't think so." Yawning, he slouched down in the seat again, snagged the cap forward over his eyes and promptly went back to sleep.

His renewed silence suited Meredith. While his closeness still made her uncomfortable, she managed to avoid any further looks in his direction. Instead, she occupied herself with her thoughts as the launch chugged across the three-mile-wide stretch of open sea toward their destination on the horizon.

They were conflicted thoughts. Had been from the moment she had received the phone call yesterday in her London hotel. It had been years since Meredith had last heard that voice, but she had immediately recognized it. Had listened while the caller told her she'd gotten Meredith's hotel number from the television station and that she and her husband were no longer living in Devonshire. They were in Cornwall now, and they needed Meredith. Would she come?

Meredith had made a vow long ago to use her science to help whoever suffered from strange occurrences to understand and deal with them. How could she refuse an earnest, even desperate appeal for her services? The answer in this case was that she darn well could have and should have.

So why didn't I refuse? Meredith asked herself now. Was it because the trouble Lord and Lady Danely were experiencing, when it had been briefly explained to her over the phone, was just too intriguing to resist? Well, there was some truth to that since their problem had some very provocative aspects to it.

Or was it because she'd realized that the time had come to confront issues that had never gone away, never softened?

But none of those answers satisfied Meredith. She really didn't understand exactly why she had agreed to come. It certainly wasn't because she owed the caller anything. She *didn't*, she insisted to herself, wanting to believe it. Telling herself there could be no obligation in that direction, not with all that had happened.

All right, so she didn't know why she was here. But there was one thing she was very clear about. None of this was going to be easy. For one thing, she didn't know if she could address those issues from the past when, and if, the time came. Didn't know if she even wanted to address them. Not when they were so painful.

And for another, there was the man at her side. Jackson Hawke. Meredith didn't trust him, and continued to feel he was hiding something. She was still convinced that, although she'd been necessary to him in order to secure this case, he resented her being there. Underneath all that seductive banter of his, her presence worried him somehow.

Well, he bothered her, too. When she had finally tracked him down at his own hotel yesterday evening to inform him she was accepting the case, she'd ended the phone call with a brisk "We are not rivals in some competition. I expect you to keep your distance and let me conduct my own investigation while you conduct yours."

Considering at the moment how that sinful body of his was still in contact with hers, in fact leaning closer to her by slow, tantalizing degrees, this was pretty ironic. He was going to be a problem. Definitely.

Another few seconds, and he would be sprawled all over her. And while that presented some very tempting possibilities, she didn't think she wanted to risk it. Before anything could happen, she nudged his shoulder with her own.

He came awake again with another yawn, pushed the baseball cap to the back of his head, and looked around. "Where are we?"

"Almost there. If you didn't get much sleep last night, then what were you doing all morning?"

"Wishing I could have been seeing the sights from the chopper that brought me down from London last night, instead of which—"

"Wait a minute, let me get this straight. You came to Cornwall by helicopter?"

"That's right. A buddy of mine flies one for this company, and if you hadn't wanted us to travel separately—"

"Never mind." She didn't want to go there again. "You were saying about the morning?"

"Got dragged around to the local art galleries. Dave is a painter."

Dave being the brunette's husband, Meredith figured. "I see." Meredith could certainly understand the lure of Cornwall for an artist. The scenery was spectacular, and the island looming ahead of them was no exception.

It was a small island, probably only several square miles in area, and most of that was steep granite with Croft Castle crowning its pinnacle. It looked to Meredith like the perfect image of an English castle with its turrets and battlements. Definitely a romantic sight.

All of that changed in the next moment as a bank of cloud passed over the sun. Then Croft Castle abruptly became a massive, forbidding pile of rock. Was it just her imagination, a result of the shadows cast by the cloud cover, or had the castle taken on a sinister quality?

Meredith couldn't help shivering. Jackson noticed her reaction and misunderstood it.

"Cold?"

"A little, now that the sun's gone under."

"I've got an arm here ready to keep you warm," he offered.

"I'm not that cold, thank you."

"We don't have to be enemies, Meredith."

"We don't have to snuggle, either, to be friends."

"Friends, huh? That's progress, anyway."

"It could be, if you had an open mind about my work. Which you don't," she reminded him.

"Maybe I can work on that. But spooks?" He shook his head. "I don't know."

The sun came out again, warm and friendly. Croft Castle was no longer something dark and eerie. Meredith decided that she had let her imagination get the best of her. Not like her. She was always so levelheaded when she approached her subjects.

All the same, she removed her gaze from the castle, turning her attention to a scene that was more cheerful.

Below the mount, tucked into the curve of a little bay, was a fishing village. Its stone cottages, some of which were painted white and others whose walls were hung with slate tiles, had window boxes and tiny gardens. Here was the riot of color that Meredith had looked for in London. Even the boats drawn up on the slope of the shingle beach were bright with color.

The launch crawled across the blue-green waters of the harbor, arriving at another stone quay where a dark green Land Rover that had seen better days was waiting to meet them. Its driver came forward as they climbed from the launch.

"Had a smooth crossing, did you?" he greeted them.

His hearty manner was genuine enough, though Meredith sensed there was something stressed about it. Understandable, if this man with the neat, ginger mustache was who she assumed he was.

"It's not always the case," he said. "We can get some rather heavy seas at this time of the year. In any event, we're very glad you're here. Guy St. Denis," he introduced himself, shaking their hands.

As she had supposed, this was Lord Danely. His casual garb, cords and a baggy sweater, couldn't conceal the bearing of a man with his aristocratic lineage.

Meredith had expected to…well, not dislike him. That wouldn't have been fair, just because she had issues with his wife. But she had thought she would feel uneasy in his company and instead found herself unable to resist his genial welcome.

All of this, of course, had absolutely nothing to do with Lord Danely's reluctance concerning her work, which she was prepared to respect. And which was an entirely separate issue, anyway.

There was no one with him. He didn't miss the anxious gaze she cast in the direction of the Land Rover. "Judith is waiting for us up at the castle," he said, his tone solemn now as he examined her. Given their connection, which was only by marriage, it wasn't surprising he should be as curious about her as she was about him.

Jackson Hawke was much too intelligent not to feel the constraint of this meeting. Meredith could see it in his puzzled gaze as it shifted from her to Lord Danely. But she didn't bother to enlighten him, and was glad he didn't ask.

"Well, then," Lord Danely suggested, resuming his attitude of amiable host, "shall we collect your things?"

The pilot helped them to move their belongings from the launch to the Land Rover. Meredith was aware, during this transfer, of the tang of the sea, the mild air and the sun warming the cobbles of the lane. This was the weather she had wanted in London and she wished she could enjoy it as much as it deserved. She couldn't. Not when the knowledge of the woman waiting for her up at the castle had her suddenly tense. And wondering again if she had made a serious mistake in coming to Croft Island.

"You two ride up front," Meredith urged when the vehicle had been loaded. "I'll sit in back with the luggage."

The arrangement would relieve her of the necessity of chatting with Lord Danely on the drive to the castle. She wanted to be quiet, wanted time to find her courage for the meeting with his wife.

Jackson couldn't have understood her need, but he must have sensed it. She was grateful that he came to her rescue when Lord Danely, who had insisted they must call him Guy, looked like he might question her decision.

"Sounds like a good plan. You can play tour guide for me, Guy. We ready to roll?"

They were, but the Land Rover had barely turned up the village street when its progress was halted by a boat being moved out of a repair yard.

Jackson used the opportunity to question Lord Danely about the island. "The folks here? They all in the fishing business?"

"Not much of that anymore, I'm afraid. A number of the cottages were left vacant when our people moved away to find work on the mainland. Things did brighten when the holiday trade became important. That's an inn over there. Pub keeps a good bar. One or two of the cottages opened shops, another a tea room."

"So the boats—"

"Offer excursions for the trippers along our Cornish coast. Sight-seeing, picnics in sheltered coves. That sort of thing. And the castle, when we turned it into a hotel, was a draw. But, of course, now…"

The whole operation here was seriously threatened. That's what he was telling them, Meredith thought, unable to ignore either the conversation or the tone of concern in the front seat.

The boat on its trailer cleared the street, allowing the Land Rover to proceed. They passed out of the village and almost immediately began to climb a steep, winding lane bordered thickly on one side by banks of rhododendrons in full bloom and on the other side offering a view of the sea that was equally breath-taking.

Then, as their vehicle rounded a sharp turn and crested the road, Croft Castle rose suddenly in front of them. From this angle, she was unable to see the original keep. That ancient fortress was tucked behind an impressive modern wing. Or at least it would have been modern when it was added to the castle, probably sometime late in the seventeenth century, judging by its style.

Climbing from the Land Rover when it rolled to a stop, Meredith eyed the tall structure. Her attention was drawn immediately to a series of what looked like life-sized stone figures high above them on the roof.

"They're all turned in the same direction," she observed.

"Yes, they face the keep," Guy said, joining her in the cobbled forecourt. "Those are Croft Castle's guardian angels."

Angels? If he hadn't told her, she wouldn't have guessed they represented angels, even with their folded wings. They looked so dark and brooding crouched up there at intervals along the stone parapet.

What were they meant to guard against? Meredith wondered. And what imaginative ancestor of Lord Danely's had installed them? And why?

Her hand shading her eyes against the glare of the sun, she was fascinated by them. A second later, she gave a little start. It was absurd, but she could swear that one of those figures had just moved.

It had to be an illusion, a trick of the blinding sunlight. But it was a strange, unnerving sensation, even for someone with her experience. She glanced quickly in the direction of the two men. They were no longer interested in the figures ranged along the parapet. Nor was Meredith. The front door had opened. A slender, silver-haired woman emerged from the castle. Lady Danely.

She came down the steps to greet them. Meredith could see by her nervous smile that Judith St. Denis was as anxious about this meeting as she was.

They didn't embrace. Both of them knew better than that. They simply stood there for a long moment regarding each other, and she wondered if the other woman was experiencing the same churning emotions.

Then, drawing a quick breath and releasing it slowly, Meredith offered her hand. "Hello, Mother," she managed in a steady voice.

Chapter Three

And just what in sweet Hades, Jackson wondered, following them into the castle, was that all about?

Mother and daughter? Yeah, apparently so. And why had both Meredith and their hosts neglected to inform him of this little connection? An oversight? Uh-uh, he didn't buy it.

There was something funny about their relationship all right. He didn't have to be a private investigator to see that. No affection in their meeting. In fact, it had been downright strained.

And it continued to be awkward, which Jackson guessed was why they were getting this little tour of the wing that was the occupied portion of the castle, serving as both hotel and home for its owners. The tour was meant to ease that stiffness, he supposed, but it was turning out to be as formal as the rooms themselves.

Entrance lobby with a grand staircase. Drawing room, library, dining room. All of them imposing with their Jacobean this and their Gothic Revival that. But Jackson didn't need to see any of this elegance. He had already gotten the picture here.

Things like a battered Land Rover. A couple of blank spaces on the walls suggesting that paintings might have been sacrificed to keep them going. And no staff in evidence. Hadn't Guy said he would later bring in their luggage himself, carry it to their rooms for them?

Then there was the castle itself. It hadn't been inhabited by the St. Denis family since sometime in the nineteenth century but this wing had all the fresh look of a luxury hotel. Meaning that its owners must have sunk all they had in bringing it to life again, including modern comforts for their paying guests. Guy had even indicated as much. Something about moving back to Croft Castle after having lost the family's principal seat in Devonshire.

Jackson understood their financial desperation all too well. Wasn't he fighting a similar battle? What he couldn't figure out was the problem Meredith and her mother had with each other and it didn't look like anybody was going to enlighten him.

Fair enough. He had a couple of worrisome secrets of his own that he intended to keep to himself. For now, anyway. And that included the way he felt about Meredith Allen. He didn't want her on this case. Didn't want the constant temptation of her. Her kind of woman was dangerous to him. Hadn't he learned that painful lesson back in the States?

But what was he to do? This case was vital to him. It meant his survival if he succeeded in solving it. His ruin if he didn't. And Meredith came with the deal. Without her, Lady Danely would never have persuaded her husband to enlist the services of both her daughter and the private investigator Lord Danely himself, preferred.

No problem, Jackson thought. He could work with Meredith.

Sure you can. That's why you have to fight like hell to keep from wanting her every minute you're around her. Like now, for instance.

If he kept on eyeing her like this, his lust wasn't going to stay a secret much longer. He was close to betraying himself with an embarrassing arousal.

Whatever his struggle, Jackson couldn't help himself. As ordinary as that denim shirtdress was, she looked damn alluring in it. Probably because of the slit in her skirt, which offered enticing glimpses of her thighs when she moved. Those silky thighs had him imagining the lush territory above them. And Jackson's imagination was very good when it came to such areas.

There was one thing in his favor where his resolve not to get involved with her was concerned. Meredith had about as much use for him as he had for her ghosts. She'd made that all too clear back in the States when she'd refused to let him get anywhere near her, even though he had been unwisely hot for her then, too.

Except Jackson could have sworn she'd been checking him out on the launch. Maybe, but where the subject of her ghosts was concerned, she could be a real pain in the butt. Oh, yeah, it was going to be a lot of fun, their being thrown together like this on the same case. A miracle if they didn't kill each other. Still, when he considered that shapely little backside…

The backside was currently preceding him in the direction of Lord and Lady Danely's private, ground floor apartment.

"I thought we'd tell you what's been happening in the castle while we have tea," Judith said, leading the way into a sitting room that was only slightly less regal than the rest of the place.

Jackson had been wondering when they would get around to the reason why he and Meredith were here.

A tall woman in a coverall, its pattern so jazzy it made his eyes ache, was waiting for them with a trolley loaded with goodies. Judith introduced her as Imogen, the cook who had accompanied them from Devonshire.

Guy had already explained toward the end of the tour that the only other help was a daily who came up from the village and a man who handled the yard work as needed. Jackson had the impression that they'd had to let other staff go when the guests stopped coming. And currently there were no paying guests at all in the castle.

"Imogen has done us proud," Guy said, indicating the spread on the trolley after the cook had retreated.

Jackson wasn't much for tea, English or otherwise, but the West Country specialty of clotted cream and strawberry jam heaped on split scones appealed to him.

"Imogen works magic with her Aga," Judith said, passing the plate of scones to her daughter.

"That's a type of English stove, isn't it?" Meredith responded.

Mother and daughter were still being nothing but polite to each other, Jackson noticed. And wary. He was getting a little restless with all this careful courtesy, eager to get down to business.

Apparently, Meredith was equally impatient to undertake their investigation. A few sips of her tea, and she was leaning toward Lord Danely with an earnest "I'd like to hear about your ghost."

"*Alleged* ghost," Jackson corrected her from his own chair. Might as well make that clear from the start, he thought, though he had to admit that if any ghost was going to pick a house to haunt, this was the place for it. Magnificent or not, the castle had all the required macabre elements, including those ugly stone gargoyles on the fireplace staring at him malevolently.

Meredith frowned at his remark, but she offered no argument.

Guy, standing by the fireplace, set his cup on the stone mantel. "Jackson already heard some of the story when we talked on the phone, but I'm sure he, too, would appreciate a full account now."

Oh, yeah, he'd heard all right, Jackson thought. Enough, anyway, to leave him totally confounded by the source of the strange occurrences at Croft Castle.

"Actually," Guy began, "before the trouble started, we were rather proud of our resident ghost. There aren't many stately homes in England that can claim the company of so distinguished a guest."

"Distinguished how?" Meredith asked.

"Our Edward was one of Britain's many royal Edwards."

"A king? And he died here?"

"A prince who would have been king if he had survived. And, yes, he died here at Croft Castle. That is, if one is to believe the tale passed down to us by the ancient chroniclers, most of whom were monks writing long after the events they described."

He doesn't like this, Jackson thought, realizing that Guy looked embarrassed about the whole thing. He doesn't believe in this ghost any more than I do, probably feels trapped by the situation. And helpless.

Meredith, on the other hand, was fascinated. Jackson noticed how she had her head tipped to one side as she listened intently.

"Edward Atheling," Guy continued reluctantly, "was, in any case, a very real prince. History knows him as Edward the Exile, one of the sons of the ruling Saxon king, Edmund Ironside, who was sent to live on the continent after his father died. Eventually, his uncle, Edward the Confessor, came to the throne. And since that Edward had no issue, and our Edward did, he was recalled to England as the rightful heir."

"But if I remember my history," Meredith said, "it was Harold Godwinson who grabbed the crown after Edward the Confessor died, and William the Conqueror who took it away from Harold. So what happened to your Edward's issue?"

"That would have been his son, Edgar. A Saxon faction proclaimed him as the true heir, but in the end he was made to submit to William the Conqueror. Edgar lived, but he and his descendants were forgotten, and our Edward became no more than a footnote in history. Who knows what that history would have been if Edward Atheling *had* ascended the throne."

Jackson could have contributed a little something of his own to that footnote, and it wouldn't have been half bad. But he kept silent.

"A lost king," Meredith murmured, "who died at Croft Castle."

Guy nodded. "Murdered, actually. Or so claims the legend."

"And what is that legend?" Meredith urged.

Ah, now we get to the good stuff, Jackson thought.

"According to the story," Guy said, "a storm blew the ship bearing Edward back to England off its course. It landed here on the island where he was welcomed by the Saxon baron who built Croft Castle. One Sir Hugh Gwinfryd."

"An ancestor of yours?" Jackson asked.

"Good Lord, I should hope not. By all accounts, Sir Hugh was an unsavory character. A vile man reputed to be a practitioner of the Black Arts. They say the huge dogs he kept were hounds from hell. Gifts from Satan himself, with whom Sir Hugh had a pact." Guy shrugged. "All nonsense, of course."

Yeah, but it makes great storytelling, Jackson thought. He could see that Meredith certainly thought so. Those gorgeous eyes of hers were glowing with eagerness as she spoke to Guy.

"So your family…"

"Has no direct connection with Sir Hugh, I'm happy to say. Croft came to my people as a share of the spoils from the Conquest. And by then Edward was long dead. Murdered by his host. It was said that Harold Godwinson paid Sir Hugh an enormous sum to rid him of his rival to the throne. There is, however, another version of the story."

"The bawdy one that our guests seem to prefer," Judith said, helping herself to more tea from the silver pot. "Or did."

Jackson was more than ready to hear it. Guy obliged him.

"Our Edward, so the tale goes, was a remarkably handsome fellow with an appetite for carnal pleasures. And in the best tradition of such legends, Sir Hugh's young wife was a beauty ripe for seduction."

"The inevitable happened," Jackson guessed.

Guy smiled. "With the usual result. Sir Hugh caught them together in the act of—I believe the polite term would be flagrante delicto—and promptly dispatched Edward with his sword. The common reaction of a man who was cuckolded in those days."

"And Edward has been haunting Croft ever since," Meredith said, ignoring the tea that was growing cold at her elbow.

"*Allegedly* haunting," Jackson corrected her again, hating to spoil the satisfaction that was gleaming from those eyes, whose color he wished he could appreciate, but needing to keep this whole thing on a level of reality.

"Certainly not a serious haunting," Judith said. "Not until just lately, anyway."

"But before your current trouble," Meredith wanted to know. "Tell me about that."

"You must understand," Guy informed her from where he continued to stand by the fireplace, "that until these last few weeks, we had no activity whatsoever. Edward was just a harmless legend to entertain our guests. Prior to that…well, my family hasn't lived here for over a century, so the tales are very old. And," he added firmly, "they were never more than just that. Tales."

"Of what?" Meredith persisted.

"Nothing violent or evil," Judith explained. "Things such as women reporting their breasts being touched when no one was near them or swearing they felt little puffs of air in their ears, like a warm breath. And then there was the medieval-style banquet Guy's great-great grandfather recreated for his guests. A flask of mead and a plate of oatcakes, both favorites of Edward according to legend, mysteriously disappeared from the table."

Jackson laughed. "Sounds like Edward was busy satisfying those appetites of his."

"In other words," Meredith said, "he's always been a benign ghost, but now—"

"Now," Jackson cut in, "somebody is using the claims of overimaginative women to blame Edward Atheling—long in his grave, I might add—for their human shenanigans."

Meredith turned to him in exasperation. "We don't know

that. We don't know it isn't Edward himself." She gave her attention again to Guy and her mother. "Was there ever an actual sighting?"

"An apparition, you mean?" Judith shook her head. "No, nothing like that."

"So he's never materialized."

"And won't," Jackson insisted.

Meredith said nothing this time, but when those fabulous eyes of hers flashed their fire at him, he got the message. "Yeah, I remember. I need to keep an open mind. But I can do that better by hearing what you folks *do* know for certain."

Guy, suddenly looking tired, came away from the fireplace and sat down. His wife gazed at him in concern and took up the story. She's trying to spare him, Jackson thought, and he wondered about that.

"It was only small things to begin with," Judith said. "Like Imogen one morning finding the utensils in her kitchen all out of place, as if someone had moved them around during the night. Then on another morning we discovered the pictures in the drawing room hanging upside down on the walls and every lightbulb in the library blown."

"Pranks?" Jackson asked, helping himself to another scone, which he lathered with the thick cream.

"That's what we thought at first. Just harmless pranks. But then the mischief turned nasty. Guests complained of foul odors in their rooms, and when we searched them we turned up rotting fish and seaweed."

"Gifts from the sea, huh?" Jackson seemed to be the only one interested now in the scones. Probably not very smart of him, he thought as he spooned jam on top of the clotted cream in what had to be a lethal combination. The things must be loaded with calories, never mind all the grams of fat. He'd just have to work it off. Maybe take a run down that mountain and back in the morning.

"Not entirely. On one occasion a half-eaten rat was left on

one of the pillows of a couple who then checked out immediately." Judith shuddered over the memory.

"You have any enemies?" Jackson questioned her. "Someone who might have a reason to want to put you out of business?"

Judith shook her head. "No one. At least no one we know of. It's hard to imagine that anyone—"

"What about your staff? Could one of them have a grudge?"

"That's not likely. They're all loyal, trusted people, including the ones we had to let go."

"The light," Guy prompted his wife. "Tell them about the light. That's when all this rot about a ghost started to be spread around and the guests stopped coming."

"We never saw it ourselves," Judith said. "None of the windows in our rooms here look out toward the original part of the castle. It was several of our guests who reported seeing it across the rooftops late at night from their bedrooms upstairs."

"What kind of a light?" Meredith asked. And Jackson knew, *just* knew, she was already convinced it was some kind of spectral glow.

"Nothing bright," her mother explained. "Well, it couldn't have been since there's no electricity over there. Whatever it was, they said it seemed to drift from window to window in the old keep and then vanish altogether."

"You investigate?" Jackson asked, catching jam that was dripping out of the side of his scone sandwich.

"We did, of course," Guy said.

"And found nothing," Jackson surmised.

"True, and what makes it so hard to explain is that the keep is tightly locked at all times. After all, it is tenth century, and though the roofs have always been kept in repair, the place is in a derelict state, so we have to be careful."

"Meaning your nocturnal visitor is somehow finding his way in and out without a key."

"If he isn't mortal," Meredith argued, "that wouldn't be a problem."

Jackson managed to hold his tongue this time, mostly because it was occupied with the scone. But Guy, preferring Jackson's contention, didn't.

"Well, it is just conceivable…" He hesitated and then offered them a possibility. "The Cornish coast has an old history of wreckers and smugglers. Never any evidence that my ancestors were involved in such operations, but the family did seem to grow mysteriously wealthy early in the nineteenth century. And if they were concealing contraband from the excise officers…"

"I see what you mean," Jackson said. "They'd have to have some undetectable way of moving the loads into the castle and a safe place to store them until they were moved out again."

"It is certainly a tempting explanation," Guy agreed, "but if such passages and rooms are here at Croft, I've never discovered any sign of them."

"Doesn't mean they don't exist and that somebody else hasn't learned where they are and is using your ghost for his own benefit."

"What are you suggesting?" Meredith challenged him. "That someone is getting into the old keep by a secret means and is searching for—what?"

"Maybe contraband that's still hidden here. For all we know, it could be a fortune in Napoleon brandy."

Meredith didn't tell him what she thought about this speculation. She didn't have to. Those expressive eyes of hers were all over him again, letting him know she was none too happy with his theories.

Jackson wasn't serious about the brandy. However, a maze of secret passages somewhere in the castle was certainly a possibility. If it existed, it could be anywhere. But to begin with…

"I'd like to have a look at that old keep," he said, taking a last bite of his scone and setting the plate aside.

"And so would I," Meredith said, for once agreeing with him. But not for the same reason, Jackson knew. She was still on the trail of that ghost of hers.

Judith got to her feet. "Yes, we realized you'd want to examine that part of the castle, but I thought we'd show you Mrs. Forbes-Walsh's room first."

Ah, that famous room where the poltergeist had been so busy, Jackson thought. Not that he was ready to believe a poltergeist had been responsible for what might have happened there. On the other hand, he supposed he had to be grateful for whatever did occur since it had played a major role in Lord and Lady Danely hiring them.

The four of them left the sitting room and made their way to the stairway.

"Except for recovering Mrs. Forbes-Walsh's things," Judith explained on their way up, "we left the room just as we found it. We had to pack for her. She refused to go back into the room."

What was that old British saying? Jackson asked himself. About keeping a stiff upper lip? That's what Lord and Lady Danely were doing all right. But he could tell—and he supposed Meredith could, too—that the couple was deeply worried. Praying that he and Meredith could help them. Jackson was hoping for that, too. Otherwise… But there was no percentage in worrying about that until he had to.

They went along a broad corridor and stopped at a door at the end. Judith produced a key. "No one's been in here since we lost Mrs. Forbes-Walsh."

She unlocked the door and spread it open, moving back to allow her daughter and the private investigator to enter. Jackson issued a long, slow whistle as he stepped through the opening after Meredith.

Talk about a room being trashed!

It looked like a storm had blown through the place. Furniture had been overturned. Drawers had been yanked out of tables and chests, their contents strewn across the floor. They now kept company with books and shattered ornaments that had been swept from shelves in some kind of weird frenzy.

After a single, sweeping glance at the shambles, Meredith turned to him with a dry smile. "What was that you were saying earlier about a very human mischief? Well, even you have to admit that no mortal is responsible for this."

BUT JACKSON HAD refused to admit any such thing. Meredith, still fuming over the stubbornness of the man in the face of such obvious evidence, unpacked her things behind the closed door of the spacious bedroom they had given her.

Rigged, he'd maintained. Somebody could have rigged the room beforehand. Jerked a few strings from wherever this *somebody* had been concealed—just enough, say, to convince Mrs. Forbes-Walsh that the objects flying through the air were the work of a spook—then proceeded after the dowager had fled in terror to make a thorough job of the destruction.

Hey, it wouldn't be the first time this kind of thing had been pulled. That's what he'd maintained.

Even after his advocate, Guy, had indicated that Mrs. Forbes-Walsh had sworn she'd heard a mocking male laughter from an invisible source, Jackson had gone on maintaining there could be no connection here with a ghost.

So, okay, he'd finally been willing to concede, maybe it had somehow been psychokinesis-related. A very *human* form of psychokinesis.

Yes, *as if,* Meredith thought, collecting what she'd need for a shower and heading for the bathroom. Oh, sure, there were documented cases where individuals seemed to have some subconscious energy to move objects without touching them. But in nearly every instance they turned out to be emotionally disturbed young people. And there were no young people, disturbed or otherwise, at Croft Castle.

And why am I letting Jackson Hawke upset me like this? she wondered. It was bad enough that every time she got near him she became aware of his potent masculinity. Did she have to let him go and bother her even when he was a safe distance away behind the door of his own room across the hall? Presumably catching up on some of that sleep he had lost last night.

She intended to lie down herself for a couple of hours, though for a different reason. She needed to be rested for what she planned tonight. But first she wanted that shower.

The old keep had been laden with the dust and cobwebs of years of neglect, and Meredith felt grimy after their tour through it. Their inspection of the place had yielded no result. But tonight, she promised herself, could be another story.

Reaching the bathroom, she paused just inside the door to listen. A wind had risen and was wailing around the old stone walls of the castle. It made a strange sound. Like the call of a mournful voice.

Was that what made her suddenly uneasy? So unsettled that she found herself locking the bathroom door behind her? It was a silly precaution, she decided as she stripped off her clothes, stepped into the tub and drew the curtain behind her.

All right, she thought, adjusting the shower head, so it wasn't the wind or even Jackson Hawke, arrogantly, dangerously sexy though he was, that had her all on edge. These were probably just devices to keep her mind busy so she wouldn't have to think about her meeting with her mother.

It had been harder than she'd anticipated seeing her after all these years. What her mother herself was feeling Meredith didn't know. She was a stranger, after all, little more than a memory. One that hadn't seemed to change much over the years. Judith had always been a striking, self-possessed woman, and still was.

Meredith realized they would have to sit down and talk. But she wasn't looking forward to that. Abandonment wasn't an easy thing to discuss. Or forgive.

That would have to wait, however, because after dinner Meredith was going to mount a late-night vigil in the ancient part of the castle where the lights had been seen. She was more convinced than ever after their tour through the keep, where

Guy had pointed out that its only two outside doors were barred from the inside and had remained so after each of his investigations, that something supernatural was responsible for those lights.

Ironic, she supposed as she lathered herself under the spray, that she'd go and lock a bathroom door behind her while planning to spend the night alone in what was reputedly a haunted castle.

But it wasn't the same thing at all, because Meredith's past investigations had convinced her that people could be a threat. Ghosts weren't. Not when you respected their existence. Besides, this wouldn't be the first night she spent in a building with a bad reputation. After all, this was her job. And hadn't she survived every one of those nights without being in any way harmed?

No, she thought, she wasn't afraid of ghosts. What she did fear, however, as she turned under the invigorating stream of water, was her own treacherous imagination. Now why did she have to go and have this sudden, erotic vision of Jackson Hawke sharing the shower with her? Where did that come from? The image of those big hands of his slowly, sensually soaping her flesh, then his slick hardness pasting itself against her while—

What on earth are you doing? Stop thinking about him. Think about something else. Something safe and pleasant. Like wondering how Rand and Joanna are doing back home.

Angry with herself, Meredith quickly rinsed herself off and turned off the spray. There was a sudden silence. Even the wind had died down to the merest whisper.

For a few seconds she found herself listening again, as though expecting something. Then, refusing to give in to her imagination, she swept back the curtain.

The small bathroom was filled with the steam from her shower. She was stepping out of the tub when she saw it. Three words drawn in the moisture that fogged the mirror above the sink.

HAIL AND BEWARE

Meredith froze, staring at the message scrawled on the misted glass. The bathroom door was locked, the single window shut and fastened. That could only mean—

Another realization abruptly checked her excitement. She was standing here completely naked, and if she wasn't alone in the bathroom, if a pair of unseen eyes was at this very second feasting their gaze on all her exposed flesh—

Meredith snatched the thick bath sheet from the heated bar over which it was draped and hastily wrapped it around herself. And that's when the knockings began.

Chapter Four

Hardly daring to breathe, her head tipped over to one side, Meredith listened intently. Nothing.

Had she been mistaken? No, she couldn't have imagined it. There had definitely been a series of soft, rhythmic rappings. Now there was only this disappointing silence, but still she waited.

There!

The knockings came again, and this time she was almost certain she could detect a deliberate pattern. Several strong taps, then a pause followed by three more taps. Was it a communication from the same ghostly hand that had drawn the message on her mirror?

Meredith could tell now that the source of those rappings came from outside the bathroom. Oblivious to her state of undress, she unlocked the bathroom door and went into the bedroom.

The disturbances were louder here, but this wasn't their origin. They seemed to be echoing from inside the wall itself in the direction of the hallway.

Clutching the bath sheet around her, her heart beating rapidly with excitement, Meredith rushed out into the hall. And almost slammed into Jackson Hawke, whose knuckles were about to perform another staccato on the wall paneling beside her bedroom door.

"You."

Using his outstretched fist now as a support instead of a hammer, he leaned against the wall and eyed her in the bath sheet. "That sounds like you were expecting someone else. Looks like it, too."

Ignoring his suggestive observation, she demanded an explanation. "What were you doing out here making all that racket?"

"Testing the paneling."

"Why?"

"To see what's solid and what might be hollow."

"Not those secret panels again."

"Why not? Somebody is getting in and out of this place, and they don't seem to be using doors. So why should a secret passage be any harder to swallow than—"

He broke off, an expression of sudden understanding lighting those bold blue eyes that continued to look at her, not as if they were seeing the bath sheet but everything that was beneath it.

"Ah, that's why you raced out here in nothing but that towel. You thought it was your ghost talking to you."

Annoyed by his perpetual arrogance, Meredith made the mistake of blurting, "He *did* speak to me."

"I don't blame him, not if you were parading around looking like that. Or were you in an even more enticing state?"

Meredith turned around and marched back into her bedroom. But Jackson slipped in behind her before she could shut the door in his face.

"He issued an interesting invitation, maybe?" he persisted, following her on her way back to the bathroom.

"What he issued was a warning. Not that I expect you to believe me." She told him about the message on the mirror.

He joined her in the bathroom, where he examined the mirror. "Nothing there now."

"Well, of course there isn't. The steam has dried off. But it *was* there." She waited for him to scoff at her claim, and when he didn't, she was encouraged to go on. "Look, I know you think this is all crazy, but I believe in his presence. What's more—"

She stopped in midsentence with the realization that Jackson wasn't listening to her. He was still busy focusing that brazen, hot-eyed gaze of his on the sight of her in the bath sheet.

Meredith hadn't taken the time to dry herself off after her shower. The bath sheet had absorbed all the wetness, and now its damp folds were molded to her body like a second skin. She was conscious of the thing clinging to her provocatively, leaving very little to the imagination.

"Are you enjoying yourself?" she challenged him.

"What? I'm listening. Go on. This is fascinating."

"Fine. We'll talk, then. *After* you get out of here. And close the door behind you."

He went without an argument, though she didn't trust the grin on that wide, sensual mouth of his. When the door had shut behind him, she discarded the towel and bundled herself into her floor-length terry-cloth robe. Safely covered, she left the bathroom. She found Jackson leaning patiently against the bureau, hands tucked into the pockets of his black jeans.

"You were saying?" he drawled.

"Yes, about Edward Atheling. And I'm more convinced than ever that it is he."

"Good. Then we don't need to waste time trying to prove his existence. We can move on to the business of why we're really here, which is to learn just what's been happening at Croft Castle and why."

He might be ready to dismiss the presence of Edward Atheling, but Meredith wasn't. "Granted, but I'm prepared to believe that mystery is connected with the past. Edward's past and that his message wasn't just a warning, it was also a greeting. A *friendly* one."

One of Jackson's thick black eyebrows arched cynically

"Friendly, huh? Aren't you the same woman who was trying to tell me it was your ghost who destroyed that guest room and chased off its occupant?"

"I've been thinking about that. He's been peaceful all these years, so why should he turn malicious now?"

"You're the psychologist. You explain it."

"What if it was an act of desperation, his method for convincing a reluctant Lord Danely to bring us to the island?"

"You saying old Edward is trying to tell us something?"

"Maybe."

"What?"

"That we're both of us right. That he is here but not responsible for the evil in this place. That the other force *is* a human one and that Edward—as much as we do—would like to see it dealt with and defeated."

"That's something I can work with, anyway."

As long as I don't have to believe in your ghost. That's what Jackson was telling her, Meredith realized. She was prepared to accept his compromise. For now at least.

He stood away from the bureau. His hands, still buried in his pockets, stretched the already taut fabric of his jeans across his groin and lean hips, making a tantalizing, altogether masculine sight. Meredith was relieved when he turned away and sauntered in the direction of the door.

"And if I'm going to make any progress toward a solution," he said over his shoulder, "then I need to snatch a few hours of sleep. Holler if you get any more ghostly visitations. Otherwise, I'll see you at dinner."

He left, closing the door behind him.

Meredith, too, needed to rest. But instead of stretching out on the bed, she went to the window and looked out. She couldn't see the guardian angels on the roofs from here, but she could picture them up there. And she wondered.

Had one of them this afternoon not been stone but something else? The image perhaps of Edward Atheling? She hadn't told Jackson about that. He wouldn't have bought it, anymore than he'd bought the ghost writing on her mirror.

She went on wondering. Could Edward, too, be guarding against some ancient curse at Croft Castle?

Warm as her thick terry-cloth robe was, Meredith couldn't prevent the shiver that seized her. But then she knew her shiver had nothing to do with temperature.

MEREDITH CHECKED THE contents of the canvas carryall to make sure it contained everything she would need. Satisfied that it was all there, she drew on a thick sweater. The keep was unheated, and she would need both the sweater and the woolen slacks she wore for warmth.

She glanced at her watch. It was just after eleven o'clock. Time to leave. Picking up the bulky carryall, she dipped the lights and cautiously cracked the bedroom door.

The hall was dark except for a single lamp that cast a feeble glow at the far end of the passage. When she listened, the only sound she could hear was the hollow ticking of the grandfather clock at the head of the stairs. The stillness told her that everyone else in the place must be in their beds and hopefully asleep by now.

Pulling the door back, Meredith slipped into the gloom of the hall, then turned to ease the door shut behind her.

"I was beginning to wonder when you would turn up."

Meredith whipped around with a little squawk of alarm. He must have been lurking close by, so undetectable in that black apparel of his that he had blended in with the heavy shadows.

"What are you doing sneaking up on me?"

"Funny. I was under the impression you were the one doing the sneaking. I don't know why since there isn't anyone to disturb. We're the only ones on this floor, remember."

"You were waiting for me. How did you know—"

"What you were up to? It didn't take much detecting, Meredith. I heard you asking Imogen for a thermos of coffee, and then there was that little chat you had with Guy after dinner. I guess all that whispering meant you were asking him for the key to the keep that's never out of his possession. Besides…"

"What?"

"I may not be certain of the color of your eyes, but the gleam of anticipation in them was pretty easy to read. We ready to roll?"

There was no contest, Meredith decided. Jackson Hawke easily qualified as the most overbearing man she had ever encountered. "You're not going anywhere with me."

"Aw, now, Meredith, you didn't think I'd let you spend the night alone in that keep?"

"I don't need a protector. I can take care of myself."

"Uh-huh. You got a gun in that mysterious bag of yours?"

"Of course I don't. Handguns are illegal in England."

"Well, there you go."

"Listen—"

"Yeah, I know. You weren't planning to shoot a ghost over there. You were planning on communicating with one, because this is a friendly ghost. He's also the ghost that told you to beware, which makes him a smart spirit."

Meredith knew he was right. The lights observed late at night in the old keep might not be spectral at all but human in origin. *Dangerously* human.

"You said it yourself this afternoon," he reminded her. "Two forces at work in the castle, one ghostly and one very real."

"I also said I wanted us to conduct separate investigations. I won't have you—"

"Sneering over your ghost. So, all right, I'll keep my mouth shut about Edward Atheling, but I am coming with you."

She wanted to go on arguing that his presence wasn't necessary, but he was so insistent it would have been useless. And, admittedly, foolish of her. There *was* a risk in this vigil, and also…well, she couldn't deny the appeal of his strength if it did become necessary for him to defend her. Not that she wasn't capable of protecting herself. Still…

"I suppose I can't prevent it."

"That's my girl."

"I am not—"

"Your girl. I'll try to remember that, though the cleft in that stubborn little chin of yours doesn't make it easy. Along with a few of your other assets."

"And that's another thing. You have this aggravating habit of finishing my sentences for me." The carryall was growing heavy. Meredith paused to shift it to her other hand. "I would appreciate it if you would stop anticipating me."

"Sure. You mind telling me what you're carrying in that bulging bag of yours?"

"Necessities. Can we please go?"

He accommodated her, and moments later they were on the ground floor and moving along another dim passage. There was a stone archway at its end that framed a stout door, its oak surface scarred by time. When they reached it, Meredith produced the key that Lord Danely had given her and fitted it into the heavy lock.

The lock had been maintained, allowing the key to turn smoothly. But the hinges of the door hadn't been oiled recently. They creaked eerily when Meredith spread the door inward on the blackness beyond.

Jackson had a flashlight. Its beam revealed the interior as they stepped through the gothic arch, closing and locking the door behind them. They were in the ancient keep now. This was the chapel, Meredith remembered.

There were carvings everywhere. The figures in them that had appeared so pious and friendly during their daylight visit were another matter late at night. They looked menacing in the glow of the flashlight, with eyes that seemed to follow them as Jackson led the way along the aisle that ended at a second arch and another door.

This one was unlocked, and when they passed through the portal they found themselves in the Great Hall of the original fortress.

"Damn effective, isn't it?" Jackson muttered.

Meredith knew what he meant. The vast, echoing hall, raw and dank with age, was a loathsome place with rusting weapons on its walls, the smell of dust and decay, and suspicious droppings everywhere on the stone flags of the floor.

The origin of those droppings manifested itself a second later when something swooped over her head. Bats! Lord Danely had warned them the creatures found their way through the louver from which the smoke of the central hearth had once escaped high in the open roof.

Meredith shuddered. She could tolerate all manner of ghosts, but bats were something else. Fortunately, the Great Hall, which was apparently infested with them, was not her destination. The light that had been observed had its source in another section of the castle.

She was relieved to put the Great Hall behind them as they mounted a flight of spiral stairs located within a corner tower.

Over the centuries there had been many improvements to the old keep before it had been abandoned altogether when the newer wing was built. Before that desertion, a Long Gallery had been constructed on an upper floor sometime during the Tudor era. It was this once fashionable addition to the castle at which they arrived when they finally exited from the dark tower.

"Moon's up," Jackson said as they paused to catch their breath. The climb had been a steep one through several levels.

The windows that had been so few and small elsewhere in the keep were in abundance here. Banks of them were located in alcoves along the entire length of the outside wall of the Long Gallery. It was in these windows that guests had reported seeing the strange, moving light late at night.

Those same windows now admitted the glow of the moon, permitting Meredith an adequate view of the Long Gallery. The broad, elaborately paneled corridor stretched in front of them like a gloomy tunnel. At its far end, more than a hundred feet away, it turned, wrapping itself around that side of the keep.

The gallery was unfurnished except for several faded, threadbare tapestries sagging on the inner walls. Meredith decided they couldn't be very valuable or they would have been removed ages ago along with most of the other furnishings in the keep.

"Where do you want to settle?" Jackson asked.

"This should do," she said, indicating the first of the shallow alcoves on their left. "We can see most of the gallery from here without being easily noticed."

"Make yourself comfortable, then. I'm going to check that short extension around the corner down there."

He strode away, the beam of his flashlight receding into the distance. Meredith made use of his absence, unloading the contents of the carryall on the floor of the embrasure. By the time Jackson returned several minutes later, she had everything in place and was already seated on the blanket she had spread on the boards.

"Everything is quiet down there," he reported. He played the flashlight over her arrangement. "Yo, what's this? A picnic?"

"I've experienced enough all-night surveillances to know how to arm myself for them."

"I'm impressed," he said, dropping on the blanket beside her. "What all have you got here?"

He poked through the provisions she had brought with her. The thermos of hot coffee, a selection of snacks, a battery-powered lantern which she would light only if it became necessary, a camera, her pocket recorder and a notebook and pen.

"You plan on documenting this stakeout?"

"It's what a good psychologist does."

If I get the chance, she thought. There was nothing certain about their vigil. It was founded on little but guesswork and speculation. Which meant anything could happen here tonight. Or nothing at all.

"Hey, a spare blanket," he said. "Do I get to bundle in it with you if it gets too cold?"

"I wouldn't count on it."

Actually, although she didn't reach for it, she could almost use that extra blanket now. The Long Gallery was like a tomb. Not a very clean one, either. There was dirt and cobwebs everywhere. There were also unpleasant rustling sounds behind the paneling.

"Mice," Jackson said.

Given the choice, Meredith thought, she'd take a mouse over a bat, although she would prefer to encounter neither.

"Cheerful place, huh?" he remarked. "All it needs is the spooky sound of an organ."

There was no organ. There was only the silence. Even the mice in the paneling were quiet now. Jackson had switched off the flashlight, leaving them with nothing but the moonlight and the shadows.

Would those shadows remain undisturbed? Meredith wondered. Or would their long, patient wait be rewarded?

A board somewhere creaked suddenly, startling her. She knew it was only the sound of the old flooring settling itself, but she unconsciously shifted closer to Jackson on the blanket. And instantly wished she hadn't, because she was now aware of the heady scent of him. She tried to describe it to herself and decided it was a blend of soap, a hint of spicy aftershave and something that was distinctly him. It was all male, and it tugged at her treacherous senses.

Meredith tried to excuse her action with a quick apology. "Sorry. I don't know why I'm so jumpy. I've spent all kinds of time in places reputed to be haunted, and I was never nervous." She hesitated before adding, "But this is different somehow. I can sense…well, a genuine evil in this old keep."

The instant the impulsive explanation was out of her mouth, she regretted it. He was sure to respond with one of his usual quips. But he didn't.

"Yeah, I know. I can feel it, too."

She glanced at him in surprise, but it was too dark to read

his expression. Still, what she had heard had been spoken with sincerity. This was an unexpected facet of Jackson Hawke. The man was actually capable of a sensitive understanding.

Meredith should have moved away from him on the blanket. But, wise or not, she stayed where she was. His stalwart nearness was comforting. And so was his deep voice when he spoke to her again in a low tone.

"Look, there's no reason we shouldn't talk. It could be a long night. Why not pass it with each other's company?"

She appreciated his suggestion, particularly when she guessed his intention was actually to settle her nerves.

"Fine," she agreed. "Providing we stick to whispers that won't risk disturbing a possible visitor."

"Whispers it is, then." He stretched back on the blanket, turning his long form on his side with his elbow propped on the floor, cheek in hand. "So, to quote a line from an old Cary Grant movie: 'Tell me, how does a girl like you get to be a girl like you?'"

"Excuse me?"

"Chasing ghosts like this. Or, in this case, whoever is masquerading as one."

"Oh. Well, it was because of my father. He was a history professor."

"Was?"

"He died last year. We were very close, so his loss has been terribly hard."

Meredith paused. She seldom spoke of her relationship with her parents, particularly in regard to her mother. The circumstances were too private, too poignant. On the the other hand, there was no reason why Jackson shouldn't know about her special connection with her father.

"It's not unusual," she went on, "for that kind of closeness to result when one parent leaves and the other remains to raise their child. It was that way with my father and me. I went everywhere with him, including the Victorian bed-and-breakfast we stayed at in New England while he was researching a book. That's where it all started."

"And this was when?"

"Oh, I must have been eight or nine. Young enough to be susceptible to the tale someone told me about a ghost who haunted the old house. I woke up that night in the room where I was sleeping, convinced the ghost was there with me and absolutely terrified. My father came, and I'll never forget how he told me that, if ghosts do exist, we shouldn't be frightened of them. That they probably mean us no harm and if we could only learn to communicate with them, think how much we'd learn about the past."

"Made an impression on you, huh?"

"It wasn't what most fathers would tell their daughters in a situation like that, but my father was unique. And, yes, that was the beginning of my interest in the subject of ghosts. Of course, later on Rand was also an inspiration."

"Rand? Who's Rand?"

"Just a sort of friend who once helped a woman he cared about deeply to deal with what she was convinced was the ghost of her ex-husband." Careless of her to go and mention Rand when she had no intention of explaining her secret vice to this man. To forestall his possible interest in that direction, she changed the topic. "What about Jackson Hawke? What intriguing little tidbits can he tell me about himself and *his* family?"

His silence told her he wasn't about to be forthcoming about himself. Whatever mystery there might be in connection with him, and she felt there was one, he obviously preferred to safeguard it by turning the subject back to her.

"This interest in ghosts. Is that why you became a psychologist? So you could help people yourself to deal with whatever they think is haunting them, like your father helped you to understand it?"

"Well, I had intended to become a parapsychologist, but a psychologist seemed more useful."

Meredith was impressed by his perceptiveness. Why hadn't she recognized this quality in him before? And why hadn't she realized that, beneath Jackson Hawke's take-charge, sexy brashness, was a man who actually had potential as a friend instead of a rival?

That was before he went and spoiled everything she was beginning to like about him with a blunt "What does the psychologist have to say about her mother? And why didn't she tell me when we were hired for this case that her mother happened to be Lady Danely?"

Jackson had just trespassed on forbidden territory. What made it worse, Meredith thought, was her suspicion that he *knew* this was a subject she didn't want to discuss. But apparently that didn't matter to him.

"The pschologist has nothing to say about her mother," she informed him sharply.

"How about *to* her? Hell, Meredith, you're the one who's supposed to know all about human relationships. Can't you see she's hurting? I could see it every time she looked at you."

"You don't know anything about my mother. Believe me, she isn't vulnerable where her daughter is concerned."

"It's that bad between the two of you, huh?"

"Could we talk about something else, please?"

"Sure." He sat up on the blanket and leaned toward her provocatively. "How about us?"

"And here I thought you were a man who dealt only in realities. There is no *us*."

"Maybe not, but the other day outside your hotel, when I asked you to go to dinner with me and told you it was more than just business, I meant it. Hell, Meredith, I was thinking back in the States about asking you out. Would have probably if we hadn't always been at odds with each other."

"Why?"

"Why not? Could be we would have enjoyed each other's company, and neither one of us is attached. You *aren't* attached, are you?"

"No." And she hadn't been since Joe Cardoni, the sports broadcaster from whom she had parted amicably after realizing in the end that they'd had absolutely nothing in common beyond mutual lust. Meredith was not about to repeat that mistake, and where Jackson Hawke was concerned, it would be so easy. "Can we just forget it, because I've got to tell you this conversation is in danger of turning from whispers to shouts."

But Jackson wasn't about to let it go. He inched closer to her. So close that she could feel his warm breath on her face. "There," he said, his voice slow and husky, "this should guarantee that we keep it nice and soft."

She had the uneasy feeling it wasn't the volume of their conversation he was talking about.

"Where was I? Yeah, trying to tell you why I was interested in developing something between us. Think it could be because I happen to find you a damn desirable woman? Or maybe it's because I like the way that mouth of yours can go from tight and stubborn in one second to…well, let's just say a challenging invitation in the next."

She was in trouble here, Meredith thought. His own mouth was a scant inch or two from her own, and even in the weak glow of the moon she could see the mesmerizing fire in his eyes. Could feel the heat of his hard body so close to her own. Could almost hear the sizzle of his intention to kiss her. And if that happened—

But it must not happen. As much as she longed in this tantalizing moment to learn more than just his scent and his heat, yearned to know the taste of him, as well, to experience the flavor of his mouth on her own, she refused to be overpowered by his sensuality. Joe Cardoni hadn't hurt her. But instinct warned her that Jackson Hawke could, and seriously so, if she made the mistake of getting involved with him.

Meredith scooted away on the blanket just far enough to put a safe distance between them. "That might be nice. If," she added, "we didn't have a vigil to keep."

And weren't in conflict over the nature of this job, she thought. But she didn't have to put that part into words. He must have already understood this himself, because to her relief he surrendered the moment. Even in the dim light, she could have sworn there was a look on his face of a man who has just come to his senses after recklessly risking himself. It was an odd reaction.

All that mattered, though, was she was safe from the temptation of him. For now, anyway. She had the feeling they would get back to this subject again before their work here at Croft Castle was finished. And maybe the next time she wouldn't be able to resist him. Not with a man who was as relentless as Jackson Hawke was when it came to getting what he wanted.

"Not much of a vigil," he complained, "with nothing happening here. Look, I got a couple of hours of solid sleep this afternoon. I'm good for the rest of the night. But there's no sense in both of us staying awake. Why don't you just curl up and grab a nap? I'll call you if anything happens."

Sleep? There was absolutely no way she could go to sleep, not after that intimate interlude they had just shared. "Thanks, but I'm not in the least tired, either."

MEREDITH COULD FEEL herself smiling as she drifted slowly back to consciousness. An expression of her contentment, of course. And why not when she was so snugly warm within the folds of the blanket wrapped around her?

She didn't want to leave the cocoon. Wanted to go on being peaceful and drowsy. That was before she became gradually aware that her sensation of security wasn't entirely due to the blanket.

Someone else shared the cocoon with her. She felt his solid length pressed against her back in spoon-fashion, one arm draped protectively around her waist. Her serenity vanished when she felt something else that was hard and hot squeezed against her bottom.

Alarmed, Meredith freed herself from the blanket and bolted to a sitting position. The accusation with which she'd been about to blast her companion expired when he mumbled something without stirring. Jackson remained innocently asleep. Though if the evidence was to be trusted, he was still capable of an unmistakable arousal.

Shoot! She had no memory of nodding off, of having the spare blanket tucked around her. Well, around both of them as it turned out. So much for their claims that neither one of them was remotely sleepy.

How long had they been asleep? It was too dark to see her watch. The moon must have set, because even that pale light was gone. That meant it was very late, that hours could have passed. In which case, if anything *had* happened, they had missed—

Her self-reproach froze without completion.

The blackness was no longer black. Down at the far end of the tunnel that was the Long Gallery appeared a faint glow. Meredith sucked in her breath as the glow strenghtened, forming itself into a floating light that was attached to nothing. Because whatever was responsible for it seemed to be without any real substance. And soundless.

It was so chilling a sight that for a moment Meredith was paralyzed. And then, overcoming her fascination, she leaned over Jackson, whispering in his ear an urgent "We have company!"

He was instantly awake and, to her relief, fully alert, demanding no explanation. Scooping up the flashlight, he scrambled to his feet. Meredith rose beside him.

Swift and quiet though they had been, their presence must have been detected. The strange light, which was five or six feet above the floor, wavered and then stopped. For a moment it hung there, pulsing, as if cautiously listening. And then slowly it began to back away, retreating down the gallery.

"Oh, no, you don't," Jackson muttered.

He launched himself in the direction of the now rapidly fleeing light. And Meredith, not pausing to grab up the lantern, followed him. As fast as she was, his long legs outdistanced her.

There was no sign of the light now, not so much as a glimmer. It was so dark again that she didn't know where she was. She was about to call out when, with a startled gasp, she collided with a tall figure. A pair of strong arms reached out to catch her.

"Steady," Jackson whispered.

"Where are we? Why did you stop?"

"Because I ran out of gallery. This branch of it anyway."

He took her hand and guided it toward what he must have already felt himself. It was the corner of the wall where it turned a right angle into the shorter section of the Long Gallery. There was no glow around that corner. The light had vanished altogether.

"Either he's doused his lamp and is hiding down there," Jackson whispered, "or—" He broke off with a decisive "Get behind me. I'm going to risk the flashlight."

Meredith was too eager for results to argue with him. She permitted his body to shield her as he switched on the flashlight and swept its powerful beam along the shorter branch of the gallery. Peering around Jackson, she could see that it was hollow, empty.

"Gone," he said. "But where the hell did he get to? There are no exits in there, no doors at all. I made sure of that when I checked this branch earlier. There's only one way in and out of the Long Gallery, and we were camped next to it. So, unless he slipped by us in the dark, and I don't think he could have without our—"

"Jackson," she cut him off solemnly, "there is another explanation."

He immediately understood her. "No, Meredith, whatever the illusion of that light, it was not some disembodied wraith

able to pass through solid walls. Whoever is playing our phantom is real."

"You can't be certain of that."

"Wanna bet?"

He lowered the flashlight, aiming it at the floor in front of
them. And that's when Meredith saw it, a thread whose ends
had been tacked to the skirts of the paneling on either side and
then stretched across the width of the gallery several inches
above the floor. The thin barrier, invisible in the dark, was no
longer taut. It had been snapped in the center and now lay in
halves on the boards.

"A ghost didn't break that thread, Meredith."

This, then, was what he had been doing earlier in this wing
of the gallery—laying a trap for their nighttime visitor to prove
his human existence. It was a trick Meredith had used herself
on past occasions, and she couldn't deny the evidence of it.

"So where did he go?" Jackson wondered, registering his
frustration.

"Look," she whispered. "Down there."

There were three more tapestries hanging limply on the
paneled walls of the extension. A lower corner of the center
tapestry stirred slightly as they gazed at it, as if disturbed by a
current of air behind it.

"Gotcha," Jackson said with satisfaction.

Chapter Five

"Here, take the flashlight while I see what we've got." Jackson passed the flashlight to Meredith, adding a brusque "And keep back, will you. This clown could be behind there just waiting to leap out at us."

I swear, Meredith promised herself, *protective or not, if he barks one more order at me, I'm going to haul off and smack him.*

"Then be careful," she advised him, holding the flashlight while he cautiously approached the tapestry.

She watched tensely as he seized an edge of the dust-laden tapestry and eased it aside, as though he were lifting a flap. Even from several safe yards away, Meredith could see what the tapestry had covered. There was a narrow gap where a cleverly hidden door in the paneling had been left slightly ajar.

"He was in such a hurry," Jackson surmised, "that he neglected to close it tightly behind him. And then it must have drifted open, because I can feel a draft through the crack."

The same current of air that stirred the tapestry, Meredith realized. *If it hadn't, we wouldn't have known the door was there.*

Remembering Jackson's fixation with secret panels, she immediately amended that thought. *With or without the stream of air, he would probably have discovered the concealed door after tearing down every tapestry in the place and examining* the paneling until he found it, even if it took him the rest of the night. But this way—

Meredith caught her breath as he yanked so fiercely at the edge of the tapestry that one end of it was ripped from its hooks. It flopped down and out of the way, permitting them full access to the door.

Flattening himself against the wall beside it in readiness to handle any possible assailant, Jackson reached out and punched the door with his fist. The blow sent it squealing inward on a well of blackness. She was able to breathe again when nothing flew out at them, neither bats nor a phantom figure.

Jackson peered around the edge of the portal. "Looks clear," he reported.

Trusting that it was safe, she joined him at the opening. But the opening to what? she wondered, gazing into a sinister darkness that the beam of the flashlight did little to relieve.

"Guess I wasn't so wrong about secret panels in this old pile, huh?" he boasted.

"All right, we now know how he's getting in and out of the castle. And since you're so amazing, would you like to tell me who he is and what he wants?"

"Maybe I can before I'm finished. You want to wait for me back at the alcove?"

"You're not going in there after him!"

"Only way to learn the answers, which is why I'm here."

"And me," she reminded him. "Lead on."

"Meredith, you don't have to do this. I don't *want* you to do it."

She wasn't so sure herself whether she wanted to join him in that eerie blackness in pursuit of someone who could be desperate and dangerous. Maybe even armed. But she had agreed to help Guy and her mother, and if this was the only way…

"I appreciate your concern, Jackson, but it isn't your decision. And we're wasting time. Let's go."

She was afraid he would argue with her. Even more afraid

he might say something like, "It's your funeral." And considering where they were going, *funeral* was not a word she wanted to hear.

But all he did say after taking the flashlight from her was, "Then stick close to me. And whatever you do, don't let this door swing shut behind us. We don't want to get trapped in there."

Trapped was exactly what she did feel within seconds of following him through the opening and along a narrow, claustrophic passage located inside the walls of the ancient structure.

It was the kind of place that made Meredith think of every old movie melodrama she had seen, every Nancy Drew mystery she had read as a girl. A secret passage that smelled of damp and mold where a phantom could be lurking in the darkness, waiting to pounce.

It was also the kind of place you expected to never experience in reality. And yet here she was actually inside such a passage. Or, as it turned out, a whole bewildering maze of them. The thick walls of the castle proved to be honeycombed with passages and chambers.

After they had twisted and turned for several minutes, climbed and descended, Meredith whispered a worried "Do you have any idea where we are?"

"Kind of."

Which meant he didn't, and they were lost. That was bad enough, but she didn't care for the way the flashlight seemed to be growing dimmer. The batteries had to be weakening, making her wish she'd gone back for her lantern.

"If that flashlight quits, and we're in total darkness—"

"Don't worry," he assured her cheerfully, "we'll get out of here before then. Whoever built this thing would have provided it with entrances and exits, and we're bound to find one of them."

"Unless it was built to trap his enemies." Leaving them to rot into skeletons, she thought with a shudder. Fortunately, they encountered no skeletons or a lurking phantom, though there were no shortages of cobwebs and grime.

"Not likely. I think Guy was right about his ancestors and that some of them were involved in smuggling. This thing was probably built to hinder excise men in case of any surprise raids. They would have been so confused that the delay would have given the smugglers time to move their contraband and escape. And somehow our nighttime visitor stumbled onto what was lost and forgotten for a couple of centuries."

And has been using this maze to enter and leave the castle, Meredith thought. It was a plausible explanation, but if it was any of that old contraband he was searching for, there was no sign of it. All she and Jackson found in the chambers that must have once stored it were a few empty, abandoned casks, gray with age.

"You do realize," she pointed out, "he must be long gone by now."

Making this a useless pursuit, she thought, but she didn't say it. Jackson was so convinced of results he had them pause every few minutes to listen for any sound of their quarry. But all they heard were the faint whispers of the chilled air that streamed along the passageways, which were like echo chambers for them. It made the drafts sound like hushed, mournful voices.

"I know it's silly," she confessed, "but I feel these currents are talking to us. If only we could understand—"

"Listen!" Jackson interrupted her sharply, holding up his free hand for silence. "Hear it?"

"What? I don't— Yes!"

And she *could* hear it now, the unmistakable sound of activity somewhere below them. The beam of the flashlight in Jackson's hand cut a swath through the darkness in front of them, revealing the corner of another shallow stairway several yards away around the curving wall of the passage.

"He hasn't left the castle," Jackson whispered. "He's down

there messing with something, which means he doesn't know we're here. This is my chance to take him."

"Jackson, no! This is too dangerous! He could be just waiting to ambush us!"

"Not you, Ms. Allen. You're waiting right here. Don't worry, I'll come back for you. Just stay where you are and keep still."

"Jackson, don't you dare—"

Too late. He was already gone, his long legs carrying him swiftly out of sight around the bend. And since he had taken the flashlight with him, leaving her in complete blackness, there was no way she could go after him. Not without risking her neck on a dark stairway.

Damn the man for abandoning her like this! She spent a moment silently cursing him for his reckless action and then a much longer moment worrying about him.

What was happening down there? She could see nothing, hear nothing. She strained her ears, but there was no noise at all. Not until eternal seconds later did she detect a far-off, startled yell followed by a muffled curse and the sounds of what must be a struggle. Then silence again, total and ominous.

Meredith waited for a few tense seconds more before—unable to bear the stillness any longer—she called out an alarmed "Jackson!"

It was rash of her to betray her presence like that, to risk an attack in the darkness. She didn't care. She had to *know*. But not even the whispering air answered her this time.

What if Jackson was lying unconscious down there? Hurt and in need of her? She had to go to him! If only she had brought that lantern! But as it was...

There was no help for it. She would have to feel her way. Not by groping blindly, either. The wall. She would use the wall to guide her.

But when she placed her hand flat against the wall on her left, she encountered moisture that must have seeped through the stones. It made a slimy sensation against her palm. Never mind. Vile as it was, the contact was necessary.

She found she could tolerate the oozing wall as she moved forward, taking care not to stumble over the uneven surface of the floor. What was less easy to withstand was the fear that, in the tradition of one of the those old melodramas, a pair of hands would reach out from the inky blackness and close around her throat.

Don't be a fool, Meredith. You stand a better chance of taking a nasty tumble down those stairs.

Where was the flight of steps? Shouldn't she have reached it by now? She had felt the wall curving around to the left in the direction of the stairway. Wait a minute. Hadn't the flashlight indicated that the passage swung off to the *right* and that the stairs were located there? No, she must not have remembered correctly, because her toe suddenly felt the edge of the first step.

Careful now.

Keeping her hand on the wall, she slowly descended the shallow flight. When she judged that she was about halfway down, she paused to listen again. Silence.

"Jackson," she whispered, "where are you?"

There was still no answer, nor any sound of breathing except her own. And something else. There was no light. Shouldn't she have seen the glow of Jackson's flashlight by now?

Summoning her courage, she went the rest of the way down. The passage turned here, like a gallery in the blackest of caverns. And that's when she heard it! Not the whisper of the moving air or the noise of a scuffle. This was something else.

For a moment, she was unable to identify it. And then she realized what she was hearing was the faint, but unmistakable, boom and hiss of the surf. It was coming from somewhere beneath her, slow and steady. What's more, she swore she could smell the sea.

Did this portion of the passage overhang the sea? Perhaps, but even so, how could she so clearly hear and smell it through the thickness of the wall? Unless...

Excited by the possibility of an opening, either a door or a window, Meredith moved forward in search of it. And paid the penalty for her carelessness by dropping feetfirst through a gap in the floor.

Crying out in terror, scrambling to save herself, she managed to halt her plunge by locking her arms over what felt like a pair of parallel timbers. After the painful jolt of this jarring contact, it took her a horrified moment to fully understand the situation. The planks, between what must be a pair of joists to which she clung, had evidently rotted away, leaving an opening in the floor. From the waist down, there was nothing between her and the surf far below.

Her plight was a serious one. She couldn't go on hanging here. Her arms were already tiring with the effort of supporting herself. Nor could she trust the joists not to collapse under the stress of her weight.

Gymnastics had never been her strength. And that was just as true now as she exerted her dwindling energy in a desperate attempt to lift herself out of the hole. But no matter how she strained and squirmed, eyes squeezed shut with the effort, she was unable to lever herself over the lip of the gap.

What are you going to do, Meredith? What can you do to save—

She gasped, her eyes flying open to the gleam of a light. And the equally startling pressure of a pair of arms, which had reached down from somewhere behind her to encircle her waist like a steel band.

"Stop wriggling," commanded a deep voice.

She did, and within seconds she was dragged out of the hole and deposited on a solid section of the floor. When she had recovered her wind, she found her rescuer hunkered down beside her. He had retrieved the flashlight from where he had placed it on the boards and was using it to check her for any signs of injury.

"You all right?"

"A little tender under the arms, but that's all. Not like Joanna, who had practically the same thing happen to her and ended up in the hospital."

"Joanna, huh. Would that be another friend like the mysterious Rand?"

"You could say that, I guess. Thank you for coming to my rescue."

"You're welcome, and why didn't you wait where I left you?" Jackson demanded.

"Why didn't I— Listen, from what I heard, I thought maybe you were the one who could use some help."

"Yeah, well, I didn't. I would have had the bastard, too, if he hadn't knocked the flashlight out of my hand when he jumped me from behind. I had him pinned down, but without a light, he managed to give me the slip in the dark. By the time I found the flashlight and got it working again, he was gone and you were yelling."

"Did you get a look at him?"

"Not a glimpse."

"Too bad." Meredith looked around. "Where are we, anyway?"

"Another chamber, I guess. How did you wind up here?"

"By trusting the wall I was holding onto in the darkness. Big mistake. It looks like it led me down the wrong passage."

Jackson played the flashlight in a slow arc. "And into a dead end. Come on, let's see if we can't get out of this maze before these batteries quit altogether."

They were threatening to do just that, Meredith realized as they retraced their route to the other chamber where Jackson had battled with their visitor. There was another passage here along which he had apparently escaped. It sloped steadily downward as they followed it.

"We must be at ground level by now," Jackson said.

"And still not out of here, and if that flashlight gives out—"

"It already has."

Meredith came to a stop. "You're right. There's a glimmer but it isn't from the flashlight."

"Daylight. It must be finding its way through cracks in the masonry."

Along with the outside air, she thought. No wonder there were drafts in the passageways. "Daylight already?"

"This time of the year the nights aren't all that long at this latitude. And we spent a good chunk of this one curled up together on that blanket."

Meredith didn't want to be reminded of that treacherous episode. She quickly changed the subject as they moved on, just in case Jackson should be in the mood to discuss the intimacy they had shared. "Are you sure our man came this way? Because if this isn't the route to an exit, I don't relish going back."

"I don't think we'll have to. Look up ahead. That's more than just a glimmer."

It was true. There was a glow of daylight in front of them that strengthened as they advanced, promising the end of the passageway. Meredith hesitated as they approached the rectangle of light.

"What if he should be waiting out there?"

"Not a chance. He's long gone by now. He wouldn't want to risk daylight and being recognized. All the same, you wait here and let me check it out."

"You are *not* abandoning me again. If you're worried, just lead the way, and I'll follow at a safe distance."

She did, and when she caught up with Jackson, who signaled that it was all clear, she found him at the end of the tunnel where it spilled over into an enclosed pit a few feet below them and several yards in diameter.

"That's where the light is coming from," he said, indicating a crude iron grille that covered a hatch on the opposite side of the pit.

The hatch, just above the bottom of the circular pit, wasn't large enough to admit anything like a strong glow. But after the darkness of the passageways, even this dim light seemed intense. And very welcome to Meredith, as was the pit itself when she and Jackson climbed down into it.

She felt as if she had just emerged from the depths of a coal mine, even though she was still at the bottom of its main shaft. That was what the lofty tower, whose stone walls rose around them on all sides, felt like.

"What is this place?" Jackson wondered, gazing up into the hollow gloom.

Meredith had learned enough about castles from her father to know exactly where they were. "A garderobe."

"And that would be?"

"You don't want to know."

"How bad can it be?"

"Well, let me put it this way. A garderobe was the medieval answer to plumbing."

"You mean we're standing at the bottom of—"

"Exactly what you think, yes. And that hatch over there allowed whatever poor soul was assigned the duty, to get in here and periodically clean out the contents of the pit."

"Handy."

"I imagine our phantom thought so, too, when he somehow discovered it."

"Yeah, it has to be the way he's been getting in and out of the keep. Let's see if it will do the same for us."

Jackson went to the iron grille and tried it. It swung open with little effort. A moment later, to Meredith's immense relief, they crawled through the hatch. Though the garderobe must have been abandoned for centuries, it definitely had an unpleasant connotation, and she was glad to put it behind her.

They found themselves on the floor of a shallow well that

had permitted access to the grille. Its rim was overgrown by shrubbery that had concealed the existence of the sunken hatch.

The sight of the sun, just beginning to peek over the horizon, was so brilliant after the long darkness of the maze that Meredith was blinded by it as they clambered out of the well. Jackson helped her to her feet.

She shivered, hugging herself against the chill air of the morning but glad to be in the open again. "It's early, but with any luck Imogen will be up and in the kitchen. Otherwise, I don't know how we're going to get back inside the castle."

"We'll rouse someone to open up."

They found a path that led in the direction of the restored wing at the front of the castle. Meredith remembered something as they followed it.

"You said our phantom was messing with something down in that chamber. Any idea what it was?"

"I think he must have been testing the walls."

"What for?"

"To see if there might be something behind them. Whatever he's hunting for, he hasn't found it yet or he wouldn't have kept coming back to the keep."

"Well, right now all I'm looking for is a hot shower."

"And I want a telephone."

She turned her head, gazing at him in surprise. "You're going to call someone at this hour?"

Jackson nodded. "A friend in London. He won't thank me for getting him out of bed, but I need what he might be able to give me. If he can provide it," he added mysteriously, "we could have some idea what's going on here."

And for the moment that's all a frustrated Meredith could get out of him.

Chapter Six

"Fine weather this morning."

"Yes, it is," Meredith agreed.

Having showered away the grime of last night's ordeal, stolen another hour of sleep and changed into clean slacks and a fresh top, she had come down from her room to be met by Imogen passing through the lobby with an empty tray in her hand.

Pleasantries exchanged, Meredith waited for the cook to move on. But Imogen continued to stand there, blocking her route.

"Nice change after the nasty stuff we've been having. Warm, too, which is why."

Meredith had already decided that Croft Castle's cook might be a treasure, but she was also an eccentric with a habit of approaching her topics in an oblique manner.

"Yes?" Meredith inquired, thinking there might be a message here.

"Why I've served up breakfast on the terrace," Imogen said with a suggestion of impatience, as though it shouldn't have been necessary for her to explain this to Meredith. "Lord and Lady D are already there. Know the way, do you?"

"I think so. Through the dining room, isn't it?"

"Right. I'm off to my Aga, then. Mind you watch the French door. Has a habit of sticking if you don't give it a good tug."

Imogen hurried off in the direction of her kitchen, leaving Meredith to find her way through the dining room. The French door opening onto the terrace required no attention. The view past the low stone wall rimming the edge of the terrace, with its mass of potted geraniums, did. It presented an eye-filling sight, the sea far below a crinkled blue chart spreading to the horizon.

Hard to credit the reality of all this sun-washed magnificence after the evil in the castle. Particularly on the heels of last night, Meredith thought.

Guy and her mother were seated at a glass-topped table. They traded cheerful good mornings with her when she joined them, but she could see they were anxiously waiting for her report.

"What can I give you?" Judith asked, indicating the array of covered dishes on the table. "Imogen has provided us with a full selection."

"Just coffee, please. We had something in the kitchen earlier when Imogen let us into the castle."

"Yes," Guy said. "I'm afraid you gave her a bit of a start when you rapped on the window like that."

"I'm sorry about that, but with the doors all locked we had no other choice."

"Jackson not with you?" His gaze traveled in the direction of the French door.

Meredith shook her head. "I knocked on his door before I came down, but there was no answer. It was a long night, so I suppose he could be catching up on his sleep and just didn't hear me." But she wondered about that. It wasn't like him not to have been alert to a summons. She also wondered about that phone call he'd wanted to make.

"A long night," Judith said, sounding tense, hopeful, "and you ended up outside the keep. Does that mean…"

"That it was more than just a long night, yes. It was an eventful one, as well."

Between sips of her coffee, Meredith went on to recount their vigil in the keep and the events that followed. Her mother and Guy ignored the eggs growing cold on their plates while they listened intently. She ended her tale with a reluctant admission.

"It looks like Jackson was right about the mischief in the castle. Most of it, anyway, must have been the work, not of a ghost, but of whoever we chased through that maze. I suppose his furtive activities were meant to ruin you. If you were forced to close your doors and go away, he'd have the opportunity to search the place without fear of discovery. Exactly what he's looking for we have yet to learn. Assuming this is all more than just theory, that is."

Guy frowned. "I blame myself," he said. "If I had thoroughly explored the keep, I might have found those passages myself, and all of this needn't have happened."

Judith reached across the table and placed a reassuring hand over her husband's. "Darling, it isn't your fault. You've been so busy trying to make a success of the hotel, there hasn't been time or thought for anything else."

"There is certainly one thing I can and will see to," he said decisively. "That hatch to the garderobe must be sealed to prevent this blighter from ever using it again."

But Meredith feared his action wouldn't be enough to discourage their stealthy intruder. That he would find some way to go on searching for what he so earnestly wanted until he found it. And if there was any possibility…

She hated to bring it up when Guy already had enough to worry about, but she had to know. "There's something I've been meaning to ask about the keep," she said as casually as possible. "Are there any cellars underneath? You didn't indicate anything like crypts or a dungeon when you toured us through the keep yesterday, but there must have been a place for the original kitchen, and I didn't see any sign of it."

"Well, you wouldn't have. It was the custom when the keep

was built to locate the kitchen in a separate structure. One imagines the arrangement was meant to prevent the risk of fire and objectionable cooking odors. Most of such buildings have long since vanished, often without a trace, and that seems to be the case here at Croft."

No cellar, then, Meredith thought. But the smugglers who had constructed those passageways must have had some secret means of moving their contraband in and out of the keep. The hatch in the garderobe surely couldn't have been sufficient for that, and yet she and Jackson had discovered no other entrance into the maze. She'd have to ask Jackson what he thought.

Ask Jackson? Just when did you start thinking of the two of you in terms of a team?

But Meredith didn't want to examine this baffling, potentiallly dangerous riddle. Or to keep wondering where he had gotten to, as though he was starting to mean more to her than he should mean. Damn the man for his talent of insidiously stealing into her imagination.

Guy glanced at his watch and got to his feet. "We have a yardman who comes up from the village twice a week. He should have arrived by now. I'm going to get him on to sealing that hatch, and then I'll attend to recovering your things from the Long Gallery."

"But you've hardly touched your breakfast," Judith said.

"No time, love."

Meredith was grateful for his preoccupation with the hatch. It kept him from questioning her interest in a possible cellar. Had he stopped to think about it, he might have realized she was checking for any other way in and out of the keep that could be used by their adversary. And she didn't want Guy being concerned about something that was no more than speculation at this point.

Either her intuition or her training in pscyhology, perhaps a combination of both, must have suggested to her that Guy was vulnerable. She knew she was right after he hurried away and her mother leaned toward her, confiding her own concern.

"I worry about him. His health isn't good, but he refuses to rest. He suffers from angina, which is why…"

"What?"

"It's so imperative," she implored, "that you and Jackson solve this trouble as quickly as you can."

A life and death situation? Is that how her mother saw it? Meredith didn't realize the matter was this urgent.

"We'll certainly do our best," she promised Judith. "Is Guy at serious risk?"

"He could be. He's having more tests next week to determine if there's been any damage since his last visit to the doctor. It's all the stress, you see. Losing the family seat in Devon was hard on him, and now there's all this new trouble, along with the drain on our finances. He wouldn't thank me for telling you this, but we've already had to part with several of the more valuable heirlooms we brought with us to Croft."

"I'm sorry," Meredith said. "I can't speak for Jackson, of course, but as far as any fee for my own service is concerned, I don't want you to think about it. If we're successful with our investigation, and after you've had a chance to get back on your feet…well, we'll see."

"That's very good of you." Judith hesitated before confessing, "But I'm afraid Guy wouldn't accept such an arrangement. He's so terribly proud. It's essentially why we've avoided calling in the police. There are no officers here on the island. If anything serious happens, the police have to come from Trefarro on the mainland. That always causes a stir, and Guy fears the publicity."

"I understand."

More than I want to, Meredith thought, unable to help her pang of resentment. Her mother was capable of this total devotion to her husband, and yet she had demonstrated none of that devotion to her daughter. Had, instead, walked out on her when Meredith had been scarcely old enough to remember her. But she did remember Judith, or at least the hurt of not having her there while she had been growing up, and that was the problem.

Did Judith sense what she was feeling? Was that why she tried now to soften the strain between them with a quick "As anxious as I am for you to clear up this trouble, I do want you to be careful. It could be very dangerous."

"We'll be cautious."

Judith nodded, was silent for a moment, and then surprised Meredith with a sympathetic "I was sorry to hear about your father."

"Thank you," Meredith said, but she was unable to elaborate on what his loss meant to her. It was too personal, too private when this woman was, after all, almost a stranger to her.

Judith made another effort. "I want you to know, Meredith, that in spite of everything, I've always been very proud of your achievements."

"How could you—"

"Your father. Didn't you know that he kept me informed of your progress with regular letters and snapshots? It's why I was able to recognize you on that television program."

No, Meredith didn't know. This was a complete surprise. Why hadn't her father told her that he had maintained contact with her mother?

Would it have made a difference if she had known? Would mother and daughter be able to share something now other than this cautious, polite conversation?

Talk to her.

That's what Jackson had urged last night in the Long Gallery. And he was right. Meredith did need to have a frank discussion with her mother about things that had to do with separation and forgiveness. Or, in this case, an inability to forgive. Was the moment ripe for making an effort to mend those old hurts?

Meredith would never know, because that moment was lost to them when the missing Jackson suddenly appeared. There was nothing ordinary about his arrival on the scene.

Even Judith caught her breath when he loped into view around the corner of the building. As for Meredith's own response…well, if she hadn't already been seated, her need to do so would probably have betrayed her reaction to the sight of him.

Dressed in nothing but running shoes and a pair of brief, black shorts, he was magnificently masculine with a sheen of perspiration on his broad shoulders and naked chest. He trotted up the steps to the terrace and came to a halt.

Meredith couldn't take her eyes off of him as he bent over, planting his big hands on the knees of his muscular legs, gulping mouthfuls of air in an effort to recover his wind. She watched the sweat trickling from his underarms and down his temples from the thatch of his tousled, dark hair. And against her will, she thought of that sensual interlude they had shared last night in the Long Gallery and how the very scent of him had left her weak and vulnerable.

Did Jackson guess how the tantalizing sight of him like this affected her? Is that why he lifted his head and grinned at her knowingly? Damn him for his conceit.

Ambling across the terrace, he turned one of the chairs around at the table and straddled it, revealing a pair of hard thighs. Perspiration had pooled in the hollow of his throat where a pulse beat a rhythm that was potently erotic. Meredith forced her eyes away from the expanse of all that slick flesh.

"Excuse my appearance, ladies," he apologized. "Running down and back up that mountain out there was tougher than an obstacle course."

No wonder he hadn't answered her knock on his door, Meredith thought.

"Which explains your disappearance," Judith said. "Can I get you some breakfast?"

Jackson shook his head. "Don't want to spoil my appetite. I was thinking Meredith and I would have an early lunch down at the inn."

Risking her composure, which seemed to suffer every time she looked at him, Meredith gazed at him in surprise. Lunch in the village? What was this all about?

"That is," he added, "if our absence won't upset any plans."

"Of course not. I'll just let Imogen know there will only be Guy and me for lunch. Excuse me." Judith rose from the table and headed for the French door.

Watching her go, Meredith didn't know whether to regret a lost opportunity or to be relieved that she had another reprieve from a conversation with her mother that was bound to be difficult. But sooner or later…

"You get a chance to fill Judith and Guy in on everything that happened last night?"

Meredith turned her attention back to Jackson. "Yes. Guy is off seeing about getting that hatch permanently sealed. And what's all this about lunch at the inn?"

He leaned toward her, resting his bronzed arms on the back of the chair. "The more I think about it," he explained, "the more convinced I am that what's been happening here is connected somehow with the past. This is a chance to learn about that past by checking out the locals, asking a few questions and hearing what they can tell us. But if you don't want to join me…"

"It's my investigation, too."

"Great." He pushed himself to his feet. "Give me an hour. I need a shower and a change. I also need to call London back. My contact up there should have had time by now to dig up what I asked him for."

That mysterious communication with London. Was he ever going to explain it to her? Apparently not at this moment since he turned his back on her and strode toward the French door, affording her a view of his tight shorts molded to a mouthwatering, male backside.

Jackson paused at the door, looking over his shoulder with a teasing "You find any more ghostly messages on that bathroom mirror of yours?"

She gave him no answer. Chuckling, he went on into the castle. He left Meredith wondering about the wisdom of accompanying him to the village.

"THEY'RE SO BRILLIANT they almost hurt my eyes to look at them!"

But Jackson wasn't looking at the banks of rhododendrons that made a solid wall along the side of the road. He was far more interested in the way that angelic face of Meredith's positively glowed with enthusiasm as she stood there admiring the masses of flowers that covered the shrubs.

She fascinated him when she was like this. Hell, she fascinated him in any mood, and if he didn't watch himself—

A bee zoomed past her ear on its way to the blossoms. Jackson watched Meredith lift a hand protectively to her head, her fingers absently combing through her hair. He would like to sift through that silky halo himself.

Face it, given half the chance, he would bury himself in more than just her hair. Starting with her sweet mouth and moving on to her small, but lush, body. Oh, yeah, he had some very hot fantasies about that body. They involved those smooth arms and legs wrapped around him while she went all wild under him. He could get hard just thinking about it, so urgent was his desire for her.

What are you doing, man? Is your memory so poor you've forgotten what can happen if you go on getting yourself worked up over her like this?

But this isn't Chicago, and Meredith isn't April Paulson. Maybe you don't have to be so worried. Maybe you and Meredith could get together without someone getting hurt.

Don't be an ass. Someone always gets hurt.

There was no way around those memories, he realized. Not when a woman like Meredith would demand more than just lust in a relationship. She would want honest, genuine emotions. Deserved them. And where his track record with commitment was concerned, he didn't know if he was capable of such emotions.

Besides, she didn't trust him. Well, why should she when he was keeping secrets from her? Meredith was intelligent. She must have sensed he hadn't been entirely open with her. He would be, though. He would share with her everything he'd been withholding, only not just yet. Not before he was reasonably certain she wouldn't turn and run when she heard those secrets. Because he needed her here. Without her, Judith and Guy might not let him go on with the case.

If only this yearning for her wouldn't keep getting in the way. It was an ache that seemed to be getting worse. And complicating it was her awareness of him. He hadn't missed her interest, either last night or earlier this morning on the terrace.

"Absolutely luscious," Meredith said.

To his foolish regret, Jackson knew she was still talking about the rhododendrons and not any portion of his anatomy.

"Have you ever seen flowers so deeply red? I wouldn't have believed—" She broke off and turned to him apologetically. "I'm sorry. I forgot."

She was referring to his color blindness. "It's all right, Meredith. You don't miss what you've never had."

"Yes, that's what they say."

The way she said it, with a kind of sadness, made him wonder if she was thinking now not about his color blindness but about her mother.

They moved on, in no hurry to reach the village. It was still early, probably another half hour or so before they could expect to get lunch at the inn. Rounding a bend, they stopped again where a pair of pine trees framed a view of the harbor below.

"Beautiful, isn't it?" Meredith murmured. "It's hard to believe there could be evil in a place like this."

She had given him the opening he'd been waiting for. It was time to unload the one secret he could safely part with now. If you could call it a secret.

"You ready to hear about those two phone calls I made to London?"

"Phone calls? Oh, yes, I forgot about them."

"Uh-huh."

She laughed, a throaty sound that had his guts tightening. Damn, the woman did things to him without trying.

"All right," she confessed, "so I've been dying to know."

"I didn't think there was any point talking about it unless I got some results, seeing as how the subject has been, uh, a little contentious where you and I are concerned."

"Edward Atheling," she said without hesitation. "Does that mean—"

"Don't get excited. This has nothing to do with ghosts. I'm talking about history, which is the specialty of my source in London. He works in the research division of the British Museum, where he has access to ancient documents. I asked him to dig up what he could for me on Edward Atheling."

"Why, if you don't believe in him?"

"In his ghost, Meredith, not the man himself. I never questioned the reality of his existence in—what century was it?"

"The tenth. Go on."

"I wanted to try to verify what Guy told us about him in connection with Croft Castle and what bearing, if any, that might have on the present. Turns out that Edward Atheling *did* die at Croft. And get this. One of the records claims that Prince Edward had a casket of royal jewels with him when his ship landed on the island. The casket disappeared after his death."

She stared at him. "Are you saying…"

"I'm still speculating at this point, Meredith, and that's all. But what if this part of the story is more than just fiction? What if that casket exists and was concealed somewhere in the old keep?"

"And *that's* what our culprit is searching for!" She was thoughtful for a few seconds. "But the casket wouldn't have to actually exist if—"

"Whoever learned about it *believes* it does. Right."

"A fortune in lost jewels. I suppose it's possible." She was silent again, gazing down into the harbor where a sailboat was heading for the open sea. "If this is the explanation, Jackson, that puts us one step closer to the solution. I just hope we can get all of the answers before my mother and Guy have to close their doors. I think that financially they're even worse off than they're willing to say."

Jackson could relate to their need. Though he didn't want Meredith to know it, he was dealing with his own desperation in that area.

"Amen," he said to himself.

THEY WERE STROLLING along the cobbled lane of the picture-book village, with its ivy-clad cottages and bow-windowed shops, when Meredith came to a sudden halt.

Jackson was puzzled. "What is it?"

"I don't believe it!" she said. "It isn't possible!"

They had stopped outside a shop that looked to Jackson like a combination of post office and general store. Something on the other side of its front window had captured her attention. With a little squeal of excitement, she parted from him without explanation and dashed into the shop.

What in the name of—

Concerned, he followed her into the shop. When he caught up with her, she was standing by a rack from which she had seized a magazine. "It's true!" she said. "My eyes weren't playing tricks on me!" Her fingers were actually trembling as she held the thing reverently in her hands.

"A magazine? You had me wondering if I was maybe going to need my martial arts training over just a magazine?"

"It isn't just a magazine. It's an *American* magazine, and to find a current issue of it in England in a remote—"

"Meredith," he interrupted her in disbelief as he looked down at the magazine over her shoulder, "this is a digest for soap opera fans who want to catch up on the episodes they've missed. You can't possibly be interested in it."

When her only answer was to stubbornly tighten her grip on the magazine, Jackson realized she was serious about her discovery.

"Don't tell me," he groaned. "You're *one* of them."

She swung around and confronted him defensively. "All right, so I'm a psychologist, and I have an addiction to a soap. There's nothing wrong with that because whatever the critics say, the soaps deal in their own way with universal truths about people."

"Wait a second. Let me see that thing." Without waiting for her permission, he snatched the magazine out of her hand to peer down at the young couple featured on its cover. "Joanna and Rand from *Beautiful and Reckless*," he read. "Characters in a soap? *These* are the friends you were talking about last night?"

Jackson lifted his eyes to meet her gaze accusingly. But Meredith was no longer looking at him. She was staring at something behind him.

"He's watching us," she murmured.

"Who?"

Mystified, Jackson looked over his shoulder. At the far end of the shop was the gaunt figure of a man somewhere in his early thirties. He wore walking shorts, a camera bag slung over one bony shoulder, and a surly expression on his narrow face.

"He isn't watching us. He's examining that display of film."

"He was watching us before you turned your head," Meredith insisted. "I think he followed us into the shop."

"What makes you say that?"

"Maybe because I noticed him when he passed us out on the street a while ago. And even then…"

"What?"

"He was eyeing us. Not a very friendly kind of eyeing, either. I don't know why he should be interested in us, but I just have a funny feeling about him."

Jackson knew there was nothing he could do about the guy. Whoever he was, he had a right to be in the shop, and there was no law against staring. In any case, the fellow had turned around and was on his way out of the shop.

"Forget about him," Jackson said. He knew that she wouldn't. To be honest about it, neither would he. Not entirely anyway. Not if it should turn out that they had a genuine reason to be worried about the stranger. But for now...

"Come on, buy your magazine and let's get out of here. I'm hungry. And stop looking at me like that. I'm sorry if I was less than tolerant about your secret addiction." Actually, he was pleased. Surprising or not, it added another interesting depth to a woman who, wisely or not, appealed to him more with each passing hour he spent in her company.

He checked the street in both directions when they came away from the shop, but there was no sign of the gaunt figure.

JACKSON WONDERED HOW many inns in England were called the George. A lot of them from what he had observed since he had arrived in the country. It must have been a popular name when these old inns were founded, and this one was no exception.

Nor was the George a disappointment when he and Meredith entered the place. The bar, which served pub lunches, boasted a wide hearth, a low ceiling crossed by heavy oak beams and the requisite settles and dartboard on one wall.

Jackson knew inns to be promising sources of local information, and he was hoping that would hold true here. Maybe from the landlord himself. He was tending the bar when they arrived. A burly, balding man with a ruddy complexion and a generous smile, he had the hearty manner that American visitors expected in English innkeepers and didn't always find.

"Colin Sheppard," he introduced himself. "Welcome to the George. Always glad to see new faces, we are. What can I get you?"

Not the useful information he and Meredith were looking

or, Jackson realized. The bar was already beginning to fill up. He knew that Colin Sheppard would be too busy serving his customers to talk to them. Maybe later.

They ordered the plowman's lunch, cider for Meredith, and a pint of the local brew for Jackson. Taking their drinks with them, they seated themselves at a corner table to wait for the arrival of their lunch.

They were barely settled when a young woman with what Jackson thought from the brightness of her hair had to be red hair, and with more freckles than he could remember having seen on anyone, wandered over to their table.

"You're the American couple Lord and Lady D have staying up at the castle, aren't you?"

"We're not a couple," Meredith hastily corrected her, to Jackson's amusement. "We're just both here at the same time. I'm Meredith Allen and this is Jackson Hawke."

"A pleasure, I'm sure. Lord and Lady D may have told you about me. Gwen Sparrow? I clean for them three mornings a week. Do some cleaning for a few others on the island, too."

This is more like it, Jackson thought. A cleaning woman who got around and looked like she wouldn't mind sharing what she knew. "Can we buy you a drink, Gwen?"

"Now that's real friendly. Not like some Yanks I could mention." She jerked her head in the direction of a table near the door. "Keeps to himself, that one does."

Jackson twisted his head around to discover that Gwen Sparrow was referring to the man with the brooding face who had been staring at them back in the shop. At the moment those hollow eyes seemed to be interested in nothing but the glass of ale over which he was hunched.

When had he turned up? Jackson wondered. Was he haunting them or was his presence just a coincidence? After all, it was a small village with only one inn, and he was entitled to be here.

"A fellow American, huh? Is he planning on being here long on the island or just passing through?"

"I couldn't say, I'm sure. Calls himself a nature photogra
pher and carries that camera everywhere, but he doesn't seem
to point it at much, and with all the sea birds around—"

"You know his name?"

"Now, one of the girls did mention it when he registered here
at the inn. Wallace, I believe it is. Archie Wallace."

The name wasn't familiar to Jackson. He sought Meredith'
gaze across the table. She answered his silent inquiry with
slight shake of her head that indicated she had never heard the
name, either. The hostile Archie Wallace was a subject that
might bear investigation, but he was a subject that would have
to wait.

"So, Gwen, how about that drink?"

"I wouldn't say no to a half pint." Jackson had risen to hi
feet with her arrival at their table and was prepared to head fo
the bar. But she forestalled him by hailing a passing barmaid
"Here, Sheila, a little service, if you please."

When Gwen had been installed at the table, her drink deliv
ered along with their lunch of thick, crusty bread, cheese, slab
of ham and generous portions of fruit, Meredith turned to her

"How do you like working at the castle, Gwen?"

Jackson applauded Meredith's studied nonchalance, know
ing it was meant to elicit the kind of information they were both
looking for.

"Lord and Lady D are ever so nice, but that cook of their
is a silly old trout." She leaned toward them, lowering her
voice to a confidential level, although she couldn't possibly b
overheard with all the buzz of talk in the now crowded room
"Mind you, I wouldn't go anywhere near the place after dark
Not with all that's been happening up there. Gives me the
willies just to think about it. Well, it would, wouldn't it?
mean, having a ghost like that."

"Have you ever seen any sign of Edward Atheling?" Mere
dith asked her, spearing a chunk of melon with her fork.

Gwen looked blank.

"That's the name of the ghost who's supposed to be haunting Croft Castle. He died there centuries ago."

Jackson wished Meredith would forget about all this talk of ghosts so they could concentrate on the real problem at Croft Castle. The flesh and blood one. But he could have hugged her a moment later when her pursuit of the subject unexpectedly paid off.

"I wouldn't have gone back if I had," Gwen said. "Imagine a bloke hanging around after he's in the grave." She sipped her ale thoughtfully. "Ages ago, you say? Well, I wouldn't know about that. But if it's that kind of thing you're after, you want to go and talk to Simon Boynton. Always digging up old muck about the island, our Professor Boynton is."

"What kind of stuff?" Jackson questioned her, tucking into his lunch.

"Ancient lore, he calls it. Forever writing papers about it since his retirement here. I'm sure I don't know who'd want to read them, and I nearly told him as much the day I tried to dust this moldly old volume on his desk. That office of his is a rare treat to clean, anyway, what with stacks of files everywhere and a typewriter that should have gone to a museum, but you'd have thought the bleeding thing was the crown jewels the way he carried on so when I picked it up."

"What kind of book?" Jackson pressed her.

"I wouldn't know, now, would I? In Latin, he said it was, and he was translating it into English. Must be something about Croft, or he wouldn't have it. Ask me, it belongs on the fire instead of locked up in that bookcase where he mostly kept it."

"Why do you say that?" Meredith asked her around a mouthful of ham and cheese.

Gwen shook her head. "Dunno. It just made my flesh crawl touching it."

Jackson made up his mind. "How do we find Professor Boynton?"

"His cottage is at the end of the lane down around the next

corner. You'll know you're there by the two yews out front clipped up like a pair of guinea hens. Look out for Sybil, though."

"And that would be?"

"His daughter. Nasty when she's in the mood, and she mostly is. Hates having to live down here and wishes she had the money to go back to London. She can have it. I got out of the place myself because it's too bleeding expensive. Well, cheers." Gwen lifted her glass and drained it.

Twenty minutes later, Meredith and Jackson were back out on the street and headed in the direction of Simon Boynton's cottage.

"Will he or won't he?" Meredith pondered out loud.

Her question needed no explanation. Jackson understood what she was asking. "If Boynton is any kind of authority on the history of Croft Island, and we're enthusiastic enough about his work, he'll talk to us. Whether he'll be willing to part with anything useful is something else."

Meredith nodded. "My father could be sensitive about his research."

"How about ancient books? Was he reluctant to discuss those? Because I'd just love to know what's so important about this one and why Boynton is guarding it."

Chapter Seven

Like all of the buildings on Croft Island, the cottage was stone with a slate roof. Nothing distinguished it from its neighbors except for a front door painted a cheerful blue and a pair of topiary guinea hens flanking a wooden gate opening onto a flagged walk. As Gwen Sparrow had promised, the hens identified the place as the Boynton cottage.

Meredith could hear a woman's voice as they neared the front door located at one end of the small building. It sounded harsh and demanding and seemed to come from inside the cottage itself. Puzzling, since the door was closed and all the windows along the front were shut. She decided the voice must be drifting through an open window around the side.

Seizing the knocker, Jackson rapped smartly on the door. There was a brief silence, and then the door was jerked open. A young, dark haired woman stood there inside a small entry, her hand over the mouthpiece of the phone she was holding.

"What is it?" she barked without a greeting.

She'd be attractive, Meredith thought, if she didn't have that scowl on her face along with too much makeup. The makeup and her clothes seemed far too sophisticated for a place like Croft Island. Was this Simon Boynton's daughter, Sybil? Must be.

"We'd like to see Professor Boynton," Jackson explained.

"My father isn't here."

"When do you expect him back?"

"I wouldn't know, I'm sure. He's up in Truro involved in more of that bloody research of his at the library there. Might be back tomorrow."

She was impatient to have them gone, clearly wanting to get back to her phone call.

"We'll try then."

"Suit yourselves." Without bothering to ask their names, she shut the door in their faces.

Before Meredith could express her opinion on the rudeness of Sybil Boynton, Jackson dragged her around the corner of the cottage. His finger at his mouth signaled his desire for her silence.

He *wouldn't*, she thought.

But knowing Jackson's brashness when it came to getting what he wanted, she shouldn't have been shocked by his intention to eavesdrop on what sounded like an urgent phone conversation.

"No, I don't expect you to turn up here at the cottage. I know better than that."

Meredith had been right. A window, beside which they flattened themselves against the wall, was cracked wide enough to permit them to overhear Sybil inside the cottage.

"Meet me along the beach by those big rocks. We won't be seen there. Yes, of course, after dark. When can you get away?"

There was a pause in which the speaker must have suggested a time for their rendezvous.

"All right, ten-thirty. And you'd better be there."

There was an unmistakable threat in Sybil Boynton's parting words. The silence that followed indicated she had ended the call. And Meredith couldn't get away from the scene fast enough.

Fearful of being observed from one of the cottage windows, she cut through an opening in a tall hedge at the side of the property, trusting that Jackson was close behind her. He was, and he halted her flight on the other side of the hedge.

"Slow down. She can't spot us here."

It was true the hedge now screened them from view, but Meredith wouldn't feel safe until they reached the lane and put distance between themselves and the Boynton cottage. Which they did a moment later, and only then was Meredith willing to talk.

"That was a risky thing to do."

"Yeah, but informative."

"You wouldn't have thought so if she had discovered us out there and called the police."

"From the tone of that phone conversation," Jackson said, "I somehow don't think the sour Sybil would have done that."

Meredith had to agree that there had definitely been a secretive quality about the conversation. "Whatever it was about, I don't see it has anything to do with us and our investigation."

"Maybe. Maybe not. But you could hear the determination in her voice even before she opened the door to us."

"Yes, and it could have been the determination of a woman desperate to meet her lover. Possibly a married lover, which would explain why they'd have to meet in secret. And don't tell me I've been watching too many episodes of *Beautiful and Reckless*, because that's just what it sounded like."

"Oh, there was a show-up-or-else threat, all right, but that could have meant a whole lot of something besides romance." Jackson was quiet until they rounded the corner into the high street, and then he turned to her with an enthusiastic "You up for another evening of on-the-spot investigation?"

Meredith looked at him suspiciously. "What does that mean?" And then it occurred to her what it *did* mean. "If you think I'm coming with you down here tonight to spy on Sybil Boynton's meeting with—"

"That's not a mystery that interests me, Meredith. Except for how it affects the mystery that *does* interest me. Or have you forgotten why we called at the Boynton cottage?"

"To ask the professor about the book Gwen Sparrow told us about, of course. But since Simon Boynton won't be back be-

fore tomorrow, I don't see what one has to do with the other."
And then suddenly she *did* see, and she was appalled by his
proposal. "You can't be serious! Eavesdropping is one thing,
but to break into that cottage while Sybil Boynton is off somewhere on the beach—"

"It's an opportunity too good to miss. Hell, that book might
contain what we're looking for. Just think about it, Meredith.
The key to unlocking the secret of Croft Castle."

"It's in Latin. I don't know about you, but it's not exactly a
first language with me."

"Yeah, but he's translating it into English. The manuscript
must be there in his office, and I want a look at it."

"It's a long shot and I don't want any part of it."

"Suit yourself."

They were silent as they left the village behind them and
began to climb the lane back to the castle.

He's reckless, Meredith thought. He's just asking to be
caught. The whole thing was irresponsible.

*But suppose he does find something, and you're not there
to share in it? He'll be impossible if he ends up solving the case
himself. Anyway, no one promised you there wouldn't be risk
in this investigation. There's always a certain risk in any of
your cases, isn't there?*

"I suppose I don't have any choice but to come with you,"
she relented. "You'll need someone as a lookout."

"Right" was all he said.

They were silent again. Meredith wished she could silence
another voice. The one inside her head that taunted her with a
much more provocative reason for surrendering to his intention to invade the Boynton cottage tonight.

*Admit it, having Jackson Hawke's company on that adven-
ture in the keep last night was exhilarating. And you don't
want to miss out on sharing another one.*

She was a fool. She'd been a fool last night, and she was being
one right now to be so aware of him walking close beside her.

He had changed out of his shorts for their visit to the village, but his outfit was still far too revealing. Jeans that hugged his hips and a black T-shirt molded to his chest and powerful shoulders. She had noticed how the other women in the inn had eyed him, had caught Gwen Sparrow admiring him.

Meredith knew he couldn't help how he looked, but did he have to dress like this? As if he was deliberately using every opportunity to take advantage of her growing weakness for him. A weakness that, with the vast differences between them, could go nowhere.

She was glad when they reached the castle. It was a chance to put distance between herself and temptation. That was before her gaze was captured by the crumbling stone figures of the angels mounted high on the parapet above them. She could detect no sign of movement among them today, but their presence made her uneasy. Why had Lord Danely's ancestor placed them there facing the old keep? What vile, ancient thing were they meant to guard against?

"WANT TO JOIN ME?" Jackson asked, his hand on the knob of his bedroom door.

His invitation was issued in a voice so slow and husky that Meredith was angry. Not with him but with herself for being so susceptible to him that she actually found herself considering his seductive offer. Until reason kicked in, that is.

"You never give up, do you?"

"I love that wicked mind of yours, Meredith."

"What's that supposed to mean?"

"That my invitation was an innocent one. I don't know about you, but at some point early on in my investigations, I like to get everything on paper."

"Why?"

"Helps me to understand what I've got so far, what I don't have yet and what I ought to be doing to get it. It's time for me to sit down at my desk in there and do that. I just thought that, since we're both working on this case, my notes could benefit from your contribution. But, hey, if you've got something else in mind for us, I could be persuaded—"

"Very commendable, but you might have explained all this before you asked me to join you in your bedroom."

He laughed softly, and she knew his omission had been deliberate. "So, are you interested?"

"Yes, I believe in organization. But I intend to make my own notes in my own notebook in my own bedroom. Maybe we can compare later on. See you at dinner?"

Not waiting for his answer, Meredith parted from him in the hall, went into her bedroom and closed the door. She had lied to him. Although she did have a notebook in her luggage, it was her practice to record everything on tape. Which she could be doing now, since she had also brought a pocket recorder with her.

But until Jackson's suggestion, the idea hadn't crossed her mind. Nor was she in any mood to be professional now. What she ought to be doing, she told herself, was sitting down with her mother for that discussion she kept avoiding. There had been no sign of Judith or Guy when they let themselves into the castle, but her mother must be somewhere nearby.

But Meredith made no effort to go and find her. Later, she promised herself, while at the same time reproaching herself for her cowardice. Knowing it was fear because of what she might hear from her mother. Or what she might say herself.

What did she so often urge her clients to do? Trust. Yes, well, it was one thing to offer that psychological advice when you weren't personally involved. And quite another to apply it to yourself.

Better lie down then and try to catch up on your sleep. You'll need it if you're in for another late-night session chasing after answers with Jackson.

But Meredith knew she was far too restless to sleep. Maybe the wind was responsible for that. It had risen again and was moaning around the old walls of the castle. A sinister sound that she knew was capable of playing tricks on the imagination.

Meredith understood better than anyone how the mind could deceive when circumstances and setting fostered it. Was she a victim of such conditions herself? Had she gone and convinced herself of the presence of Edward Atheling at Croft Castle simply because she wanted to believe it? Was that why she prowled around the bedroom now, unnerved by the wail of the wind because it seemed to be a voice calling out to her? And had that message scrawled on her bathroom mirror yesterday only been some form of illusion, as Jackson had implied?

If all of this was true, then it was time for her to dispel her fantasies. Starting with that mirror.

Marching into the bathroom, Meredith leaned over the sink and gazed closely into the glass.

Come on, Edward. If you're here, talk to me.

But as forcefully as she willed it, no communication formed itself on the glass. There was nothing there but the reflection of her own face. She watched the determined expression on it relax as it turned into a look of disappointment, altering finally to reluctant acceptance.

So she had been wrong after all. There was no ghost.

Well, since she was here anyway, she might as well start being practical and make use of the sink. The palms of her hands, sticky with the perspiration of her nervous effort, could use a wash.

Meredith turned on the taps, lathered her hands with the bar of scented soap, scrubbed them clean, and dried them on the hand towel. The action was symbolic somehow. Feeling as though she just made a fresh beginning, she automatically glanced into the mirror to check her hair. And was startled into a gasp by the reflection of Jackson's face gazing over her shoulder.

She hadn't heard him. He must have arrived while the water had been running. Meredith swung around to confront him.

"You might have knocked instead of sneaking up on—"

There was no one there. Jackson was not standing behind her. She was alone in the bathroom. A quick glance through the open doorway indicated an empty bedroom. The door to the hall remained closed.

What on earth—

Heart pounding, she whirled around to face the mirror again. The image was no longer in the glass. Gone! The only reflection there was her own, her face suddenly pale, visibly shaken.

Dear God, what had she just experienced?

Trembling now, Meredith sank down on the lid of the commode. She sat there in stunned silence, struggling to compose herself, striving to sort it out.

Had she been hallucinating? No, the face had been there, all right. She was sure of that. Clear and real. Jackson's face.

Or one close enough like it to be his double, her mind whispered to her.

The image had been a fleeting one, but she tried to remember details. The features had been the same as Jackson's. Strong, good-looking. But the hair— Yes, the hair might have been different. Longer maybe, more untamed. There was something else. Blue. She had the impression of a blue garment, maybe a kind of tunic. Jackson never wore anything but charcoal or black.

What did it mean? Who had she seen in that glass?

Her shock receded, and in its place was rooted a suspicion that grew into a near certainty. But was it possible? Yes, why not? It had to be the explanation, and what's more she had the feeling there was a way to confirm it.

Coming resolutely to her feet, Meredith left the bathroom and her bedroom and crossed the hall to Jackson's room. Had she stopped to think about it, she might have validated her next action with the excuse that surprise is the best method for obtaining results. In her excitement, however, she was wasn't thinking at all. Which was why she burst into his room without pausing to knock. And ended up being the one who was surprised.

She found Jackson emerging from his own bathroom and in the act of reaching for his robe, which was draped over a chair. He was completely naked.

Brief though the sight of him was before she spun away, her cheeks flaming as she turned her back on him, Meredith knew the hot image was burned forever into her brain. For the rest of her days she would see him like that, all splendid, well-endowed male.

Jackson himself seemed in no way troubled by the situation. "Change your mind about joining me?" he drawled, not bothering to conceal the underlying meaning in his chuckle that followed.

There was a tightness in her throat that had her croaking her apology. "I'm sorry, I thought— Why aren't you working at your desk? You said you'd be working at your desk."

"I will be. After I get dressed. I took a shower."

"Didn't you already take a shower this morning?" Did the man have an obsession about being clean?

"I do my best thinking under a hot spray. Revives the brain. Okay, it's safe now."

Meredith faced him again. Even though he was clad now in the robe, with its belt snugged securely around his waist, her memory of the hard body that was just beneath it left her unsettled. But still determined.

"Let's have it," he said.

"And what would that be?"

"Whatever it is that had you rushing in here like this."

"I'm not hiding anything, but I think you might be," she challenged him. "I've just had a demonstration of Edward Atheling's presence."

"Another one?" he said, one of his thick black eyebrows lifting skeptically. "What was it this time?"

"Something much more interesting than a warning." She went on to tell him about the face in the mirror.

He was thoughtful for a few seconds, and then he nodded slowly. "All right, let's not argue about it. Let's suppose this vision was more than imagination. How can you be sure it was the ghost of Edward Atheling?"

"I can't be certain, of course. Except for one undeniable thing."

"Which is?"

"What I haven't told you yet. That face in the mirror, Jackson, was a dead ringer for you. Would you care to offer an explanation for that?"

His face registered no emotion. But his silence was answer enough.

"It's true, isn't it?" she said, unable to help the note of triumph in her voice. "You're a descendant of Edward Atheling. And what's more, you knew he was your ancestor, didn't you?"

"A *possible* ancestor," he conceded.

"More than just possible. The resemblance, even after all these centuries, is so remarkable it can't be just a coincidence. I knew you were holding back something from all of us, and this is it."

"Yeah, well, my mother will be happy to hear it."

"What has your mother—"

"She's into genealogy. Claimed we were descended on her side from the lost king, Edward Atheling."

"And that's what brought you to Croft Castle."

"That is *not* what brought me to Croft Castle, Meredith. A case that needs solving brought me here, and I would appreciate it if you would keep this ancestor-of-my-family stuff just between us."

He's embarrassed about his connection to ancient royalty, she thought. That's why he kept it a secret.

"It has nothing to do with the case," Jackson insisted.

"I think it does. I think Edward is still trying to tell us he's innocent and that he wants his descendant to find the actual culprit. If you'd had a receptive mind, he would probably have shown himself to you to prove his existence and not to me."

Jackson shook his head. "You're forgetting what Guy told us."

"Which is?"

"Edward liked women." His voice deepened to a husky drawl. "And if he *is* still hanging around the place, I'd say he has damn good taste in his choices."

When had he closed the distance between them? Meredith wondered. He was standing so close to her now that she could feel his warm breath caressing her face. She could have backed away. She didn't. She was mesmerized by those cobalt blue eyes that held her own gaze like an embrace.

"Remember what else Guy said?"

She shook her head.

"That Edward had carnal appetites. And you know what, Meredith?" He leaned into her, his voice slow and raspy now, his mouth hovering just above hers. "I think I've inherited them."

She should have stopped him. Why didn't she stop him? Too late. His mouth was no longer hovering. It had swooped, a hawk capturing its prey. And Meredith was that willing prey.

His kiss was light and easy at first, his lips teasing hers with lazy nibbles. And then it deepened, becoming a hungry business that involved his tongue stroking hers, his hands skimming the sides of her breasts while he groaned with pleasure.

Meredith responded with an equal abandon, her senses on fire as she inhaled the clean scent of him, tasted him in her mouth all hot and wet. Felt his demanding hardness squeezed against her as she melted under his onslaught.

The long searing kiss threatened to escalate into something so urgent there would have been no retreat from it. She was actually on the point of burrowing inside his robe, running her hands over his strong, naked flesh, when he abruptly ended the kiss. To her dismay, he pulled away from her, as if cautioning himself that she was a risk. The loss of him was immediate and disappointing. Wise, yes, but hard to bear when she still longed for him.

"Lady," he growled, "you just dazzle the hell out of me."

Meredith might have responded with a confession of her own about what that wicked mouth of his did to her. Instead she murmured something inane about seeing him at dinner, turned and walked away.

She went back to her own room in a daze. Shutting her door and leaning against it weakly, she thought about Jackson and his kiss. Why had he suddenly rejected her like that and then turned around and said what he had about her dazzling him? It didn't make sense. Unless he was as confused as she was about their feelings for each other.

On the other hand, is it just possible that those differences between the two of you aren't so vast after all?

For a moment she stood there dreaming about that, her lips still tender from his attention. It was when she became aware those lips were curled in a silly smile that Meredith went rigid.

What are you thinking?

Of course, they were wrong for each other. Wrong in every way. Weren't they rivals? Didn't he scorn beliefs that were vital to her, the very fabric of her life? And wasn't he forever exasperating her with his take-charge attitude?

Besides, she didn't trust him. He kept things from her, was sneaky. Like that kiss. She saw it now for what it probably was. Damn! Jackson Hawke had gone and effectively sidetracked her from a subject he hadn't wanted to discuss.

Or had that been his intention?

THE COTTAGE WAS DARK. No light in any of its windows.

That was good, Meredith thought. It meant Sybil Boynton had left and was on her way to her meeting on the beach.

What wasn't so good was the moonlight. It was bright enough that Meredith feared one of the neighbors might spot them crouched here in the shrubbery checking out the cottage.

Jackson must have sensed her uncertainty. "Nervous?" he whispered.

She made the mistake of turning her head and looking at him. His white teeth gleamed in the treacherous moonlight, evidence of the grin he wore. She didn't mind his amusement. It was the sight of his mouth that bothered her. That sinful mouth had been haunting her ever since their kiss that afternoon.

"Of course I'm nervous," she admitted. "You'll have to forgive me. I'm not used to breaking the law. Look, could we just get on with this before someone catches us out here?"

"Looks safe enough. Let's go."

Keeping to the shadows as much as possible, they crossed the garden to the back door of the cottage. Meredith welcomed the small, vine-covered porch that sheltered the entrance here. It helped to conceal their presence.

"Just how do you plan on us getting in?" She had chosen not to question him about this particular little problem until now, fearing he meant to force a door or break a window.

"By turning the knob and walking in. I'm thinking that in a village like this people probably don't bother locking their doors." He gripped the knob and twisted. It failed to yield. "Guess the Boyntons aren't the trusting sort."

"You didn't really expect them to be, not if he has valuable old books in there. Now what?"

"Plan B."

He plunged his hand into one of the deep pockets of his lightweight jacket, but it was too dim on the porch to see what he extracted. "What's that?" she whispered.

"A picklock."

Either Jackson Hawke was a very resourceful private detective, or else he had a history she didn't want to hear. One that involved burglary. "I hope you know what you're doing."

"Relax. I can tell this lock is one of those old models. They're not much of a challenge."

"Will you need the flashlight?" She knew he had equipped it with fresh batteries, but she prayed they wouldn't have to risk it out here.

"It's a question of touch, not sight. Just give me a minute here."

That minute seemed to stretch into an eternity as Meredith, listening tensely to the soft rattle and scrape of the tool in the lock, waited for a result.

"We're in," Jackson finally announced with satisfaction.

And sure enough, the door had soundlessly, miraculously drifted open. But on what? Meredith wondered, gazing into the well of blackness beyond.

Jackson had to have better night vision than she did, because he drew her inside without hesitation, shutting the door behind them.

"Where are we?" she asked. There was a small window, and the moonlight stealing through it revealed bulky shapes, but she wasn't able to identify them, even after her eyes adjusted to the darkness.

"Looks like what the English call a scullery. Try not to bump into anything. I don't want to use the flashlight unless we have to. This way." He led her through a doorway into a larger room. "Ah, this is better."

And it was. There were more windows there, generous ones that allowed Meredith to see they were in the kitchen. Jackson had paused to get his bearings. That's when Meredith heard it. Or thought she did. A noise that, for want of a better definition, sounded like a soft clicking. It seemed to come from somewhere overhead.

"Hear it?" she whispered, clutching at his arm.

"What? I don't hear anything."

"Listen!"

They stood there in a taut silence while Meredith, with the breath stuck in her throat, wondered if the cottage was deserted after all. Maybe Sybil Boynton was still here. Or maybe her father had returned unexpectedly.

"Meredith, there isn't anything."

It was true. The cottage seemed to be perfectly still now.

"Come on," he said, "let's find that office."

He preceded her through a swing door into another room. It had to be a dining room, she thought. In the moonlight she could see the sheen of polished pewter on the shadowy outlines of a Welsh dresser.

They were starting toward another doorway, this one opening onto a passage that led to the front of the cottage, when Meredith heard it again. A series of slow, rhythmic clicks. Unmistakable this time and sounding like they were headed their way from the floor above them.

"There! You can't tell me you don't hear a clicking this time!"

"Meredith, it's a grandfather clock. Probably on a landing around the turn of what looks like a stairway down there at the other end of the hall. These old clocks can sound like Big Ben in an empty house."

She wasn't so sure he was right. She could have commented that Rand had made a similar, smug judgment in an episode of *Beautiful and Reckless*, and that he and Joanna had paid the penalty for his error. But she knew Jackson wouldn't appreciate any more analogies from her favorite soap opera.

All right, so she was imagining things.

Except it turned out she wasn't, as they both learned a moment later. They had prowled a short distance along the passage, where Jackson paused to check out a sitting room off to the right, when the clicks grew louder, closer. And then stopped.

Meredith plucked at his sleeve with a whispered, "Your grandfather clock just walked down those stairs."

Pulling back from the sitting room doorway, he swung his attention in the direction she indicated. "What are you—" he started to ask, and then froze.

Wisely froze, just as she had done. They stood there staring at the two eyes that glowed at them out of the dark. Jackson couldn't know it, but they were the fiery red that only an animal's eyes could reflect at night.

They belonged to a massive hound. Moonlight seeping

through a small window at that end of the passage picked out the shape of him. Meredith remembered what Guy had told them about the demon dogs Sir Hugh Gwinfryd kept at Croft Castle. Dogs that legend claimed were gifts from Satan. This one confronting them was so terrifying he could be one of those hounds from hell. Maybe was, for all she knew.

Would he attack them? They were strangers who had invaded his home. He probably would, though he had growled no warning yet. Like them, he remained motionless and alert at the foot of the stairs. But that changed in the next second. He began to advance toward them slowly, his nails clicking on the bare floor boards. Making the same sound Meredith had heard from the start.

"Stay behind me!" Jackson ordered, stepping protectively in front of her, shielding her with his body.

Meredith would have preferred that they turn and run. But Jackson was probably right to hold his ground. Not only would flight have been an invitation for a frenzied assault, it was unlikely they could have made it to safety.

She could feel Jackson's body, which was pressed against her, brace itself. Trembling, she waited for the savage howl that would signal the animal's charge as it launched itself at the target that was Jackson's throat.

What she heard instead was the rumble of low laughter. And what she felt was Jackson's body slowly relax. He'd been gripping the flashlight in his hand, probably intending it as a weapon of defense. Now, switching it on, he shaded its glow to prevent the light from being observed outside.

"It's safe to look, Meredith."

She peered cautiously around his bulk. Their enemy was down on his haunches in front of Jackson, his tail thumping on the floor in accompaniment with his soft whimper. The gleam of the flashlight identified him as a Great Dane.

"Some watchdog you are. What? You want your belly scratched?"

The animal had rolled over, presenting his underside. Jackson hunkered down and accommodated him. The Great Dane was ecstatic.

"That's lovely," Meredith pointed out, "but do you, uh, think we could do what we came here to do before Sybil Boynton returns and finds you and her dog bonding?"

Obliging her, Jackson stood. The Great Dane sprang to attention, prancing happily out in front as he led them down the hall. As if understanding what they wanted, he trotted straight to a door opposite the stairway. It opened into what had to be Professor Simon Boynton's office.

The Great Dane would have kept them company inside the room, but Jackson gently nudged him away. "Sorry, fellow. You'll have to wait outside."

Looking mournful, the dog took up a post at the foot of the stairway as they entered the office, shutting the door behind them. Jackson had turned off the flashlight, plunging them back into semidarkness.

"We'll never manage a search in here by moonlight," Meredith said. "Do you think we can risk a lamp if we close those drapes at the windows?"

Jackson agreed. Seconds later, with the heavy drapes tightly drawn, they located a lamp on the desk and switched it on. There were other lamps in the room, but they didn't dare to use that much light. Meredith was sorry about that. They might have helped to make the place less sinister, though she doubted it.

The office was cluttered with an assortment of strange collections that gave her the creeps. Prints on the walls that depicted dark, gothic ruins, grotesque masks ranged along the fireplace mantel, a shelf with stuffed birds whose eyes seemed to stare at her menacingly.

"Cozy," Meredith said.

Actually, it was. Where the temperature was concerned, anyway. The room was warm. Glowing embers on the hearth indicated a recent fire. Odd, since Boynton wasn't here and his daughter had planned to go out.

"Don't like the looks of this," Jackson said. He was crouched down in front of a glass-fronted bookcase, examining the lock on the door that stood ajar. "It's broken, forced open."

Meredith remembered Gwen Sparrow telling them Professor Boynton kept his valuable volumes, including the ancient one they sought, locked in a bookcase.

"What are you saying? That someone was here before us and took the book?"

"Maybe. Or maybe his daughter had some reason to break the lock and help herself to it. Not that it would have done us much good if it's in Latin. It's that translation we want. Let's try the desk."

They looked through the papers stacked beside the old upright typewriter, searched the drawers, but nowhere was there any sign of the professor's translation of the book. Nor did a cabinet beside the fireplace yield the manuscript.

"Gone," Meredith said. "Do you suppose the professor took it with him?" Though that wouldn't account for the broken lock, she thought.

Jackson didn't answer her. He was crouched down again, this time in front of the fireplace. She watched him extract a tiny scrap of charred paper from the side of the grate.

"What is it?" she asked.

"All that's left of what I think might have been a carbon copy of the manuscript. It has that fuzzy look of carbon. And look at this." He held the scrap out to her. "See them? The words *Croft* and *Gwinfryd* down here in the corner."

"Meaning?"

"There was a reason why there was a fire built here. Someone used it to destroy the carbon of that manuscript. Maybe the original of the translation along with it. Or else he took that with him together with the book itself."

"We can't be certain of that."

"No, but it all points to that. Which means whatever the book and the translation contain is dynamite."

Meredith shivered. "Could we get out of here now and talk about this somewhere else? There's an aura in this room I just don't like, not to mention that Sybil could come back at any second and find us here."

"Give me a few more minutes. There's a couple of places I still haven't searched. If you're worried, keep a lookout at the door."

"Hurry, then."

Meredith took up a nervous post by the door, cracking it so that she would be able to listen for any sound at the front door. The crack disclosed the sight of the Great Dane stretched out at the foot of the stairway, head on his paws. She could hear Jackson moving around the office behind her. Then there was a long silence.

"What's taking you so long?"

She turned her head to find him in front of one of the two windows. There was a wide window seat there they hadn't earlier investigated. He was standing over it, holding the hinged lid up in one hand as he gazed down into the cavity below it.

For a moment he didn't answer her. And then, his attention still focused on what the window seat contained, he said slowly, "You don't have to worry about Sybil Boynton coming back. She never left the cottage."

Chapter Eight

"What are you talking about? Are you telling me—"

Meredith was unable to finish her question, and Jackson damned himself for saying anything at all. Even in the weak light and with the width of the office between them, he could see the horrified expression on her face as she understood what his words implied. Why hadn't he waited to inform her of his discovery until he'd closed the lid and taken her out into the hall, away from the scene of atrocity.

"Meredith, don't!"

But he was too late to stop her. She had already swiftly crossed the room, needing to see for herself what was stuffed inside the window seat. He would have lowered the lid, but she prevented that, her hand closing insistently over his.

For a long, appalled moment she gazed down into the window seat. It wasn't a sight for anyone with a sensitive imagination.

The welt on Sybil Boynton's throat indicated she must have been garroted with some kind of cord twisted around her neck. Her tongue protruding from her mouth was evidence of how she had gasped for air during the final seconds of her strangulation. And her eyes...well, they were still open, staring up at them in frozen terror.

"That's enough!" Jackson said, his voice unintentionally gruff with anger over the brutality of the woman's death.

"But shouldn't we..."

He understood her whispered plea. "Meredith, she's beyond our help."

Freeing his hand from her grip, he slammed the lid on the window seat and turned to her. She looked awful.

"Come on, let's get you out of here."

Arm around her waist, he led her out into the passage, hooking his foot around the edge of the door and pulling it shut behind them. The Great Dane scrambled to his feet, seeking their attention.

"Not now, boy." Poor thing. He hoped the animal hadn't been devoted to Sybil Boynton. "You going to be okay?" he asked Meredith.

"Yes," she murmured.

Jackson released her, but he could see she wasn't okay at all. She leaned weakly against the wall. He would have put his arms around her, as much for comfort as support, but she waved him away.

"Please, could we just go?"

"Meredith, we have to call the cops."

"I know, but let's find a phone somewhere else. I can't—can't bear to stay here."

He nodded. Though he'd brought his cell phone with him from London, it hadn't been working when he'd tried to call his friend this morning at the British Museum. He'd been forced to use the phone in his room up at the castle, but now…

He made a decision. "The inn is nearby. They'll have a phone there, and you could use a drink if we can beg one." Hell, they could both use a drink.

She waved her hand in the direction of the dog. "What about…"

"He's all right. Probably used to being left on his own."

Jackson realized that someone would have to care for the animal until Simon Boynton returned, but that could wait.

Meredith offered no objection as he ushered her through the cottage and out the back way. He didn't bother trying to relock the door behind them. The cops would need to get in when they arrived. They weren't going to like it when they learned how he had picked that lock and entered the cottage. Yeah, well, he'd deal with that, too, when the time came.

The lighted windows of the George were a welcome sight when they reached the inn a few minutes later. A young man, who from the looks of his uncertain gait must have put more than a couple of drinks under his belt, emerged from the entrance. He nodded to them as he passed them in the street.

Jackson thought he looked familiar. And then he remembered he'd been the pilot of the launch that had brought them to the island.

They encountered another familiar face in the lobby of the inn. An unfriendly one this time. He was coming down the stairs from the guest rooms overhead, but he stopped midway on the flight when he saw them. He stared at them with that surly expression on his face, and then he swung around abruptly and retreated up the stairs.

The American photographer, Jackson thought. The cleaning woman had told them his name. Archie Wallace? Yeah, that was it. Well, Wallace wasn't important. Finding a telephone was all that mattered. There was no one at the front desk, but the barroom off the lobby was still lighted.

No patrons there, though, when they entered the place. The sole occupant was Colin Sheppard, who was behind the bar loading glasses onto a tray. Jackson knew that Meredith needed to sit down. She didn't argue when he parked her at a table.

"I'll try not to be long," he promised her.

The bluff landlord greeted him with a smile when he approached the bar. "If it's drinks you're looking for, sir, I'm afraid I can't serve you. After hours, you see, and the English pub laws are strict about that."

"It's a telephone I need more than anything."

Jackson's manner must have telegraphed his urgency. That,

and the forlorn sight of Meredith over at the table, had the land-lord immediately concerned.

"Is it a medical problem, sir? We have a doctor retired to one of the cottages out on the edge of the village. The old gentle-man no longer has a practice, but in an emergency—"

"This isn't that kind of emergency," Jackson grimly inter-rupted him. "This one requires the police."

Without asking for an explanation, the landlord promptly placed a telephone in front of him on the bar. Jackson appreci-ated his restraint, though he knew the man must be as curious as hell. Well, he would find out soon enough. The murder of Sybil Boynton would be all over the island by tomorrow.

"That would have to be Trefarro, sir. No constable here on Croft."

Colin Sheppard gave him the number and then discreetly left him alone to make the call, disappearing into the back regions of the inn with the tray of glasses. Jackson was returning the receiver to its cradle when he reappeared a few moments later.

"All right to wait here in the barroom? I was instructed we weren't to leave the inn until the police arrive. And, uh, is there any way you could make an exception about those drinks? We could really use them."

"You're welcome to the barroom, sir. As for the drinks—" He glanced in Meredith's direction, an expression of sympa-thy on his ruddy face. "I can't sell you the drinks, but you can have them without charge. If they should ask, mind you tell the police you were served before hours. Would a couple of bran-dies do, sir? Brandy is the ticket if it's a pickup you need."

"Colin, you're a prince."

Jackson carried the drinks over to the table where he had left Meredith. She looked less shaken, but he was still worried about her. "Here, get this inside you," he said. He slid the brandy toward her after seating himself across from her with his own brandy, though given a choice he would have pre-ferred bourbon.

She lifted her glass and drank, shuddering as the brandy went down. Jackson swallowed a healthy measure of the fiery stuff himself and then looked at her. "Better?" he asked.

She nodded. "I'm sorry for being a wimp, but it was such an awful shock."

"Yeah, murder usually is."

"Did you get the police? What did they say?"

"That it may take them a while to get here. There can't be much serious crime in this part of the country, which probably means they'll be calling officers out of their beds. Not to mention having to launch a police boat at this hour."

"So we're in for a long wait." She paused to sip more brandy. "They're not going to be very pleased with us, are they?"

"No, we could be in trouble."

"Do you think we'll be suspects ourselves?"

"Considering how we got into the cottage and what we were doing there, I'd say the CID isn't going to rule us out."

"Then we'll just have to convince them we couldn't have killed Sybil Boynton, that it's more than likely the lover she was supposed to have met on the beach did it."

Jackson shook his head. "I don't think there ever was a lover, Meredith." And why, he wondered, angry with himself, hadn't he attached more importance to that phone call they had overheard? Sybil Boynton might still be alive if he hadn't waited until now to figure it out.

"Then who was she meeting?"

"The guy she was blackmailing."

Meredith stared at him.

"Okay, so it's all just speculation at this point, but it makes sense if you think about it. Remember what Gwen Sparrow told us about Sybil? How she hated living down here and wanted money to get back to London?"

Meredith nodded slowly. "And there was the threat in her voice when she was arranging to meet him. All right, that makes a good argument for a case of blackmail. But blackmail about what?"

"Whatever is in that book."

"Convince me."

Jackson watched her tip her head over to one side in that habit she had whenever she was listening intently to someone. He hadn't stopped liking this little mannerism of hers. And a few others, as well, all of which were going to sidetrack him if he didn't watch himself.

"Suppose," he said, concentrating on a possible scenario, "Simon Boynton stumbled onto something awesome when he was doing the translation of that old book. Something he had a reason for sharing with his daughter's killer."

"Like what?"

"Like knowledge of a treasure hidden in Croft Castle."

"The jewel casket?"

"Could be."

"Go on."

"Let's say Sybil Boynton happened to read her father's translation, possibly without his knowledge or permission, and immediately realized the value of what she learned."

"And decided in her father's absence to blackmail her killer," Meredith said, following Jackson's scenario. "Which has to mean she also discovered the identity of the man—assuming it is a man, that is—her father shared his secret with."

"Correct."

Meredith shook her head. "But what did she have to blackmail him about? The secret itself wouldn't be reason enough."

"It would if he's the one who's been searching Croft Castle, and she threatened to expose him if he didn't pay up. That translation implicates him somehow, Meredith, or he wouldn't have taken both it and the book and burned the carbon. Whatever it is, it has to be worth a lot to him."

"So valuable," she said, looking sick at the memory, "that he murdered Sybil Boynton to protect his secret. Yes, all of it could have happened that way."

Jackson watched her raise her glass to finish her brandy.

Then, changing her mind, she set it down again. There was a frown on her face.

"Except for one thing. If the book does describe a treasure in the castle, why would Simon Boynton tell someone else about it? Why not go after it himself? Or why wouldn't his daughter look for it instead of risking blackmail?"

Jackson shrugged. "I don't pretend to have all the answers yet, Meredith. It's only a theory at this stage, but I still think it's a solid one." Or was it? he wondered. There was something about that legendary jewel casket that was beginning to feel not right to him.

Meredith didn't respond this time. He guessed she was keeping an open mind, a quality that probably made her a good psychologist. Well, he could respect that.

Jackson polished off the rest of his own brandy, checked his watch and got to his feet. "Think I'd better use that phone again to let Guy and your mother know what's happening. As late as it is, they're probably wondering what became of us."

The landlord had disappeared again, but he'd left the phone on the bar. Guy answered Jackson's call. He was shocked and anxious when the situation was explained to him but was prepared to offer his support.

"Forget the publicity. I'm not going to worry about that. You must tell the police you and Meredith are working for us. The connection ought to help if you're under any suspicion yourselves."

Which we will be, Jackson thought, appreciating Lord Danely's backing and well aware that, in certain quarters anyway, the peerage was still impressive enough in this country to have influence.

When he got back to Meredith, he found her asleep with her head down on her arms folded on the table. She had surrendered to the effects of the brandy and her exhaustion. Jackson didn't try to wake her. She would need to be rested for whatever ordeal they might still have to undergo in the hours ahead.

Slinging a chair around, he straddled it, intending to keep a close vigil at her side until the cops arrived. Watching over her wasn't work, it was sheer pleasure.

Even like this, head turned to one side, soft hair spilling over her cheek flushed with sleep, she bewitched him. There was a fragility in those delicate features and that petite figure that aroused his protective instinct.

Not to mention how a whiff of her warm, feminine scent tugged at his gut when, unable to resist touching her, he leaned forward to gently rub a strand of her silky hair between his thumb and forefinger. He would have been in trouble if she had awakened and found him playing with her hair. But she didn't stir.

Jackson sat back, reminding himself that all her daintiness he was admiring belied an inner strength. And a stubbornness, especially where Judith was concerned. This business about her mother and her worried him. What was the problem between them Meredith didn't want to talk about?

But then, Jackson had to admit, he was also guilty of holding back. He still feared she would walk if she knew. Sooner or later, though, he would have to take his chances and tell her.

HE MUST HAVE NODDED off himself in the chair. It was the sound of voices from the direction of the lobby that roused him. Lifting his head from his chest, he heard the landlord telling someone, "Waiting for you in the barroom, sir. You'll find it just through there."

Immediately alert, Jackson came to his feet and placed a hand on Meredith's shoulder. "The police are here, Meredith."

She looked bewildered for a few seconds when she opened her eyes, and then she nodded in understanding. She was standing beside him, a tenseness in her expression, when the officers appeared in the doorway.

There were two of them. The senior officer had a craggy, weathered face that made him look like he ought to be on the quarterdeck of a tall ship barking commands. He was accompanied by a chunky young woman with limp hair and a stolid manner.

They came forward, the senior officer introducing both himself and his partner. "I'm Detective Chief Inspector Ramsay from the Crime Investigation Division, and this is Detective Sergeant Ware, who will be taking down your statements."

Impressive, Jackson thought wryly. All he could manage was a simple "Jackson Hawke."

"And I'm Meredith Allen," Meredith added before Jackson could introduce her.

DCI Ramsay eyed her, and Jackson thought he could detect a touch of resentment in his sharp gaze. "Yes, Lady Danely's daughter."

That sounded like Guy hadn't waited, that he must have rung up Ramsay's superior and the detective wasn't happy about pressure from high places. Jackson was sure of it when Ramsay suggested they group themselves around the table. They'd be questioning us separately otherwise, he decided.

Once seated, Ramsay offered a terse apology. "I'm sorry you were kept waiting so long, but it was necessary to examine and secure the scene at the Boynton cottage."

He's probably got a team there right now going over the place, Jackson thought, and he isn't going to like it when he hears we contaminated possible evidence by searching that office before we discovered the body.

He was right. After relating their stories, the particulars of which DSI Ware recorded on a notebook computer, Ramsay gazed at him severely.

"Need I tell you, if either of you go anywhere near that cottage again, you will see the inside of an English jail."

"Right. Anything else, Inspector?"

"Yes. Would you care to tell me why I shouldn't be charging both of you with the murder of Sybil Boynton?"

"I can think of a couple of reasons," Jackson said mildly.

"For one thing, if we had killed her, we wouldn't have stuffed her body in a window seat and then turned around and phoned the police."

"Never mind identifying ourselves and waiting here for you to turn up," Meredith added.

"There is another little argument in our favor," Jackson pointed out. "We had no motive."

"Quite," Ramsay said dryly.

But Jackson knew what he was thinking. That a couple of cunning killers might have contacted the police in order to divert suspicion from themselves and that he only had their word for it they had no motive.

He'd probably have us in the police launch and on our way to the mainland right now, Jackson thought, if it wasn't for our connection with Lord and Lady Danely, but unless they could prove who *had* murdered Sybil Boynton and why—

As though the inspector read his thoughts, he leaned toward Jackson with a warning. "I want you to bear something in mind, Mr. Hawke. You risk losing your license to operate in this country should you interfere in our investigation."

"Understood." He'd just have to be damn careful that DCI Ramsay didn't learn of his activities. Not until he delivered Sybil Boynton's killer, anyway. "But, uh, Inspector, could I just suggest that you check the telephone records? They could tell you who Sybil Boynton rang up or who rang her."

Jackson knew he had probably gone too far when Ramsay's eyes turned as hard as Cornish granite. "Thank you for pointing that out, Mr. Hawke, but we do know how to perform our investigations."

DSI Ware commanded his attention with a murmured "Sir?"

His patience fast waning, the inspector turned to her. "What is it, Sergeant?"

She leaned toward him, speaking in an undertone. He nodded before addressing Meredith and Jackson again.

"We'll need to locate Professor Boynton as soon as possi-

ble. A library in Truro, you said. Was his daughter any more
specific than that?"

They shook their heads. DCI Ramsay pushed back from the
table and got to his feet.

"I expect the two of you to remain available, should we need
to talk to you again."

Meaning he doesn't want us to leave the island, Jackson
thought.

Meredith stopped the two officers as they turned to go.
"What about the Boynton dog, Inspector?"

"His name is Cicero, Ms. Allen, and the neighbor who informed us of that has agreed to care for him until Professor
Boynton's return."

The two officers departed. When they were alone in the
barroom, Meredith looked at Jackson, her face betraying her
anxiety. "Do you think he believed us?"

"Hard to say. At least he didn't charge us."

"But this could turn out to be serious for us, couldn't it?"

"Only if the actual killer isn't caught. And I promise you,"
he said, his voice hard-edged with anger, "whatever it takes
I'm going to get that bastard."

After Ramsay's warning, he thought Meredith would be
alarmed by his intention, try to argue him out of any further
pursuit of their investigation. But she was silent for a moment
and then she looked away and nodded slowly.

"It's no longer just a matter of solving the mystery at Croft
Castle, is it? It's come down to a question of proving our inno-
cence. And there's something else."

He waited for her to go on. When she turned back to him,
he could see the fear in her eyes.

"He was dangerous enough before, but now he's gotten desperate. And since he's become a cold-blooded murderer, and
must be someone right here on this tiny island, that puts all of
us at risk. Yes, he has to be caught."

But not tonight, Jackson thought. It was long after midnight. Time he got both of them back to the castle. Guy wanted to come down and collect them in the Land Rover when Jackson used the phone again to report the outcome of their session with the police. But Meredith, standing at his elbow, declined the offer.

"I need to breathe out in the open."

Jackson decided she was right when they came away from the inn a few minutes later. The moon and stars, together with a salt-laden breeze from the sea, kept them company on their walk up the winding lane. He had forgotten, while in London, that there could be majestic skies like this.

The black, gothic pile of the castle, which reared up before them when they neared the forecourt, was far less serene with its forbidding turrets and battlements. Probably because the windows were all dark except for a few night-lights. Lord and Lady Danely must have gone to bed, as Jackson had urged them to do. Nor was there any need to rouse Imogen. He and Meredith were able to let themselves in this time with a key that Guy had provided them.

Jackson was reluctant to part from Meredith when they reached their rooms. He didn't know whether to blame that on his concern for her after what had happened tonight or the enticing sight of her in the soft glow of a lamp on a hall table.

"What?" she asked as he lingered there outside her door.

"Just wondering if you're okay."

"I'm fine, really."

She started to turn away, but he stopped her. "I'm not."

Her hand on the knob of the door behind her, she gazed at him in concern. "What's wrong? Is there something I can do?"

"Yeah, there is." Hand braced on the doorjamb, he leaned in close with the realization that he was through fighting his desire for her. Whatever the consequences, he didn't care anymore. He wanted her. *Needed* her. His mouth dipped toward hers with a sweet relief.

"Jackson, I didn't mean—"

"*I* did."

He kissed her. A long, lush kiss in which he made it his business to savor the tantalizing flavor of her mouth under his. T
relish the sensation of her alluring breasts crushed to his ches
when he pressed against her. To satisfy himself with the wo
manly scent of her in his nostrils as he inhaled deeply.

He probed and he plundered, and when he finally release
her, it wasn't enough. Not nearly enough. He wanted to go int
that bedroom with her. Wanted to bury himself inside the hea
of her body, while she wrapped herself around him and crie
out with pleasure. But after what they'd discovered in that co
tage—

No, much as he longed for it, this wasn't the right time fo
that kind of intimacy, even if she would have welcomed it. B
sooner or later, he promised himself, he was going to do mor
than just brand her with his kisses.

It was with an enormous, and very frustrated, effort tha
Jackson controlled himself. Thumb lightly stroking the side o
her jaw, he was prepared to let her go before temptation over
whelmed him again. But not without a recommendation.

"That was for me," he said softly. "Now there's somethin
you can do for yourself."

"What is it?" she asked, looking dazed by his kiss, and h
couldn't deny how much that pleased him.

"Guy told me on the phone that Judith is pretty upset by a
that happened tonight. She's worried about you, I think. Ta
to her as soon as you get the chance," he urged. "You owe th
discussion to both your mother and yourself, Meredith."

Big mistake. His suggestion earned him her immediat
anger.

"*That* again! I thought I already made it clear, this subje
is off limits to you."

"Meredith—"

"Good night."

Turning away from him abruptly, she went into her roo

and shut the door behind her. Leaving Jackson to wonder what the hell had just happened. Not with her but with him. Why should he be worried that she might be hurting? Care so much that she was vulnerable where her mother was concerned? Have this need to protect her?

Was it more than just desire he was feeling for her? Could he actually be falling for the woman? If that was true, then he was asking for real trouble, because the sparks they rubbed off of each other had as much to do with their professional rivalry as it did with lust. They might be sharing an unspoken truce where this case was concerned, but their differences hadn't gone away.

Forget it, chum. There are just too many obstacles to ever make it work.

Chapter Nine

Meredith was puzzled by the muffled roar that awakened her. Was she hearing the surge of the sea below the castle? But the sound and direction were all wrong for that. Having realized by now that the steady droning was inside the castle itself, and not very far off, either, she lifted her head from the pillow.

What time was it? Late, if the sunlight pouring through her windows was any indication. She checked her watch on the bedside table. Almost ten o'clock. She hadn't intended to sleep this long.

She was still groggy when she left her bed and padded on bare feet to the door. Cracking it, she peered out into the hall. The bedroom door directly across from her own stood wide open. The humming she heard, much louder now, originated from inside Jackson's room. Mystery explained.

Though Meredith caught no glimpse of the vacuum cleaner and whoever was wielding it, she figured Gwen Sparrow must be on the job in there. There was no sign of Jackson himself.

He was very much on her mind, however, when she closed her door and went into the bathroom. She thought about him while she showered, did her hair and makeup, and dressed. Thought how her mouth still felt swollen from his kisses last night. How her body tingled, not from the spray of the shower, but from the memory of his touch.

There was no denying the sizzle that was between them and

The Harlequin Reader Service® — Here's how it works:

NO POSTAGE
NECESSARY
IF MAILED
IN THE
UNITED STATES

BUSINESS REPLY MAIL
FIRST-CLASS MAIL   PERMIT NO. 717-003   BUFFALO, NY

POSTAGE WILL BE PAID BY ADDRESSEE

HARLEQUIN READER SERVICE
3010 WALDEN AVE
PO BOX 1867
BUFFALO NY 14240-9952

Play the Lucky Hearts Game

and get...

2 FREE BOOKS

and a FREE MYSTERY GIFT...

yes! YOURS to KEEP!

I have scratched off the silver card. Please send me my **2 FREE BOOKS** and **FREE mystery GIFT**. I understand that I am under no obligation to purchase any books as explained on the back of this card.

Scratch Here!

then look below to see what your cards get you... 2 Free Books & a Free Mystery Gift!

382 HDL D342

182 HDL D35L

FIRST NAME

LAST NAME

ADDRESS

APT.#

CITY

STATE/PROV.

ZIP/POSTAL CODE

(H-I-10/04)

Twenty-one gets you
2 FREE BOOKS
and a **FREE MYSTERY GIFT!**

Twenty gets you
2 FREE BOOKS!

Nineteen gets you
1 FREE BOOK!

TRY AGAIN!

DETACH AND MAIL CARD TODAY!

® and ™ are trademarks owned and used by the trademark

how powerfully he affected her whenever he was near. Was he only playing a game with her, or did he genuinely care for her?

He's worried about you and your mother, Meredith. Isn't that demonstration enough right there?

Then why, *why* did she go and spoil their closeness whenever he mentioned her mother? Admit it. Her anger with him over this subject was unreasonable. Unless…

Was that anger the very thing she counseled others about in her work? A defense mechanism that could be explained by fear? If so, that meant her anger was really an excuse for distancing herself from him whenever he got too intimate. But fear of what?

Meredith thought she knew. Though she found him increasingly hard to resist, Jackson Hawke was too dynamic, too assertive, overwhelming her with his sensual assaults. They were the very qualities that attracted her, but at the same time they unnerved her.

Nor did she completely trust him. There was something he was still holding back. She could feel it.

Secrets. There were too many secrets with this whole scene on Croft Island. She didn't like them. But where her heart was concerned anyway, it seemed safer to concentrate on those that were connected with their investigation.

Which was exactly what Meredith was determined to do when she answered the knock on her door and opened it to find Gwen Sparrow standing there, a carrier loaded with cleaning materials in her hand. Here was a source for further information.

"Morning, dearie," the redhead greeted her cheerfully. "Hope my vacuuming across the hall didn't go and bother you, seeing as how Lady D said to let you sleep, but when I heard you moving around in here…"

"I'm sorry. You must have been waiting to clean my room. Come in," Meredith invited her, standing aside in the doorway.

"Ta." Gwen entered, dumping her carrier on the floor.

"Uh, I don't suppose you know where Mr. Hawke is?"

"Dunno, I'm sure. He was up and gone by the time I started on his room."

Meredith didn't know how Jackson managed to thrive on so little sleep. And where, she wondered, had his restless energy taken him this morning? Maybe on another run.

"Smashing, your friend is, isn't he? A real waste, I say, if the busies end up locking him up for this here murder. I'll just start with the dusting in here, shall I?"

Gwen could have gone off to the bathroom to scrub the fixtures, or dragged the vacuum cleaner in from the hall to do the floor. But neither of those occupations would have permitted her to talk, and Meredith could see she was eager for a gossip. She obliged the woman by seating herself on the edge of the bed.

"I suppose everyone on the island knows by now what happened," she said, encouraging the woman to supply her with whatever knowledge she might have collected, hoping that some of it might be useful to Jackson and her.

"Don't get much excitement down here, dearie, so it's all anyone can talk about in the village this morning." She removed cloths and a container of polish from her carrier and began to work vigorously on a chest of drawers.

"What are they saying, Gwen?"

"The usual muck, along with wondering where the professor got to and when he'll turn up."

"Then the police haven't located him yet?"

"Shouldn't think so or we'd have heard about it. He's a law unto himself, is our Professor Boynton. Nice wood, this chest. Always takes a shine with no more than a quick wipe."

"I'm sorry for him," Meredith said. "It's bound to be a terrible shock for him when he learns of his daughter's death."

Gwen snorted. "Wouldn't count on it. Far as I could see, there was never any love lost between the two of them."

He's a law unto himself. Was it possible that Simon Boynton was in some manner connected with his daughter's death?

And where was he? If he'd gone to Truro as Sybil had claimed, then why couldn't the police find him?

Gwen had moved on to the fireplace where she began to dust the ornaments along the mantel. Her back was to Meredith when she spoke.

"On the scene yourself last night, weren't you?"

She was casual about it, but Meredith knew she longed to know whether she and Jackson *were* involved in any way in Sybil Boynton's death.

"Yes, I was there, too," Meredith said, "but Sybil Boynton was dead when we found her. Why? Are you hearing other opinions about that in the village?"

Gwen paused in her dusting to look over her shoulder. There was a concerned expression now on her freckled face. "It's all a lot of bloody tongues wondering how you ever got into the place. And seeing as how I was chatting up the two of you in the George yesterday and that the professor gave me a set of keys to the cottage for cleaning whenever he was away...well, in some minds it adds up, like."

There was no point in keeping it a secret, Meredith decided. Not when Jackson had already admitted it to the police. And Gwen was entitled to a vindication. "You tell those busy tongues we used a picklock."

It didn't seem to matter to Gwen that they had unlawfully entered the cottage. She looked nothing but relieved. "That's all right, then." Her work brought her to the wardrobe. "Collect dust something awful, these carvings do."

She was silent as she busied herself with the elaborate carvings on the wardrobe's doors, but Meredith could see her curiosity hadn't been completely satisfied.

"Is there something else you want to know, Gwen?"

For a moment the redhead said nothing, and then she turned round slowly. This time there was a sly look on her face. "It was that old book, wasn't it? The one you was asking me about at the George. That's why you were in the cottage."

Meredith considered denying it, but Gwen Sparrow was n
fool. "If I tell you—"

Anticipating her, Gwen promised a hasty, "Mum's the word
Think I want the busies to go and find out I was the one wh
told you about the book?"

"All right, then, the truth. We needed to learn what Profes
sor Boynton had discovered that was so important. But some
one else beat us to it. Probably the same someone who kille
Sybil. Anyway, the book was gone, along with the professor'
original manuscript of his translation, and the carbon copy ha
been burned in the fireplace." Meredith spread her hands in
gesture of helplessness. "And if Professor Boynton doesn'
turn up, or is unwilling to talk when he does, we'll never knov
what the book contained that's so vital."

"Willing to give anything to find out, are you?" The sly loo
on Gwen's face had been joined by an equally sly tone in he
voice.

"You know something!"

The redhead grinned triumphantly. "Thought that woul
put your knickers in a twist."

"What is it?"

"I'm not saying it's for certain, mind you, but the professo
was in the habit of keeping *two* carbons of his work."

"He was *that* cautious?"

"Had to be, he said. Once lost everything in a fire, and afte
that he made sure he not only kept the originals and ther
backup carbons in his office but that third copies were tucke
away elsewhere for sakekeeping. Silly old trout could've save
himself all that bother if he'd used a computer and disks."

"Then another copy of the translation *could* exist. Bu
where?"

"Well…"

Meredith leaned toward her earnestly. "Gwen, I know yo
don't want to get involved, but we think that manuscript con
tains something we need to help Lord and Lady Danely."

"Seeing as how it's for Lord and Lady D, then…" Her reluctance melted, at least sufficiently enough to provide the location of the possible second carbon. "Mind, you didn't hear it from me, but there's a shed at the back of the garden. Far away from the cottage, see, in case of fire. And that's all I'll say."

It was more than enough. Meredith thanked Gwen, left her making up the bed, and went in search of Jackson. She was eager to share with him what she had just learned. It wasn't until she was hurrying down the stairs that it struck her.

Eager? When had she gotten eager where Jackson Hawke was concerned? All right, so she was attracted to him sexually. No argument about that anymore. But her eagerness to be with him simply for his company was another matter entirely.

It was understandable, though. They were working on the same case. It was pretty much all they had on their minds these days. So, for that reason, why wouldn't she want to see him, talk to him? As for anything else they might have in common…well, they didn't. Did they?

It was a question Meredith wasn't prepared to answer. All she wanted to risk at that moment was a business meeting with Jackson. But he was nowhere to be found when she looked for him on the ground floor. Nor was anyone else in evidence. Not, anyway, until she checked the dining room and spotted her mother out on the terrace.

The sight of Judith standing there at the low stone wall that rimmed the terrace troubled her. She seemed like such a forlorn figure, oblivious to everything but the wide expanse of the sea.

Meredith was hesitant to join her. But Judith, turning from the view when Meredith let herself out through the French door, greeted her with a little smile. A sad one, though, she noticed.

"Good morning. Would you like some breakfast? I'm afraid Imogen has already cleared away the things out here, but she's kept a tray for you in the kitchen."

"Maybe later. I was hoping to find Jackson."

"He and Guy are searching those passages in the keep. Guy was able to round up some powerful gas lanterns. They thought the stronger light might turn up something you overlooked the other night. If you'd like to join them…"

Meredith shook her head. "I'll wait for their report."

And in the meantime, she thought, this was her opportunity to talk to her mother. Because Jackson was right. She and Judith did need to sit down and discuss their differences.

Meredith was ready to do just that now, but once again it didn't happen. Looking at her carefully, she could see that her mother was in no state to address serious issues. She seemed distracted and there were shadows under her eyes.

"Are you all right? You look tired."

"I'm afraid I didn't sleep very well last night, and then this morning… Well, I probably shouldn't have watched the newscast."

"Sybil Boynton's murder?"

Judith nodded. "They didn't identify her. The police won't release that information until her father has been located and notified of her death, but listening to the coverage was unpleasant. And Guy…Guy was terribly bothered by the mention of Croft Island."

Meredith was concerned about her mother. She was obviously as upset by the murder as her husband was. Worried by frightening events that seemed to be escalating, threatening the future of Croft Castle.

"Look," she promised Judith recklessly, "try not to fret about it, because one way or another, Jackson and I *will* clear up this mess for you." And for ourselves, she thought, remembering that they were still suspects in Sybil's murder.

"Yes, I know."

"Why don't you lie down for a while?" Meredith suggested. "See if you can catch up on some of that lost sleep."

"Thank you. I think I will try to nap."

"If you should meet Jackson on the way, tell him I'm out here waiting to speak to him."

Judith started for the French door and then turned back. "You and Jackson…you will be very careful, won't you?"

Meredith assured her that they would. She appreciated her mother's concern, but when Judith was gone, she realized they were still being nothing more than carefully polite to each other. And she wondered if this constraint between them would ever get resolved.

The minutes passed as she waited idly on the terrace. Impatient to share her news with Jackson, she thought about looking for him in the keep. But he and Guy could be anywhere in the passages, and she didn't want to risk losing herself again in that dark labyrinth.

She also considered heading for the kitchen to get that tray Imogen had for her. That didn't happen, either. Instead, she wandered restlessly from the terrace, and the next thing she knew she was pacing the cobbles in the forecourt.

Pausing, she looked up at the stone angels on the roof. They made her think of Edward Atheling. She had been visited by no further images of him. Perhaps, now that he had warned them, as well as informed them of his connection to Jackson, he no longer had any reason to make his presence known.

Her gaze traveled down the massive wall of the castle. Stone carvings framed the front door. She hadn't noticed them before. They were a strange mixture of dragons and frowning cherubs tumbling over one another. Fine work but not very cheerful.

Why was it that, even in the bright light of day, this whole place seemed menaced by shadows?

Turning her back on the building, she crossed the forecourt and seated herself on a stone mounting block. It was situated in the full warmth of the morning sun. Better. She felt better.

"You were supposed to be on the terrace. What are you doing out here?"

The rich timbre of his deep voice, already familiar to her,

was even more welcome than the sun. Swinging around on the block, she faced his tall figure looming over her. He was a startling sight, with cobwebs in his dark hair and dust powdering his clothes.

"Waiting for you to get done playing hide-and-seek in the maze. You look like something out of a grave. Any luck?"

Jackson shook his head. "Not a sign of any treasure, and we covered those passages carefully this time. Whatever our villain is after, it's either not there or hidden so well it's going to take more than a search to find it. Scoot over. I need to sit down."

Meredith made room for him on the block. He perched beside her. Since the block wasn't all that wide, his solid body was squeezed snugly against her. She made an effort to ignore the searing contact of him by concentrating on business.

"While you were exhausting yourself in the keep," she boasted, "I was collecting something useful, and I didn't have to leave my room to get it."

"Impress me."

She did by telling him what she had learned from Gwen Sparrow. "Now," she said, "if we can just get the police to investigate that shed and convince them to let us have a look at the translation, providing it's there and providing they're willing…"

Jackson shook his head. "They may already have searched the shed. If they haven't, they will before they're through. And you can forget about them sharing any of its contents with us, because they won't."

"You're right." Meredith's shoulders sagged with disappointment. "And that makes my useful information not useful at all. Damn."

He was silent. *Too* silent. She turned her head to look at him and found him looking back. There was a gleam in those cobalt blue eyes of his. She had seen it often enough to be familiar with it by now. It was the gleam of a determined warrior anticipating the hunt.

"Oh, no! You know what Inspector Ramsay said. If we go anywhere near the Boynton cottage again, we'll see the inside of an English jail. And he meant it."

"It's all a question of semantics, Meredith. And the way I define it, that shed is not the cottage."

"Yes, well, Ramsay is not going to get technical about it if we're caught snooping around that shed."

"Come on, Meredith," he challenged her, "where's your spirit for the chase?"

A grin hovered at the corners of his wide, sensual mouth. A grin that threatened her. He was dangerous to her, this man in his demon-dark outfit.

And, in case you've forgotten, he also exhilarates you.

It was an irresistible combination.

"Yes?" he said.

"Yes."

He surged to his feet, all energy again driven by a fresh purpose. "Get your purse, then, if you need it."

"I don't need— What are you talking about? We can't go down there now. We have to wait for the cover of darkness, like last night."

"And risk having the cops learn about those carbons stored in the shed and end up beating us to the manuscript? I don't think so."

"Will you stop tempting me and just *consider* what you're asking."

"You're right. I probably should be doing this on my own. No need to involve you."

"That is not what I meant. Broad daylight, Jackson. There's no telling how many minutes you'll need this time with that picklock, because the shed is sure to be locked. Or how many nervous neighbors could be keeping a watch on the place, and if they should spot us—"

"Only if we're delayed getting into the shed, which wouldn't happen if we had a key."

"And how do you propose getting one?"

"If Simon Boynton is keeping documents in there that he values, it figures he'd want the shed cleaned from time to time. And you did say Gwen Sparrow was given a complete set of keys for the property."

"You don't really think Gwen will risk her job by parting with that key?"

"Oh, I think I might be able to convince her to loan it to us for a couple of hours."

The grin was no longer just hovering. It had taken full possession of his mouth. It was the cocky grin of a masculine ego confident of his persuasive powers with a susceptible female.

"You do, huh?"

"You'll see."

And she did several minutes later when they located Gwen at the far end of the drawing room, where she was vacuuming the Persian rug.

"Look," Jackson suggested to Meredith, stopping her outside the doorway, "why don't you wait here? I don't want the poor woman to think we're ganging up on her."

"Right, we wouldn't want to overwhelm her," Meredith said dryly, knowing this was exactly his intention and that another female presence would only diminish the impact of his maneuvers.

So she remained behind, watching from the shadows in the hallway as he went to work. And Jackson Hawke was very good at what he did. Even his gait, as he closed in on his target, was calculated to command feminine attention. A kind of swaggering stride that said he meant business.

Meredith waited for Gwen to notice him. She did when he was about halfway down the length of the drawing room that stretched between them. The redhead, shutting off the noisy vacuum cleaner and coming erect, was all smiles as he approached her. Meredith didn't exist, if the woman was even aware of her lingering out in the hallway.

Meredith couldn't hear their exchange from this distance. She didn't have to. The body language was loud enough. Jackson began with a direct assault that seemed to consist of flirtation on the heels of blatant flattery, while Gwen giggled her appreciation.

She resisted, of course, when he got serious, shaking her head emphatically. But Jackson was a professional. Poor Gwen had no chance. Meredith could see her weakening as he leaned in close, turning up the charm of a handsome, compelling male who seldom failed to get what he wanted. In the end Gwen bobbed her head in agreement, lifted her purse out of the carrier of cleaning supplies, removed a key from a ring and surrendered it to him with what looked like an adoring sigh. He thanked her warmly.

The whole performance couldn't have lasted more than two minutes. Though she was a disapproving spectator, Meredith had to admit it was damn effective. She was waiting for Jackson out in the hallway when he joined her, triumphantly bearing the key.

"Got it!"

"You are absolutely shameless."

"Yeah, I know." He winked at her. "But I get results."

JACKSON HALTED THEM on the street outside the George.

"Let's stop in here."

"I thought you didn't want to lose any time getting to that shed."

"Only if Simon Boynton hasn't turned up yet or the cops aren't on the scene again. If anyone in the village has heard, the word is sure to have reached the inn."

Meredith had to agree they needed to check this out before they risked invading the shed.

Since it was still a few minutes before noon, the bar had yet to open for business. But Colin Sheppard was behind the desk in the lobby. The affable landlord greeted them with a smile tempered by regret.

"Madam, sir. A pleasure to see you out and about. Though it's not a very nice morning for any of us, is it? Terrible thing, this murder, and no help, either, to our holiday traffic."

When Jackson asked him about Professor Boynton and the police, he leaned his elbows on the front desk and shook his head.

"Shouldn't think either the professor or the police have returned to the island yet, or I would have heard. We always do at the inn. Were you needing a word with them, sir?"

"Just wondering."

"And quite right, too, after last night's business. But I wouldn't worry, sir. Our English police are very thorough, and if they believed that either of you were in any way to blame for Sybil Boynton's death, you can be certain they wouldn't have let you go."

He thinks that's why we stopped in to ask him about the professor and the police, Meredith thought. *Because we're afraid we could be charged with the murder.*

Of course, they *were* still very much concerned about this possibility. But it was just as well Colin Sheppard should believe it was their only motive for being here. They didn't want anyone in the village getting the idea that they had another agenda.

Thanking him, they started to go, but the landlord detained them with a hesitant "There is one other thing, sir."

"What's that?" Jackson asked him.

Sheppard straightened up from the front desk on which he'd been leaning. "It's a bit awkward, you see, being as how he's a guest and all. But the American gentleman staying here, Mr. Wallace…" His gaze slid meaningfully in the direction of the stairway leading to the rooms upstairs. "Well, the fact is, sir, he's been asking questions about you."

"Has he?" Jackson's eyes darkened, looking suddenly as hard as steel. "What kind of questions?"

"Having to do with your stay at the castle mostly. Are you working for Lord and Lady D? And if so, why? And what luck are you having with that work? Mind you, I gave him no answers, and I wouldn't have mentioned it, except we're all very fond of Lord and Lady D. I don't like talk about them or their guests, and I made certain he understood that. Yes, Sheila?"

The barmaid had appeared in the doorway behind the desk. "Rob is out back with the beer delivery from the launch. Wanting to know where you want it stowed."

"If you'll excuse me, madam, sir."

The landlord departed with the barmaid, leaving them alone in the lobby. Meredith glanced at Jackson. There was an expression on his face that reminded her of just how dangerous this forceful man could be.

"I don't like characters who hang around without explanations," he said grimly. "Especially ones who ask questions about me."

The mysterious, surly Archie Wallace, Meredith thought. Who was he? And why was he interested in Jackson?

"I'm going to have to have a little talk with this guy," Jackson promised, and the toughness in his deep voice made Meredith feel sorry for Archie Wallace. Their meeting would not be a friendly one. "But right now we've got other business."

Jackson hurried her in the direction of the front door. Something caught Meredith's eye, and she stopped.

"What?" he asked.

There was a board mounted on the wall beside the door to the bar. On it was chalked the lunch menu for the day.

"Cornish pasties and sherry trifle," she read. Her stomach, which had yet to be fed today, longed for the popular English fare. "It's noon. The bar will be opening. Couldn't we eat and then go on to the shed?"

"And take the chance someone will get there ahead of us? We can't wait, Meredith. Come on, I'll buy you lunch afterwards."

Providing we aren't on our way to the jail in Treffaro, she thought with a last, regretful look at the board as Jackson's urgency compelled her to accompany him out onto the street, where they turned in the direction of the Boynton cottage.

The cottage itself, when they sauntered past it a few minutes later in an effort to learn whether there was any sign of occupation, had crime scene tape stretched across its windows and doors. It had been sealed by the police. There could be no one inside.

"Looks safe," Jackson pronounced. "Now let's see if we can locate that shed."

Screening themselves behind the same tall hedge at the side of the property they had used as a cover yesterday, they made their way to the back of the garden at the rear of the cottage.

"I can see the roof of what's got to be the shed," Jackson said as they rounded the end of the hedge.

His height must have permitted him a view of that much, because all Meredith could see was the barrier that stretched between them and the shed. The area was a wilderness of tall, thick vegetation that looked impenetrable.

"We'll never get through that stuff."

Undaunted, Jackson led the way, plunging into the wall of growth. "Be grateful it's here to conceal us," he called softly over one shoulder.

She tried to look at it that way, but it was a little difficult when she had to squeeze her way past brambles that tore and scratched, wade through hydrangeas gone wild, suffer nettles that stung, battle a thicket of laurels, and smell the bitter odor of something she didn't want to even think about. Long before they reached the shed, Meredith was convinced her companion must at some time in his life have trained for jungle survival. The whole thing was nothing more than a mild challenge to him.

"Here we go," he said when they emerged at last from a tangle of sprawled vines to find themselves at the back wall of the shed with its peeling paint. "Door must be on the other side."

They worked their way around to the front of the small

building. The lush vegetation fell behind, putting them in the open. And leaving us entirely vulnerable, Meredith thought. The windows of the cottage next door looked out on the Boynton lawn, at the edge of which the shed was situated.

She could only hope, as Jackson fitted the key into the lock of the stout door, that the neighbor wasn't keeping a close watch on the place from one of those windows. Her relief was considerable when Jackson finally had the door open and they were able to scoot inside and close the door behind them.

The place was as dim as a cavern. The one small, grimy window in the back wall admitted only a weak glow. But a light bulb dangling from a cord overhead indicated the shed was equipped with rudimentary electricity. Which was understandable if Simon Boynton was storing documents in here that would need more than the inadequate daylight from a single window to be examined.

"There must be a switch," Meredith said, "but I don't see—"

"Here it is."

Jackson flipped the switch located on a side wall. The naked bulb glared with an eerie light that, while not strong, was sufficient enough to permit them to view their cramped surroundings.

The shed contained a clutter of garden tools, a bag of fertilizer and a broken chair. But it was the two metal filing cabinets that interested them.

"Locked?" Meredith wondered, following Jackson to that side of the shed.

He tried several of the drawers. "No locks. Guess he figures the lock on the door is enough. You take this cabinet. I'll take the other."

Working side by side in silence, they began to search swiftly through the drawers. All of them were packed with labeled files, some of which contained the carbons of the professor's various manuscripts.

"Here it is!" Jackson announced. "No, this can't be right. It's strictly the maritime history of Croft Island."

They went on looking without result. Could Gwen be wrong about the existence of a second carbon, or had the police been in here before them and claimed the translation?

In the end, it was Meredith who found it tucked at the back of the bottom drawer. "I think I've got it!" Coming erect with the manuscript in her hand, she read the title page to him. "*The Ancient History of Croft Castle*, as translated from the original by Simon Boynton."

"That's it, all right. Now let's see if we can learn what got Sybil Boynton killed."

Jackson started to reach for the pages that were bound together with a pair of rubber bands, but Meredith held on to them.

"Not here. Let's go down on the shore to read them. After that jungle out there and this musty shed, I need to breathe somewhere out in the open."

"Right. We shouldn't hang around here, anyway. We can always bring the thing back afterwards."

The manuscript was thin enough that Meredith was easily able to stuff it down into her roomy shoulder bag. Killing the light, Jackson led the way out of the shed and turned to lock the door.

Everything considered, all of this had been far easier than she'd anticipated, Meredith thought.

It was a premature self-congratulation. Scant seconds later, just as Jackson was slipping the door key back into his pocket, potential trouble arrived in the form of their friend from last night. The Great Dane, tail wagging, came bounding toward them across the lawn from the direction of the neighbor's garden.

"Cicero," called a woman's voice from somewhere on the other side of a dense thicket of rhododendrons, "come back here!"

Meredith and Jackson froze. The dog, too, had stopped,

wondering whether to be obedient or ignore the command. Were they about to be discovered?

"Treats, Cicero," coaxed the woman. "And if you're a good boy, walkies after."

The Great Dane, tempted by the promised treats, whipped around and raced back to the neighbor's garden. Meredith and Jackson wasted no time in leaving the scene. Ducking around the side of the shed, they lost themselves in the shrubbery.

Several minutes later they found a deserted spot on the shore. Meredith breathed deeply, welcoming the salty tang of the sea in her nostrils. They settled side by side on a flat boulder. She removed the manuscript from her bag.

"We'll get through that thing faster if we divide it," Jackson suggested.

She agreed, peeled away the rubber bands, and handed half of the pages to him. They read for some time in silence while the waves broke and ran over the shingle beach below them. The language of the book, even though translated into English from the Latin of the old chroniclers, was sometimes difficult to deal with. But Meredith persisted, and was finally rewarded.

"Here!" she said, turning to Jackson in excitement. "You better read this yourself."

Leaning over, he began to read aloud the passages she indicated from the manuscript in her lap. "'There exists about this ancient keep, hidden from pious eyes, a thing so extraordinary that to behold it…'"

As Jackson read on, his voice bit into the words. He finished on a harsh note and stared at her, his blue eyes stormy with disgust.

"A casket of lost jewels might be a stretch," he thundered, "but at least it's possible! But this—*this* is just plain nuts!"

Chapter Ten

"May I suggest something?" Meredith said.

Jackson, still fuming, eyed her with mistrust. "I don't think so."

"Why?"

"Because I know what that voice means. When you start sounding that way, all calm and reasonable, you're no longer just a woman. You're a psychologist treating an irrational subject."

"Who said anything about needing therapy for a rage disorder, even though you do look like you're ready to throw the manuscript into the sea. All I'm asking is that we both keep an open mind about this."

"An open— Come on, Meredith. The whole thing is preposterous! The gate to hell! You're asking me to be serious about the *gate to hell*?"

"Yes. Well, no, maybe not about the reality of a gate itself but certainly about the claim of it in these pages. Remember what Guy told us? How Sir Hugh Gwinfryd, who built the original castle, was a practitioner of the Black Arts and had a pact with the devil himself."

"It's only a legend, Meredith."

"One the book confirms."

Jackson's finger jabbed at the page. "And embellishes with this junk about Sir Hugh being the guardian of the gate to hell, which just happens to be located somewhere in or near Croft Castle. Satan must have dearly loved old Sir Hugh to trust him with that one."

Look, if you dare, for the portal of Hades, and you will know it when you find it.

That was the direction from the ancient chronicler. Meredith remembered the rest from those passages, as well. "Think what it's saying, Jackson. How the hidden opening to the underworld was lost after Sir Hugh's death, but—"

"'Whosoever discovers it will be the possessor of great power and wealth,'" he quoted dryly. "Excuse me for being a skeptic, but I'd like to know how that one is supposed to work."

"Not just any *whosoever*. It has to be one of Sir Hugh's descendants. The book stresses that, right here just before it adds that Croft Castle will also be restored to his family."

"So what. It's still a fairy tale."

"You're missing the point. *You* might not believe it, and *I* might not believe it, but someone on this island does. Believes in it so strongly he's convinced he's entitled to his legacy."

"And will go to any lengths to get it, including murder to protect both his search and his identity." Jackson nodded slowly. "Yeah, I see what you mean. Okay, that explains why he keeps coming back to the castle. He isn't looking for jewels. He's looking for this lost whatever."

"It also explains why neither Simon Boynton nor his daughter went after it themselves, because only a descendant of Sir Hugh can benefit from it."

Jackson was thoughtful for a few seconds. "I think I must be going over the edge myself, because this is beginning to make sense to me. Which means I might need your professional help yet, Meredith. All right, Simon Boynton stumbles onto this thing, trusts in at least the possibility of it, and tells our culprit about it."

"Someone he had a reason to believe is a descendant of Sir Hugh."

"Yeah, and maybe Boynton told that descendant because he made a deal to get a share of the promised wealth. Then, at some point he goes to Truro for research in the library there. Why?"

"Possibly," Meredith suggested, "he hopes to learn directions to the portal from another ancient book, because this one doesn't provide them, and his unknown partner certainly hasn't found the gate yet. I don't suppose when you and Guy searched the passages this morning that you…"

"Not a sign of anything like that."

They were both silent for a long moment, gazing out at the long rollers, and then Jackson shook his head. "All of this hangs together, but none of it is definite. I don't know. Maybe we're on the wrong track with this gate to hell stuff. Maybe what's so valuable is something else in the manuscript."

"I didn't find anything else that qualifies in my half of the book."

"No, and I didn't find anything in mine, either," he admitted.

"Then we are on the right track." She hesitated. "What do you think? Should we tell the police what we've learned?"

"I wouldn't recommend it. As fantastic as it is, they'd either confine us in some mental facility for observation or else clap us in jail for breaking and entering again. No, we need to keep this to ourselves until we have something more solid than the contents of this thin little book." He handed his half of the manuscript to her and got to his feet. "I owe you a lunch. Let's see if they're still serving at the George."

Meredith banded the pages together again and tucked the manuscript back into her bag. But she continued to sit on the boulder, gazing up at Jackson in sudden understanding.

"Change your mind?"

"It's not that. It's what just occurred to me."

"Being?"

"If Hugh Gwinfryd was Edward Atheling's enemy, as history claims, it explains why Edward's ghost is watching over his descendant. And that's you."

"Meredith—"

"No, don't look at me in that let's-try-to-be-patient-with-her way. Don't you see? That makes Sir Hugh's descendant your enemy, which is why Edward is concerned about you. Jackson, you've got to be extra careful from now on."

He grinned down at her in a way that made her stomach flutter with more than just hunger. "I'm much more interested in the idea that *you're* worried about me. Let's eat."

THE LUNCH CROWD HAD thinned out by the time they reached the inn. They were able to have a table to themselves in an unoccupied corner of the barroom, which gave them the opportunity to talk without being overheard.

Not that they did talk at first. They were too busy concentrating on the steaming, savory Cornish pasties that were served to them. Or at least Meredith was. Some minutes passed before she realized Jackson was no longer eating. Something was bothering him.

"What's wrong?"

He scowled into his ale and then looked up at her sharply "I don't like it."

She assumed he wasn't talking about the Cornish pasty on his plate.

"Boynton has been gone too long," he said. "Where is he that the police haven't located him? What is he up to?"

"Maybe he found something in that library he went to in Truro. Something that's put him on the trail of further research elsewhere."

"Exactly, and I want to know what that something is."

Meredith watched his jaw tighten, a sign that he'd made up his mind.

"We're going to Truro," he said.

"You want to know how to find that gate. Why, if you don't

believe in it?" He didn't answer her. "You're not still thinking about a casket of lost jewels, are you?"

He shook his head. "No, I've given up on that one altogether. It was never a strong possibility, anyway."

"But the gate is," she insisted.

"Maybe. Let's just say it's the best shot we have now for providing us with some answers. And, with any luck, those answers are going to save Lord and Lady Danely's business, as well as our own necks."

"And if the gate, or what passes for it, doesn't exist?"

"Doesn't matter. All I want is what Simon Boynton went after in that library. If it turns out to be directions to the gate, so much the better. If not, then I hope it's at least some kind of evidence we can take to the police to clear ourselves."

"Then let the police find it."

"But they won't, because even if we told them about it they wouldn't be interested. All they care about is locating Boynton, not what he's after."

She could see he was frustrated and that she was the cause of it. Well, she couldn't help that. What he proposed was out of the question.

"You're forgetting what Inspector Ramsay, in so many words, told us. That we weren't to leave the island. We've already pressed our luck as it is by disobeying him where the shed was concerned, and if we were to take off for the mainland, we could be in real trouble."

"Damn it, Meredith!" He slapped his hand on the table, no longer just frustrated but openly angry. "If you won't go with me, then I'll—"

"Go by yourself. But you won't today." She nodded toward a clock on the wall. "The launch will already have left on its afternoon crossing."

He didn't argue with her. He shoved back from the table impatiently. "If you're through eating, let's get out of here."

When they left the inn, they headed back up the road to the

castle. There didn't seem to be anything more to be achieved by hanging around the village, she thought. Jackson was silent at her side during their climb. And remote.

He was a stranger again. Or maybe he had never stopped being a stranger. She had thought she was beginning to understand him. That his restless energy was the product of a man who was dynamic by nature. Now she wasn't so entirely sure whether this was the explanation for his intenseness.

There was something else going on here. She remembered his initial explosion down on the shore when she had pointed out those revealing passages in the translation. And how angry he'd been when she resisted going to Truro. Both had been overreactions, more than just disappointment because the case had taken a wrong, unexpected turn.

"Why?" she abruptly asked him now. "Why is this case so vital to you?"

"It's important to both of us, isn't it?"

"But it's more than that for you. You seem, I don't know, *driven* by it."

"It's just determination, Meredith. It comes with being a P.I."

It was far from being a satisfactory explanation, but she could see by the stubborn line of his jaw that it was all she was going to get.

He was still cool with her when, reaching the front door of the castle, he turned to her. "I'll leave you here. I'm going back to the village. There are a couple of things I want to check out."

She gazed at him in bewilderment. "You didn't have to walk me back here if that's what you wanted to do."

"Yes, I did," he said firmly. "You want to give me the manuscript? I'll see that it gets put back into the shed and the key returned to Gwen."

The manuscript. She had forgotten about it in their conflict over Truro. Taking the pages out of her bag, she handed them to him. She thought about asking him just what else he intended to do down in the village, but she could see he was in no mood for further questions.

"Will you do something for me?" he asked her, his voice gruff.

"If I can," she said cautiously.

"Take care of yourself while I'm gone. No risks, okay?"

Not waiting for her answer, he turned his back on her and walked away. Perplexed, Meredith stood there by the door and watched his tall, stalwart figure stride across the forecourt. The man was a contradiction, angry with her and at the same time concerned for her safety. Would she ever understand him? For that matter, did she even want to understand him?

She wasn't sure. But there was one certainty. Jackson Hawke intrigued her on every level, excited her even, but there was something formidable about his hard strength that she feared.

DETERMINED TO FORGET about Jackson, Meredith went in search of her mother, hoping to finally have that talk with her. But the castle was quiet, with no one in evidence. Gwen Sparrow, who cleaned here only in the mornings, would have long since returned to the village. But she did run into Imogen, who told her that she could find Lord and Lady Danely in their apartment.

Judith answered her knock, inviting her into the sitting room with a low "Guy is lying down in the bedroom."

Remembering how her mother had expressed concern over her husband's health, Meredith asked softly, "Is he all right?"

"I wanted to phone the doctor, but he wouldn't hear of it. He insists it isn't the angina acting up, that he's just tired."

Meredith would have excused herself and left the apartment, but Guy must have heard the murmur of their voices. He wandered out from the bedroom.

"Darling, you're supposed to be resting," Judith objected.

"Don't fuss, love. Look, I can rest sitting here on the sofa.

I want to hear Meredith tell us what progress, if any, she and Jackson are making."

Judith settled close beside him on the sofa, keeping an anxious watch over him. Meredith, seating herself in a chair facing them, didn't miss the pleading look her mother sent her. She didn't want Guy troubled by further bad news.

Meredith was selective in her report, telling them about Edward Atleling's brief manifestations. That in her opinion his presence was a friendly one and that he was not the cause of the trouble at Croft. She tried to be as encouraging as possible about the rest while carefully omitting any disturbing mention of a gate to hell.

There was something she needed to learn, however, and she asked it as casually as possible. "Guy, do you know if there are any of Sir Hugh Gwinfryd's descendants on the island?"

He shook his head. "None that I've ever heard of. Good Lord, I should be surprised if any of them exist at all after all these centuries, at least in Cornwall."

"Well, it was just something that occurred to me as a possibility." She didn't explain any further than that, and Guy didn't ask.

Knowing her mother intended to remain at her husband's side, and that there was no possibility of a private session with her, Meredith left the couple and went up to her room.

She tried to work on her notes for the lectures she was scheduled to deliver when she returned to London, but she kept thinking about Jackson. Wondering where he was and what he was doing. She expected to find out at dinner, but he didn't return to the castle for dinner. Guy told her he had rung up from the village to let them know he would eat something at the inn and not to bother about him.

After dinner, Meredith left her mother and Guy over a game of cribbage, which Judith said relaxed him, and went back to her room and her notes. But she was irritated now by Jackson's long absence. He might have told her what he was up to.

She hated to admit it, but the truth was, she felt left out. Well, it was her own fault for getting involved with him. She should have maintained what she had promised herself in the beginning, a strictly professional relationship in which they conducted their own separate investigations. Too late for that now.

As the evening wore on, and there was no sign of him when she twice checked his room, she found herself worrying in earnest. Maybe he was in trouble. She thought about going to Guy and her mother, but she hesitated to alarm them with her mother already concerned.

It was after dark when Meredith made up her mind to borrow the Land Rover and drive down to the village to look for Jackson herself. She was getting her jacket when a rap sounded on her door. Hurrying to answer it, she found Jackson standing there, thumbs hooked casually in the pockets of his black jeans.

"Where have you been?" she demanded, the hot words spewing from her before she could stop them.

His familiar grin, as he shifted his weight from one leg to another, meant he had forgotten his own anger with her. "Worried about me? I think I like that."

"I worry about Joanna and Rand, too," she said, referring to her favorite soap opera characters, "so don't take it personally."

"Sorry," he apologized. "I shouldn't have walked out on you like that. I went looking for the American, Archie Wallace, to have it out with him. Didn't find him, though, and nobody seemed to know where he had gotten to."

"That was hours ago."

"Yeah, well, I hung around the inn, but he never turned up. I did learn something useful about getting over to the mainland, though. You don't have to depend on the schedule of the launch. The guy who pilots it, Rob Curzon, also rents boats. I reserved an outboard for first thing in the morning. Then I had a word with Guy just now. He and Judith keep a little car garaged over in Trefarro for use when they're on the mainland. Said I could borrow it tomorrow."

"Then you're still set on going to Truro?"

"That's the plan." He hesitated. "If you still don't want to go with me, I'll understand, but I'd feel better with you at my side. You know?"

Yes, she did know. He was being protective again. *Touchingly* protective. The last of her resistance drained away. "I suppose I'd better come. If nothing else, you'll need someone in the car with you to keep reminding you what side of the road you're supposed to be driving on."

"That's better," he said, his voice turning husky as he placed a big hand against the side of her face, his thumb slowly stroking her cheek.

Meredith caught her breath. And held it for several heartbeats when he leaned down. Close, closer still. She waited for his mouth to fasten on hers. Yearned for his kiss. And was disappointed, releasing her breath on a long sigh, when he suddenly withdrew.

He groaned. "If I start, I'll never stop. Not this time. And we both need some sleep if we're going to get out of here at first light."

It was a sensible decision. It just wasn't an appealing one.

"Damn it, I always seem to be parting from you at this door, when what I want to do is come into that room with you. But," he promised, his voice deepening to a growl, "the next time—and you can count on it, Meredith, there will be a next time—then you and I…"

He left the rest unsaid, but she got the message. It left her feeling decidedly weak after he was gone.

JACKSON CONGRATULATED himself on successfully negotiating the roundabout, one of those tricky traffic circles so common at English crossroads, and as much a challenge to American motorists as driving on the left side.

You're going to feel at home in this country yet, Hawke. Providing.

A lot of meaning in that single word. In his case, it meant *providing* he didn't wind up back in the States because he'd failed to meet the deadline of an ultimatum.

Jackson glanced at Meredith beside him. She had drifted off as the little English Ford skimmed across the moorland on its way to Truro. One of these days he was going to have to explain to her how he was fighting for his survival. That he either had to solve this case or go under.

He had almost told her yesterday, when she had demanded to know on their walk back to the castle why the Croft case was so vital to him. But he had resisted, fearing she would misunderstand his motives. He wanted to make certain of their relationship before he shared the truth with her.

Their relationship? Hell, there wasn't supposed to be any relationship. Not after what had happened back in the States with April. That's what he'd emphatically promised himself when he'd left for England. That from now on he wouldn't get involved.

Yeah, well, it was too late. He and Meredith were already involved. He had only to look at her, with her silky blond hair and full, slightly parted mouth, to know just *how* involved. The kind that tugged seriously at a man's guts. But he was afraid to trust his feelings for her. Scared he would end up hurting her, as he had hurt April.

"Where are we exactly?" Meredith asked, stirring beside him.

He'd like to know that himself. But, of course, she wasn't talking about their relationship. "Just coming into the city."

Truro was an old market town, with a soaring cathedral and enough Georgian buildings to make even the casual tourist happy. They had made good time. It was still early and the library was just opening for the day when they managed to find both it and a parking spot out on the street.

The young man in charge of the rare and ancient books department had fair hair, a pronounced Adam's apple and a pair of pale eyes that regarded them suspiciously across his desk.

"The police were here yesterday asking me this same question, although they were not interested in what Professor Boynton was researching, only in where he might have gone after he left the library. I will tell you what I told them. I don't know."

"But you could tell us what book or books he used," Jackson said. "That is, if you know."

"Of course, I know. Some of our volumes are extremely valuable. We're very particular about the handling of them, which is why I insisted on photocopying that page for him myself."

"He wanted a copy of a certain page?" This was even better than he had hoped for, Jackson thought. "How about showing us that page?"

"Are you with the police?"

"Uh, not exactly."

"Meaning you aren't. In which case I have no intention of accommodating you. Yes, madam, how can I help you?" He moved off to serve an elderly woman at the far end of the counter.

"Pompous little twit," Jackson muttered.

Meredith laid a hand on his arm. "Go over there by the door and let me handle this."

"What are you going to do?"

"Just go."

Jackson went. A minute later, when the elderly woman had departed, he watched Meredith move in on the young librarian. Damn, she was applying the same technique he had used on Gwen Sparrow yesterday to get that key! He couldn't hear their exchange from here, but he knew brazen flirtation when he saw it.

In no time at all, Meredith was sauntering toward him, a photocopy in her hand.

"What did you have to promise him to get it?" Jackson demanded, unable to help the sharp, proprietary tone in his voice.

"A night he'll never forget." The expression on his face must have hardened, even though he knew she was joking, because she laughed and took his arm. "Let's get out of here and see what my wanton seduction earned for us."

What it got them, Jackson learned, once they were back inside the parked car and he had a chance to look at the sheet, was immediate frustration.

"This is no good. It's all in Latin."

"Yes, I know," Meredith said.

He gazed at her hopefully. "Do you know any Latin at all?"

"Not enough to be able to read it with anything like fluency. But I did have three years of it in high school. Don't ask me why, except my father, being the history teacher he was, believed in a classical education, and I always wanted to please him. It was a long time ago, and I'm not sure how much I remember, but I can try."

Jackson watched her, liking the way her delicate features got all scrunched up as she concentrated on the photocopy.

"Croft is mentioned twice here in this passage, so we must be on the right track. Let's see. *Foraminis* means a kind of hole or opening, I think. Or maybe a pit. Something like that. *Inferus* means under, I know. And *terra*, of course, is ground or earth. Hold on. It's going to take me a while to figure this out."

Long minutes passed before Meredith finally looked up from the page, her eyes glowing with excitement. "I've got it, what Simon Boynton must have been looking for!"

"The directions to the portal?"

"Well, an indication of where to find it. As far as I can make out, it's somewhere deep down under the castle."

Jackson was impressed by her effort and told her so.

"Yes, but it doesn't make sense. When I asked Guy, he told me there is no cellar or dungeon under the keep. Nothing like that. It's all solid rock." She shook her head. "Maybe I didn't get the translation right."

They were silent for several seconds, and then Jackson had a thought. "Do any of the words in there stand for cave?"

She consulted the sheet again. "I don't think so, no." She looked up at him. "What are you thinking?"

"That an island like Croft could have natural caves, maybe a number of them that would have been useful to smugglers. Probably down along the shore."

"Yes," she said, her excitement peaking again. "And if caves do exist, and one of them is below the castle itself, maybe it contained more than just a way into the castle for smugglers. Like the gate to—" She broke off, frowning again. "But this possibility must have occurred to Simon Boynton, too. He was in Truro the day of his daughter's murder. We're pretty sure he didn't go back to the island. So where did he go from here, and where is he now?"

"Could be he wanted more than just an indication." Looking out at the library, Jackson considered the problem. "And if none of the material in the library there was able to provide him with exact directions, he might have had an idea where he could go to find— *Duck!*"

Alarmed by the urgency of his sudden command, she started to twist around.

"Meredith, don't look! Just get down!"

He, himself, had already bent low in the seat. Putting his hand on her arm, he drew her down with him below the level of the car windows.

"What is it?" she asked, voice hushed, eyes wide.

"Trouble, if she spotted us. It was Inspector Ramsay's partner, Sergeant Ware. She was just getting out of a police car back on the corner. Let's hope she's not on her way into the library, because if she is, your young friend in there is bound to tell her we stopped by. And since we weren't supposed to have left the island—"

"*Please*, could we just get out of here?"

"Let me check." Jackson lifted his head just high enough to

permit him a view of the street and the entrance to the library. "Gone," he reported. "Whether she went into the library or had another errand in one of the other buildings along here, is anybody's guess. In any case, she's nowhere in sight so it's safe for us to clear off. But stay down until we put a couple of blocks between us and that police cruiser."

Jackson started the engine and pulled out into the traffic. He kept an eye on the rearview mirror all the way out of the city, but there was no sign of Sergeant Ware in pursuit of them. They remained vigilant all the way back to Trefarro, stopping only long enough at a fast-food restaurant to order a carryout lunch, which they ate while underway.

The tricky part, once they reached Trefarro, was getting the Ford back into the garage and themselves down to the quay without being observed by any officer on patrol. They made it without being challenged, but neither of them relaxed until the little outboard was putt-putting across the harbor.

Hand on the tiller and his gaze on the distant Croft Island toward which they steadily crawled, Jackson called over the sound of the engine, "How would you like to go spelunking this afternoon?"

Meredith, seated in the bow facing him, didn't have to consider his proposal. "I wouldn't. Poking around a cave is not high on my list of fascinating things to do." She paused, turning around to look at the island. "But I suppose we don't have a choice if we want to solve this puzzle. So, providing it even exists, how do we go about reaching this cave? On foot?"

Jackson shook his head. "From what I've seen of the island, the beach is probably impassable in places, certainly on the castle side where the cliffs look like they fall sheer to the water."

"By boat, then."

"Why not? We've got the outboard rented for the entire day, the sea is calm, and—" he leaned over to rap his knuckles on a box stored under his seat "—I was told the emergency kit here includes a flashlight."

"All right, but let's stop at the dock first. There's a call box there. I want to find out how Guy is doing and whether he knows anything about a cave below the castle."

Jackson stretched his legs on the stone quay, watching a fisherman mend a lobster pot while Meredith phoned the castle. She was still inside the call box when a grizzled figure in baggy pants and a seaman's cap appeared. Jackson recognized him as Fred Griggs, the handyman who worked for Lord and Lady Danely a few days each week.

"Lookin' fer Rob to turn in yer boat? 'Cause he ain't here if yer are."

"No, we're going out with it again."

The old man cast a weather eye on the open waters beyond the harbor. "Yer want to be mindful then. I ain't sayin' we're in fer any dirty stuff, but sea aroun' here can change that fast."

"We're going to stick close to the shore."

"That'd be wise." Griggs began to cast off the lines of the launch.

"I thought Rob Curzon always handled the shuttle."

"Aye, he does, but I'm takin' the afternoon run today. Robbie is off somewheres else."

"I don't blame him. The island is pretty small. Must get dull for someone his age."

Griggs laughed. "Robbie? Yer don't know him then."

And that's when the old man told him something interesting about Rob Curzon.

Chapter Eleven

Meredith was so intent on telling Jackson what she'd learned from her phone call that she failed to notice the sober expression on his face.

"There *are* caves around the shoreline. More than a dozen of them, Guy thinks. Most of them are very shallow, hardly caves at all. And, yes, one of them is almost directly below the castle. But he's never visited it, because it means either rappelling down to it over the side of the cliff or reaching it by boat. So, you were right about that. One thing, though. The mouth of the cave is covered when the tide is in."

Jackson glanced down over the side of the quay, checking the barnacle-encrusted waterline. "Well, it's out now."

"Yes, but we'll need to be cautious about that. Guy didn't ask, and I didn't go into it, but I know he must be wondering why we're interested in the cave. We'll have to explain that later. Oh, I almost forgot. He's feeling much better today."

Jackson nodded. "That's good."

Meredith frowned, realizing suddenly that something was on his mind. "Have you been listening to anything I said?"

"Every word."

"Then why do you look so distracted?" She noticed he was gazing at the launch that was now underway. "I saw you talking to the pilot while I was on the phone. Fred Griggs, isn't it? What was he saying?"

"Just something about Rob Curzon."

"What about him, other than I can see he's not taking this afternoon's run to the mainland."

Still sober, Jackson turned to her. "The old man told me the island is Rob's whole life. Seems that his family has been on Croft forever, so far back that not even they know when their people were first here. I don't know about you, but I find that damn revealing."

Meredith understood then what had him preoccupied. "That mysterious descendant of Sir Hugh Gwinfryd. That's what you're thinking Rob Curzon might be, isn't it? Jackson, we can't suspect him of that without evidence. There must be others here whose families have been connected with the island for ages."

"Yeah," he said, surfacing from his reverie, "you're right, of course. It was just a P.I.'s itch, and now I've scratched it."

But Meredith knew, as they settled themselves in the outboard again, that Jackson wasn't dismissing Rob Curzon as a potential culprit. Nor, now that he had told her about the young man, was she.

It was when they were chugging around the point of the small bay that Meredith brought up another matter that had occurred to her.

"This cave," she said above the throb of the motor. "Are we just wasting our time going to it? It doesn't seem to be a secret, which means it must have been visited by others before us."

"I know. I've considered that, too. But then nobody was looking for a gate to hell, and that puts another spin on it. Anyway, right now it's all we've got."

So we go with it, she thought. It's what good P.I.s did. For that matter, psychologists, too.

From her seat in the bow, Meredith scanned the rocky coastline only yards away off their port side as they plowed steadily through a sea that was as smooth as glass. There were several gaping black holes between the boulders that could have been the entrances to caves. But none of them was the cave they were seeking. That was on the far side of the island, and they had some distance to go before they reached this area.

It was the fierce cries of a pair of gulls quarreling over some tidbit that shifted Meredith's attention in another direction. That was when she discovered it out over the open waters—a bank of fog headed their way.

"Jackson!"

"Yeah, I see it."

"Do you think we ought to turn back?"

"We'll be all right as long as we keep hugging the shoreline."

Much more swiftly than she would have believed possible given the still air, the fog enveloped them. It was thicker than a mist but not so heavy they couldn't still make out the darker mass of the island. The motor on their craft was so small it had never permitted them to travel at any kind of speed. But for safety's sake, Jackson eased the thottle back until they were no more than creeping through the sluggish, gray waters.

Even so, the sound of the engine seemed louder in the fog. The odor of the sea was stronger, too—a mixture of salt and fish and seaweed mingling with the fumes from the engine.

"It's getting worse, isn't it?" she observed.

It was true. The fog was no longer just smoke. It was a solid wall behind which the shoreline, close as it was, had vanished. Not even its dim outline was visible to her.

Jackson cut the engine. The abrupt silence seemed uncanny. "We'll have to sit it out," he decided. "I'll put out the anchor. That should keep us from drifting."

He was right. Without any bearings whatsoever, they could easily become lost in this mess and find themselves far out of sight of land by the time the fog lifted.

There was a splash as the anchor went over the side. Then, except for the gentle lap of the waters against the hull, there was only the silence again.

The fog was clammy, with an eerie quality about it. And so ense that, even though Jackson was only a few feet away in e stern, she couldn't see him. She didn't know he was moving until she felt the boat rocking as he made his way forward.

"You're cold," he said, squeezing beside her on the seat.

It was true the temperature had dropped when the sun was lotted out, but her jacket protected her against the chill. "I'm ot cold."

"Yes, you are," he insisted, sliding his arm around her waist nd drawing her snugly against his side.

"I guess I am at that."

But it wasn't his body heat that had her snuggling against im. It was something much more provocative than that. Something that had to do with the solid, protective bulk of him. The ntimate, caring contact of a man who made her feel safe and ecure. Who awakened pleasurable memories of his stirring isses. And who was also dangerous when she was still not certain whether she could trust her emotions with him.

To defuse the risk of the moment, and also because she did enuinely want to know more about this tough but tender male, he used the opportunity to question him.

"A P.I. with an itch, huh? So, just how did Jackson Hawke o about acquiring that itch?"

"I didn't. It came with the gene pool."

"I thought it was royalty that flowed through your veins."

"That's my mother's side. Or so she'd have us believe. But ith my father's family it's law enforcement. He's a county heriff in rural Illinois where I grew up, just like his father and randfather were before him."

"But you're not."

"Nope. I guess I was just too independent to be governed y the rules of formal law enforcement."

Meredith had discovered how true that was.

"Who knows how I would have ended up if my father's rother hadn't taken me under his wing. Casey Hawke. He and my aunt manage the home office of Hawke Detective Agenc in Chicago."

And Jackson's cousins operated branches of that agency i various regions of the United States. Meredith already knew this much. "So your uncle taught you the P.I. business."

"How to scratch that itch, right."

"Uh, speaking of that. The *fingers*."

His arm around her waist had shifted while they talked, hi hand climbing insidiously up her rib cage under her jacket. Hi fingers were now in contact with the side of her breast, wher his thumb moved in slow, seductive circles.

"Too friendly, huh?"

"Considering the circumstances, I would say so." To *treacherous* a temptation was more like it, with that skillfu thumb of his arousing her. Still, Meredith couldn't help won dering what it would be like to have Jackson Hawke mak love to her while they were buried like this in the fog. But in small rowboat? Decidedly uncomfortable.

"Did Uncle Casey also give you lessons in sneakiness?" T her relief, his arm slid back down to her waist. She might no have found the will to resist him if it hadn't.

"Learned that one for myself about the time I discovere girls were more than just nuisances. But he did help me to fin my special calling when he handed me my first case. Clien wanted proof that his mother was being defrauded by a mediur who claimed he could materialize her late husband for her. got that proof, along with a reputation for debunking fak ghosts."

Which eventually landed him in the role of my rival, Mer edith thought, remembering their past conflicts back in the State

When she'd heard that he was being sent to England to ope the first overseas branch of the agency, she had believed sh was rid of him. Now, ironically, here she was huddled besid him in the fog, sharing his warmth and eager to know every thing about him.

Why? Why was it so important for her to understand him? But she needn't have asked herself that question. She knew the answer.

"You were successful back in the States," she conceded. "So why didn't your aunt and uncle keep you there? Why did they want to send you over here?"

He hesitated. "They didn't. I asked to come."

"Oh?"

Somewhere out in the fog that licked at them, a gull cried mournfully. It was a haunting, disturbing sound. Jackson's arm tightened around her waist.

There was silence again. She waited for him to go on, but he didn't. She could feel his restraint and sensed the subject had suddenly become uncomfortable for him, perhaps even painful.

He might never have talked of it, but, shrouded as they were in a world where only the two of them existed in this time and space, confidences were natural. At least that's what she thought at first.

"There was a woman back home," he finally said. "April Paulson."

Entitled to it or not, Meredith felt an immediate pang of jealousy. Even worse, Jackson's arm dropped from her waist as he inched slightly away from her on the seat. It was a loss that hurt more than she was willing to admit.

"You don't have to talk about it," she said.

"Yes, I do. It's time you knew about it."

Then it wasn't just the setting. He *wanted* her to know. Her spirits lifted. "You were involved with her."

"Not in the way you think. April's husband, Len, was my best friend. He was also a Chicago cop who worked on the streets."

"That couldn't have been the safest of jobs."

"It wasn't. That's why Len had me promise that, if anything ever happened to him, I'd be there for April and his kid."

"And did something—" Meredith couldn't bring herself to say it.

Jackson said it for her in a husky voice. "Yeah, he was killed in a drug bust."

"Leaving you to look out for his wife and child."

"A little boy, Kevin. I spent a lot of time with him and April in those weeks after Len died, helping her to get back on her feet. The thing is…"

He paused again, and Meredith knew this was a struggle for him. She also thought she understood now why he had put distance between them. It was nothing personal, nothing to do with the two of them. It was simply his method of dealing with an emotional issue, not trusting himself to be intimate with her while discussing an anguish connected with another woman.

"The thing is," he continued, "April came to misunderstand my attentions."

"She fell in love with you."

"I don't know. I think she convinced herself it was something more than friendship because she'd lost Len, and I was there with Kevin and her so much. I just knew if she went on relying on me, counting on me being a full-time substitute for Len, it could only end up with everybody losing. What else could happen when I couldn't be for her what she wanted me to be."

"So you thought it was time to put distance between you. A *lot* of distance."

"Yeah, I left April and came to England. But only after I made certain she had family and friends around her and that she was all right financially."

He was justifying his actions. He didn't have to. Meredith could see he had done the right thing. But she suspected he'd suffered guilt over what he perceived as a desertion. It would explain that reluctance to get too close to her she had sometimes sensed in him, especially at the beginning. A fear perhaps that he might end up hurting both her and himself, just as he must have convinced himself he had hurt April Paulson.

Did that make it impossible for him to trust himself to fall in love? Because, although they *had* become very close in spite of a mutual reluctance, there was the possibility that, if she dared to take it a step further and fall in love with Jackson Hawke, he would back away from her, turn and run. Or was it too late? Was she already hopelessly—

"Fog is beginning to ease up," he said.

Her mind had been so busy she had failed to notice, but he was right. The fog was no longer a solid wall. A patchy thing now, with long veils of it driven toward the mainland by a sea breeze, it was possible to once again make out the island's coastline.

"I think it's safe enough for us to go on."

Getting up from the seat they had been sharing, he moved to the stern and raised the anchor. Then he settled himself at the tiller, but just before he turned the engine over, he looked at her over his shoulder. There was a sober expression on his face.

"Thanks for listening to me," he said.

THEY RAN INTO another band of fog as they chugged around to the far side of the island. While they were feeling their way through it, Meredith thought she heard the rumble of an engine that wasn't theirs. A ghostly sound that had her wondering if she was imagining it.

"Is there another boat out here?" she called to Jackson.

Before he could answer her, a craft suddenly materialized out of the fog. A gray phantom without identity, or any figure she could make out, it sliced through the waters off their starboard side and then was gone, disappearing again into the deep mist. So brief had been its appearance it seemed more like an apparition without substance than a reality.

"Whoever he was," Jackson said, "he was in a hurry."

Maybe he had the right idea, Meredith thought. Maybe they should be turning around and following him before the fog got so impossibly thick again they'd never find their way back to port.

Within seconds of her fresh concern, their little boat shot out of the bank of fog like a missile tearing through a curtain of gauze. The change was startling.

They were entirely in the open, without a shred of fog to obscure either land, sea or sky. And there, almost directly in front of them, rose the sheer, black face of the cliff on whose high summit crouched the bulky pile that was Croft Castle's keep. From this angle, Meredith thought, the stronghold would have presented a formidable challenge to any ancient raiders who approached by sea.

"See it?" Jackson said, pointing toward the mouth of a cave located at the waterline at the base of the cliff.

She nodded as Jackson turned the outboard and headed for the cave. The waters, which had been as smooth as oil, were choppy now under the strengthening breeze.

"Kicking up just a bit," Jackson said, working the bouncing boat toward shore.

There was no beach to speak of, Meredith noticed as they neared their objective. Just scattered boulders at the foot of the cliff, some of them almost submerged. When they approached the entrance to the cave, she could see that it, too, was partly under water.

"Looks like the channel here goes straight into the cave," Jackson observed, slowing them once more to a crawl. "We'll be able to run the boat right inside."

In fact, she realized, unless they wanted to wade, there was no other way through the opening.

The gap was too narrow to navigate under power. He killed the motor and seized one of the two oars, using it like a pole to shove the boat forward. It was a tight squeeze. They bumped against one of the rough walls as Jackson guided them through the tunnel.

Once past the neck with its low ceiling, the cave opened into a sizable chamber where their boat floated on a deep, murky pool. They sat there in silence for a few seconds, needing to adjust their eyes to the gloom and because it was an eerie kind of cavern. A place where, if voices spoke at all, they would do so in hushed tones, and where the greenish light, reflected off the waters, cast strange, shimmering patterns on the walls.

"It's so quiet," she whispered, though actually that wasn't true. When she listened, she could hear the waters making soft, hollow, sucking sounds under a low ledge.

Jackson used the oar again, driving them across the surface to the back side of the chamber where the level floor was above water. The underside of the boat scraped bottom at the shallow end of the pool, its nose nudging against dry rock.

Jackson scrambled past her and out of the boat. There was a knob of rock that made a perfect post for anchoring a line. Joining him on shore, Meredith even wondered whether the groove in it was natural or if it had been cut into the stone for that very purpose.

Jackson must have been thinking the same thing. As he looped the line of their outboard around the knob and secured it snugly, he voiced his speculation about the cave.

"This pool makes an ideal spot for mooring small boats. Smugglers could have run their cargoes in here and unloaded them in secret."

"And stored them where?"

"That might tell us," he said, indicating the opening to a passage in the back wall.

Armed with the flashlight from the emergency box, they set off to explore the gallery. It sloped gradually upward, twisting and turning into the sinister blackness ahead of them. Most of it had been carved by nature, but in several tight spots it looked as though it might have been widened by ancient tools.

There were no side passages. Nothing that might have lost them in a bewildering labyrinth, like the secret passages that had swallowed them in the keep. The route was a direct one.

But a route to what? Meredith asked herself. Some lost treasure connected with the age of smuggling? Or something more awesome than that? The gate to hell. It had to be a myth, and yet—

"Up ahead," Jackson said. "It looks like another chamber."

It proved to be just that. When the passage carrying them opened onto it, Meredith could see it was smaller than the first chamber. It was also empty, as well as a disappointment in another respect.

"I don't see any other openings," she said as Jackson swung the beam of the flashlight around the cavern. "It's a dead end."

"I don't think it was always that way. Look over here."

She joined him on the other side of the chamber where he was examining what appeared to be crude steps that had been hacked out of the granite inside a shallow recess. They ascended for several feet and then ended in blank wall.

"They don't make sense."

"But they did at one time. Can't you see it?" he said, lifting the flashlight so that it shone directly on the wall.

She *could* see it now. The wall here wasn't solid, as it was elsewhere in the chamber. This section inside the recess was composed of a mass of tumbled rocks and boulders that reached from floor to ceiling without a gap.

"A cave-in," she said. "And from the looks of it, it happened long ago."

"Either that, or it was a deliberate act meant to permanently block wherever these stairs led to."

She stared at him. "Do you think…"

"That this was the entrance to Sir Hugh's gate to hell? Maybe. Or maybe it was a smugglers' passage that climbed right up into the heart of the cliff and somehow connected with the castle keep at the other end."

"It could have been both."

"We'll never know. It would take heavy equipment in here

to shift that rock, and if the passage is buried in other places along its length—"

"Listen!" she whispered.

"What? I didn't hear anything."

"Jackson, there's someone in here with us!"

"The ghost of a long-dead smuggler?"

"Stop grinning at me. This was very human. There!"

It was unmistakable this time. A soft, feeble groan that sent chills racing along her spine. Jackson heard it, too.

"It's from over there behind that mound of rocks. Stay here."

Meredith didn't obey him, though she did keep behind him as they rounded the pile of rocks. The flashlight disclosed the figure of a man stretched out on his back on the floor.

"Here, hold this while I check him out."

"Be careful," she advised Jackson as he handed her the flashlight and crouched beside the inert figure.

Her warning was unnecessary. She could see that as she directed the light at the stranger. From the looks of him, he was in no state to harm anyone. His eyes were closed and his face wore the pallor of someone who had suffered a trauma. Nor was he built for action. A small, thin man with gray hair and pinched features, she judged him to be somewhere in his late fifties. But who was he, and how did he get here?

"There's blood on this side of his skull from a wound," Jackson reported. "He was struck by something. Or someone."

Experiencing those chills again, Meredith glanced quickly over her shoulder. But there was no assailant lurking in the cave.

Jackson's examination roused the man. His eyes fluttered open. They were gray and watery, glazed with shock. "Gone?" he muttered. "Is he gone?" He obviously had no idea who he was talking to.

"Who?" Jackson pressed him.

"I—" He paused, struggling to speak. "I fear I made a grave error in ever telling him what was in the book."

Meredith and Jackson exchanged lightning glances. Professor Simon Boynton! The injured man had to be Professor Boynton!

"It was the cave-in, you see," he whispered, wanting them to understand. "We were prevented from going any farther. It enraged him. He—he seemed to think it was somehow my fault, and he turned on me. You—you will be careful of him, won't you?"

"Who was it, Professor? Who attacked you?"

"That's right. Savage brute attacked me. Insane. He's insane, of course. Why didn't I see that before? Why…"

His eyes closed again. He was still.

"No use trying to question him. He's totally unconscious this time."

Jackson felt for his pulse while Meredith gazed down at the professor in concern and compassion. "The boat," she said. "The other boat that passed us in the fog. It had to have been—"

"Yeah, the bastard who struck Boynton. He must have dragged him behind these rocks where he thought he'd never be found. Then he fled, probably believing he'd left the professor dead. Which he will be, if we don't get help for him. His pulse is pretty weak."

"Didn't the landlord of the inn tell you there's a retired doctor in the village?"

"He did."

"Then we'll have to take him there. Between us we ought to be able to carry him back to the outboard."

"He's a lightweight. I'll manage him. You just be sure I can see where I'm going."

Meredith winced as Jackson heaved the professor up in his arms, staggered to his feet and slung him over his shoulder. But the professor was oblivious to any pain and never stirred. They started down the gallery, Meredith being careful to light the way for Jackson with his load.

Simon Boynton's condition was a serious one. Could he survive the blow to his head, or would he never regain consciousness?

Dead or alive, he was a victim of the same desperate man who had murdered his daughter. But surely the professor couldn't have known about Sybil. If he had, he wouldn't have accompanied her killer to this lonely place. On the other hand, Meredith realized, if greed was extreme enough, it could forgive a lot. Even murder.

"Something is wrong," Jackson said. "Hear it?"

He was a few yards out in front of her. She caught up to him where he had stopped. She, too, paused to listen.

"Water," she said. "It sounds like rushing water."

"It is," he said grimly.

He hurried forward again, and she knew what he was thinking as she brought up the rear with the flashlight. She was thinking it, too.

Their fears were realized as they rounded the last bend and arrived in the larger of the two chambers. The pool, which had been so still when they'd left it, was no longer quiet. Waters were surging into the cave from the outside, breaking over the surface of the pool.

"It can't be just a breeze out there anymore," she said.

"It's more than a wind driving waves in here, Meredith. The tide has turned and is on its way up."

He was right. They'd misjudged the tide, perhaps because of losing all that time while stalled in the fog. Now it was rising rapidly under the force of the wind. The cave would soon be flooded. Though the spot where they stood was still high and dry, the opening was already sinking, with only a few feet of clearance between its ceiling and the water level. That was not the worst.

"The boat! Where's the boat? Jackson, it's gone!"

"Yeah, I sort of noticed that myself."

"It must have been tugged loose by the action of the waves and dragged out into the channel."

"Either that or that bastard started to wonder where we might be going after he passed us. And if he did, he could have turned around, come back here, found our boat and released it, because I'd swear I had the line tied so it couldn't work loose."

At this point what did it matter? "Jackson, what are we going to do? If we stay here, we'll be trapped, and if we go back to the other chamber and wait until Guy gets worried and sends help, it may be too late for the professor."

Jackson lowered the professor to the floor of the cave, came to his feet and peeled off his jacket. "I'm going after our boat. With any luck, it'll be drifting out there close by."

Meredith was horrifed by his intention. "You can't! You'll drown in all that wild stuff!"

"Sit tight. I'll be back before you can miss me."

Before she could stop him, he had kicked off his shoes and launched himself into the churning pool. She watched, fists pressed to her mouth, as he headed for the opening with strong, steady strokes. He battled a relentless force of wind and tide, but he was a powerful swimmer. Within seconds, he had passed through the opening and was gone.

Meredith sank to the floor of the cave, sick with apprehension as she huddled beside the prone figure of Simon Boynton. It was one thing for Jackson to overcome the waters of the pool, but out there in the turbulence of the channel... No, she wouldn't let herself imagine the worst!

...before you can miss me.

She already missed him. Snatching up his jacket from where he had dropped it, she held it to her face, sniffing its folds to detect his scent, feeling the warmth that still lingered from his body. The jacket was a silly substitute for the man himself, but it provided her with a kind of comfort. And an assurance that he would return for it. He *had* to survive and come back. Because if he didn't—

Don't let yourself think about it. Think about something else. The professor. Check on the professor.

She was leaning over Simon Boynton's body when she saw it. A folded sheet of paper that must have fallen out of one of the pockets of the professor's tweed coat.

Meredith picked it up and spread it open. It was a photocopy of a very old map. Croft Island. The cave here was marked on the map with a legend in Latin. She couldn't make it out clearly, but it might have referred to the portal to hell.

It seemed she and Jackson had been right back in Truro when they'd speculated that Professor Boynton, after leaving the library there, had gone off somewhere to seek exact directions to the gate. That's where he'd been then, on the trail of this map.

Meredith refolded the map and was tucking it into her bag when a shout had her scrambling to her feet. She'd never seen anything more welcome than the sight of the wave that carried the outboard with Jackson aboard it into the cave. Once through the opening, his body bent low to avoid the ceiling, he poled the boat rapidly to her side of the pool.

"You're soaked!"

"You will be, too," he promised. "It's very rough out there. I had a devil of a time catching up with the boat and pulling myself aboard."

It was little short of a miracle that he had recovered the boat at all.

"Let's move," he urged. "We've got to get Boynton and ourselves on board and out of here while we can still clear that opening, because the water is coming up fast."

The water was already lapping at their feet by the time they loaded the professor and their gear into the boat. Meredith settled in the bow, Jackson in the stern at the tiller with the unconscious Simon Boynton lying between them.

She held her breath as Jackson tried to start the engine. It took a few sputtering failures before it caught and held. With a roar, the outboard headed for the opening. The gap was now so reduced in height that, even with their bodies bent double, they barely scraped through.

The craft bucked and rolled as it met the oncoming break-ers outside. Bracing herself against the onslaught, Meredith sat up and gasped at the startling sight of the sea around them. She had heard that Cornwall was known for its abrupt, drastic chan-ges in weather. The claim was no exaggeration.

The sea, which had been so placid less than an hour ago, was now raging as ragged black clouds raced across the sky that now bore all the signs of an imminent storm. Nor was the channel visible any longer. The boulders that had marked it were buried beneath the surf.

"Hang on!" Jackson shouted. "This is going to be a real bat-tle getting back to port!"

She nodded, clinging to the gunwales as the outboard val-iantly fought its way through the billows. Battered as it was by the wind and tide that tossed it from side to side in the troughs, then lifted the prop of its engine clear out of the water when it crested the foam, it was a wonder the little boat made any progress at all. But under Jackson's skill and guidance, they wallowed steadily onward.

Meredith, too, felt punished by a wind that whipped her hair in her eyes and drenched her with salt spray. There was a can under her seat. She used it to bail out the water that was col-lecting on the floor of the boat.

The professor's head was being bumped cruelly against the edge of one of the two seats between which his body was wedged. Stripping off her jacket and bunching it into a pillow, she half rose out of her seat and leaned forward to cushion him with the jacket.

"Meredith!" Jackson yelled. "Sit down!"

His warning came too late. At that second a mountainous wave crashed into the side of the outboard. The boat heeled over sharply, pitching Meredith into the sea where the deep, dark waters closed over her head.

Chapter Twelve

Meredith was so stunned by the impact of the cold waters that, for a moment, she was unable to resist an undertow that seemed to be sucking her down to a certain death.

Then, as panic seized her, she began to fight back. Legs kicking away seaweed that threatened to entangle her, she stretched her body upward in an effort to reach the surface. But how long could she hold her breath? Her lungs were already on fire, and if she passed out—

A pair of arms suddenly wrapped around her. Caught in their powerful embrace, she felt herself being sped toward the light above them. Seconds later, she and her rescuer shot to the surface.

"Don't gulp," Jackson commanded. "Breathe through your nose, or you'll swallow water."

"The boat," she gasped. "Have we lost the boat?" Without it, they couldn't hope to survive for very long in this pounding sea.

"Behind you," he said. "I threw out the anchor after I cut the engine. The drag kept it from being carried too far away."

Meredith twisted around to see the outboard bobbing on the swells several yards away.

"Can you make it that far on your own?" Jackson asked, treading water as he continued to support her. "Otherwise, I can try carrying you on my back."

"I'll make it."

She was a good swimmer. Ordinarily, that was. But in these waters and without Jackson's strength to cling to, the yards seemed like light-years.

In the end, a wave carried them the final few feet, swinging them into the side of the boat. Meredith reached out, grasping the gunwale.

"Hang on," Jackson said. "I'm going to work around to the other side. I'll need your weight on this end to keep her from capsizing while I haul myself aboard."

He was gone then. Seconds later, she felt a heavy tug as he heaved himself into the boat. Then his arms were reaching over the side, pulling her from the sea. Once in the boat, she collapsed on a seat.

"The professor," she said, unable to see him since Jackson's body blocked her view.

"Still with us."

It was a miracle he hadn't been swept overboard by her carelessness, which had almost cost her her own life. And Jackson's, as well. Her fingers squeezed his hand in an expression of gratitude. "Thank you," she murmured. "That was a foolish thing to do."

"You won't get any argument from me. You should have stayed in your seat."

"I meant jumping in after me like that. Brave and wonderful, but foolish."

"You're welcome. Take your blouse off."

"Hey, I'm grateful, but—"

"Meredith, you're wet clean through and probably numb with cold. Take your blouse off, and put your jacket on. It will help. Here." He picked up her jacket from where it had landed on a seat before she went overboard and thrust it at her.

"What about you?"

"I'll be fine."

He left her and carefully made his way aft to bring in the anchor and restart the engine. Meredith struggled out of her blouse and bundled into the jacket, which remained reasonably dry. From the waist down, she was still sopping, including her shoes, but that couldn't be helped.

The wind had eased somewhat while they'd struggled in the water. But that timely, blessed lull ended once they were underway again. The wind seemed to gather new strength, the seas growing so heavy they kicked spume high into the air. The outboard was bounced around like a toy.

Meredith resumed her bailing while managing this time to stay firmly seated. From time to time, she cast an anxious gaze in Simon Boynton's direction. He never stirred and his lips looked blue. She was worried about him, but there was nothing they could do for him until they were back in port.

But could their poor craft withstand this fierce blow long enough to limp into port? How far now was the harbor? It was difficult to tell, because the light was rapidly failing.

"It's getting dark," she called to Jackson at the tiller. "The sun must have set."

"It isn't just that," he yelled back. "I think there's a serious storm on the way. This stuff, bad as it is, is only a forerunner."

Dear God, if he was right, if the wind and water got any worse, they could never hope to survive them.

She looked up. Black clouds were still scudding across the sky. Seconds later, the first drops fell. Just a drizzle at first. Then the rain increased, lashing them furiously. Wet and miserable, Meredith renewed her bailing.

"We're coming around the point!" Jackson announced.

When they swung about, the wind and waves attacked them ferociously, as if determined not to lose them. But the elements lost the final battle when Jackson piloted the boat into the lee of the little bay. The wind was still strong, the waters rough, but nothing like the blasts of the open sea.

The contrast was so sudden, so pronounced that Meredith was shocked by it. Not until they reached the quay in the harbor could she believe they were safe. She was trembling with relief when she got slowly to her feet, her legs still unsteady after Jackson killed the engine, made their line fast and came to her in the bow.

"You all right?" he asked, sliding his arms around her waist and drawing her against him.

"Sure."

For a moment, she did nothing but relish the feel of his solid body holding her securely. The rain and the cold and their wet clothes didn't matter. They were alive. And then she remembered their passenger.

"The professor," she said, pulling away from Jackson. "We've got to get him to that doctor."

"He needs a hospital on the mainland, but there's no way he can be moved to one in this weather. Yeah, we'll have to trust this retired doctor. You happen to know his name or where he lives?"

Meredith shook her head. "I can't remember ever hearing either one mentioned."

"Me, either. We've got a problem. If we ask anyone in the village, it's going to get back to the killer. And if he learns Boynton is still alive and where he is…"

"He'll try to get to him and silence him before he can talk."

Meredith gazed at the village just beyond the quay. There were lights in the windows, but the street was deserted. The harbor, too. The weather had everyone indoors, which meant Simon Boynton was safe for the moment. But they had to act quickly before their secret was discovered. Her eye fell on the bright red call box at the end of the quay.

"I'll phone the castle and ask Guy and my mother," she said. "They should be told we're safe, anyway. They're probably very worried about us by now."

"Good idea. Make sure they understand they can't mention this business to anyone, not even Imogen."

Meredith left Jackson guarding the professor and hurried away to the call box. Imogen answered her ring and went off to fetch Lord Danely. While Meredith waited for Guy to come to the phone, she checked the quay through the glass.

There was a light outside the call box swinging in the wind at the end of a pole. In its glow she saw the figure of a man in an old-fashioned rain slicker headed in the direction of their outboard. When he passed under the lantern, she recognized him as Fred Griggs, the old man who helped Rob Curzon with the boats.

Jackson must have seen the old man approaching and had headed him off midway along the quay.

She couldn't hear the exchange between the two men and Guy had picked up the phone. By the time she hung up, Jackson was alone again and had returned to the other end of the quay.

"It's all right," he assured her when she anxiously joined him. "Griggs is gone."

"He didn't get a glimpse of the professor, did he?"

"No, I managed to keep him away from the outboard, but I had a devil of a time satisfying him that both the boat and the motor were fine and that he could check them over himself in the morning when he had daylight."

"How did he know we were back in port?"

"He heard us chugging in. Said he was worried when we didn't get back before dark and was about to call the rescue station in Trefarro. Funny thing, though."

"What?"

"When I asked him if Rob Curzon had returned, he said he guessed he was spending the night with a girlfriend on the mainland."

"Maybe he is."

"I wonder." Jackson frowned, lost in thought for a moment, and then he shook his head. "You get what we need?"

"Dr. James Merrick. His cottage is near the beach, isolated from the others."

"Perfect. We'd better not lose any more time getting Boynton over there."

Jackson bore the professor over his shoulder and Meredith led the way, keeping far enough in front to warn Jackson if she encountered anyone. But they saw no one as they trudged through the wind and rain.

With the directions Guy had provided, they had no trouble finding the place. A fisherman's house converted into a small retirement cottage, it was nestled against a slope above the shore.

Lights in its windows indicated the doctor was at home. Their glow also revealed flower beds, whose contents had suffered in the storm. Meredith presumed that Dr. Merrick—a widower who lived alone, according to Guy—was an amateur gardener.

There was a tiny porch at the end of the path. It sheltered them while they waited for the doctor to answer Meredith's knock on the front door. Above the wail of the wind, she heard a dog barking somewhere in the rear of the cottage. A sharp, muffled command silenced the animal. A moment later the porch light was switched on and the door opened.

Meredith found herself confronted by a little gnome of a man, who peered at her suspiciously over a pair of half glasses. "What's this?" he demanded in a voice that could only be described as cantankerous.

"Dr. Merrick? I'm Lord Danely's stepdaughter, Meredith Allen."

"Did he send you here? I can't imagine why. Man knows I don't have a practice anymore."

"This is an emergency," Jackson spoke firmly behind her. "We have an injured man."

Meredith stepped to one side so that the doctor could see the professor slung over Jackson's shoulder. He looked, grunted, then moved aside in the doorway. "You'd better come in, then."

It was a neat cottage, its low ceilings crossed by heavy beams and its few rooms overcrowded with furniture that must have once occupied a larger home. Meredith had a glimpse of an open fire in a cozy sitting room as Dr. Merrick conducted them along a narrow passage.

"I don't have a surgery these days," he said, and Meredith knew this was the British term for a physician's office and examining room. "This will have to do. On the bed, please. Never mind the counterpane. It's seen it all, blood, dirt and tears."

He led them into a guest room where Jackson laid the professor on the bed. Dr. Merrick bent over the patient and then turned to look at them over the half glasses, a severe expression on his round face.

"This is Simon Boynton."

"Yes," Jackson said.

"All right," he said brusquely, "you can tell me later what happened. Go wait in the sitting room while I get my bag and do what I can for him."

They went. There was no sign of the dog. He must have been shut up in the back of the cottage. Meredith welcomed the fire on the wide hearth in the sitting room. She sat close to it, warming herself while Jackson prowled around the room restlessly. They didn't talk. The only sound was the popping of the fire and the moan of the wind outside.

It was some moments before the elderly Dr. Merrick joined them. "I cleaned and dressed the wound," he reported, drying his hands on a towel. "He's still unconscious, not good. Not good at all. He should be in hospital, but he'll have to remain here until the weather clears. I've seen these storms before. They isolate the island. Not even a medical helicopter can land in winds of this velocity, and certainly a boat is out of the question. That injury—how did he get it?"

Jackson explained briefly without going into details.

"The police will have to be told," Dr. Merrick insisted.

"I intend to phone them as soon as we get back to the castle," Jackson promised. "But you understand, don't you, why the professor's presence in your cottage has to be kept secret until the police get here and can protect him?"

Meredith added her own plea. "Please, you can't tell anyone, Doctor."

Dr. Merrick glowered at them over the half glasses. "Did you expect me to go down to the George and announce it in the bar? Go home, the both of you, and let me treat my patient."

Assured by the doctor that the professor would be safe with him, Meredith and Jackson left the cottage. They were on their way to the castle when Guy met them with the Land Rover.

"Filthy night," he said as they squeezed into the front seat with him. "How is Boynton?"

"Still in a coma," Jackson told him. "And unless he comes out of it, we're not going to know who attacked him."

Guy nodded soberly as he turned the vehicle and headed back up the lane. "You can tell us everything after I get you back to the castle. Judith is waiting with a late supper. Thought you'd be hungry."

Meredith was. That quick lunch she and Jackson had eaten on the road from Truro was so long ago it seemed a dim memory. So were dry clothes. They remedied that problem as soon as they reached the castle. Once changed, they joined Guy and her mother in the dining room.

Meredith let Jackson recount in further detail their adventures in the outboard and the cave while she concentrated on a bowl of steaming tomato soup and a chilled salmon salad. After the meal, Jackson scraped his chair back from the table.

"Guess I'd better not delay it any longer. I've got to make that phone call to the police, even if they can't get here tonight. Something tells me DCI Ramsay is not going to be pleased with us."

"I'll do my bit to help you explain," Guy said.

The two men went off together to use the nearest phone in the library, leaving mother and daughter alone in the dining room. Meredith expected Judith to have questions for her or perhaps to express a concern for her safety. But the older woman was silent, and when Meredith looked at her there was a coolness in her eyes, a firmness in her mouth.

"Is something wrong?" Meredith asked her.

Judith didn't answer her for a moment, and then she seemed to make up her mind. "Guy and I have been discussing it since you rang up earlier from the quay. We came to a decision about your services for us."

"I don't understand."

"I'm sorry, but we feel it's no longer necessary for you to remain at Croft."

Meredith stared at her. "Let me get this straight. You're asking us to leave?"

"Not Jackson. You. There's really no point in your staying on when we know our problem here has nothing to do with a ghost. That's evident now, isn't it? And, after all, this was the reason for asking you to come."

"But your trouble hasn't been solved. There's a killer out there who won't give up until he finds what he wants, even if we think it can't exist. And what he wants is connected somehow with Croft Castle."

"Yes, but whoever he is is mortal, not a ghost. And since Jackson is a trained private detective…well, I think we can rely on both him and the police to handle it for us."

Meredith couldn't believe what she was hearing. "You're firing me. That's what it amounts to, doesn't it?"

"If you put it that way, I suppose I am. Of course, we're grateful for how you've tried to help us, but you know what our financial situation is." Judith's shoulders lifted in a little shrug. "We just can't afford two investigators anymore."

"But I told you—"

"Yes, I remember how you offered to waive your fee, but Guy won't hear of that. Really, it's better this way, Meredith. You have those lectures coming up, and I'm sure you could use the time back in London to prepare for them."

"And what if the police won't permit me to leave the island?"

"I think they'll be reasonable about it after they have a chance to interview you and Jackson tomorrow, especially if Guy uses his influence. All you have to promise them is to make yourself available in London, should you be needed again."

Meredith gazed at her mother in stricken silence. Judith sat there across the table from her, elegant, self-contained, and remote. Just as she'd always remembered her. Nothing had changed between them. Meredith had been wrong to think it ever could.

"We're not going to talk about this, are we?"

"I don't think there's anything more to discuss," Judith said. "If the weather is clear in the morning and the launch operating, you'll be able to leave on its first run. The police should have talked to you by then."

Meredith knew she couldn't bear to go on sitting here in the dining room with her mother. Pushing herself up from the table, she managed a calm "It's settled then. I'll go to my room and pack. Tell Jackson I was too tired to wait and that I'll see him in the morning."

Would Judith explain everything to Jackson when he returned to the dining room? she wondered as she mounted the stairs to her room. Or would she let Meredith tell him herself that she was leaving Croft?

She tried not to be emotional about it as she let herself into her room, stripped off her clothes in the bathroom and stepped under the spray for a much needed hot shower. She had trained herself long ago not to be hurt by her mother's treatment of her. So why should she be hurt now?

Because for all your efforts, that hurt never really did go away, did it? It was always there underneath. You deceived yourself if you believed it wasn't.

Well, there would be no healing now between her mother and her. Judith was sending her away. She had to accept that and try to put it behind her.

The shower warmed her, but she still felt cold inside as she bundled into her terry-cloth robe. Peeling off the shower cap, she stood in front of the mirror, fluffing her blond hair. There was no friendly message on its misted surface this time, no image of an encouraging face in the glass when she wiped it dry. Edward Atheling, it seemed, had also abandoned her.

There was a little alcove just outside the bathroom. Her suitcase was there mounted on a luggage rack. She began to fill it with her things from the closet and chest of drawers.

The storm continued to rage around the exposed castle walls, the bellowing wind flinging rain against the windows. Meredith was scarcely conscious of it in her numb resignation.

She had left her bedroom door slightly ajar as an invitation to Jackson in case he should want to speak to her when he came upstairs. Finally hearing his footsteps outside in the hall, she paused, anticipating his knock. But when his own door opened and closed, she knew he had gone into his room.

He probably thought she was already settled for the night. Had her mother told him she was leaving in the morning and why? Probably not, or he would surely have stopped to speak to her.

Unless—

But Meredith didn't want to think the worst. That Jackson might actually be relieved she was going, because he couldn't handle his feelings for her. She couldn't forget what he'd told her about April Paulson while they had been stalled in the fog. And how she'd sensed he was reluctant to care for another woman, because he feared hurting her. But that wouldn't apply if a woman was important enough to him.

Was *she* important to him? Meredith didn't know. She wasn't sure of anything anymore.

She went on with her packing, moving mechanically from closet and chest of drawers to her suitcase. Trying to ignore her misery over Jackson. And not succeeding.

She finally stopped midway between the closet and the alcove. This was absurd. Whatever Jackson felt or didn't feel for her, why should she deny her own feelings for him? Though she had yet to be certain whether she was in love with him or not, she did know they were deep feelings. And that, wise or not, they had become involved.

But he might be gone from her life after tomorrow. She might never see him again. The possibility was unbearable after all they had shared. And if they weren't alone when she said goodbye in the morning—

No! She had to be with him tonight, talk to him. Just the two of them in what could be their last time together.

Dropping the garments she was carrying on top of the suitcase, Meredith turned around and marched with determination in the direction of the door. She was halfway there when doubt stopped her.

Talk to him about what? What are you going to say?

She stood there, torn with uncertainty. In the end, the decision was made for her when a firm rap sounded on her door. She went and pulled it back to find Jackson standing there in the opening.

The sight of him had her remembering how her lungs had been starved for oxygen when she'd been sucked down into the sea. She felt like that now, suddenly robbed of all air.

Freshly emerged from his own shower, he was dressed in nothing but a pair of snug jeans that rode low on his lean hips. The rest was uncovered, from his taut belly to his sleekly muscled chest, broad shoulders and a head of damp, tousled hair. All hard, hot flesh, he had never looked more tempting.

"Noticed your door was ajar and your light still on," he drawled.

"And what if it had been closed and my room dark? What if I had gone to bed?"

He shifted his weight from one leg to another, his eyes gleaming as he looked at her. And she knew he was imagining her as she was under her robe, her body naked and vulnerable. "It wouldn't have mattered. I would have been here anyway."

"Why?"

"Unfinished business."

"To tell me about the phone call to the police?"

"Not that business."

"What, then?"

"You and me."

"I don't understand?"

"Yes, you do." His voice slowed, turning so deep and raspy that the sound of it had her shivering inside her robe. "Didn't I promise you that one of these nights I wasn't going to stand outside this door and wish you a polite good evening, then watch you walk away from me?"

She seemed to recall that those partings had involved a good deal more than just polite good evenings. But she didn't remind him of that. She responded instead with a casual "Did you?"

"You know damn well I did," he growled.

"And?"

"This is that night, Meredith."

SHE DIDN'T REMEMBER inviting him into her room or either of them closing the door behind him. But somehow that's where he was, standing so close to her that she could feel the heat of his body, smell his masculine scent.

"Why *this* night?" She found the courage to challenge him, while fearing he'd been told she had been asked to leave Croft Castle and sympathy had brought him to her door. A motive she couldn't have endured.

For a moment he didn't answer her. He went on gazing at her with those smoldering blue eyes above the sexy stubble on his jaw.

"Do you know what you did to me this afternoon?" he said, his voice turning harsh with accusation. "You didn't just scare the hell out of me when you went into the sea like that. You destroyed me. You stopped my heart cold. Right in here."

He slapped his hand against his bare chest.

"And when it started to beat again, I knew it would never

be the same. That's what you did to me, Meredith Allen. You took my heart and changed it forever. Because I almost lost you. Because I realized the second I jumped into the water after you just how important you'd become to me. There. Is that answer enough for why I'm standing here?"

"It is," she said softly, her own heart swelling with the realization that he hadn't been told of her dismissal. He had come to her just because she was important to him. She mattered.

And if Meredith had any lingering uncertainties about that, he dispelled them with a demanding, but oh-so-potent, demonstration of his intentions. She didn't struggle when his arms wound around her, hauling her up against the rock-hard wall of his chest. Didn't try to object when his mouth seized hers in a deep, greedy kiss. Didn't fail to respond with little whimpers in her throat when he strained her against his powerful arousal.

His attentions gentled after that first urgent assault. Big hands framing her face, he treated her to a series of slow, lingering kisses. Kisses that involved a mating of their tongues. Inflaming her senses with a flavor that was somehow the essence of him until she swore she could hear her heart thudding beneath her ribs. Or was it his own she heard?

When his mouth at last lifted from her own, and she was able to gaze up into his face, she was startled by the look in his eyes. They had darkened to a stormy blue.

"Damn you! What am I going to do when I just can't get enough of you?"

"Did I say you couldn't have more?"

Taking his hands, she guided them to the top of her robe. He needed no further invitation. His eager fingers parted the robe, burrowed inside to the naked flesh that waited for him.

"All you want, Jackson," she promised him. "All you want…"

And that I want, she thought with a low moan as his hands cupped her breasts. Caressed them. Cherished them. And in the nd were replaced by his mouth when, lowering his head, he ook possession of her rigid buds.

Drawing them in turn into his mouth, he tugged on them trongly, devouring them with his tongue while she mewed with pleasure. Nor was he satisfied with just her breasts. Releasing them, he stood erect, pulled the robe over her shoulders and down her arms. It dropped to the floor, pooling at her eet and leaving her body fully exposed to his ravenous gaze.

"What's happening?" she whispered, confused by his intention when he sank to his knees in front of her.

"Worship," he said. "I'm about to worship a goddess."

Wrapping his arms around her hips, he buried his face into he compliant flesh of her belly. Then that skillful tongue of his went to work again, blazing a slow trail of wet heat down, down, down to the juncture of her thighs. Invading the very core of her being, plundering her shamelessly until she begged to be liberated from his sweet torment with a wild, wanton "Please, oh, please…" And was finally rewarded with a shattering release.

Her body was still shuddering with the spasms of his victory when he rose to his feet and held her tightly. Without his support, she would have collapsed. Even then, her knees bucked, her legs threatening to fail her completely.

Jackson prevented that. Scooping her up into his arms, all forceful male, he strode across the room and placed her on the four-poster bed. Then, shucking his jeans, he stretched out beside her and gathered her close.

He was both an aggressive and tender lover. He kissed her again, stroked her breasts, parted her thighs and applied his magic touch. When he joined his hardness with her softness, Meredith knew that her union with Jackson Hawke was like nothing she had ever experienced before. Full, rich, infinitely satisfying.

The storm had intensified. She was dimly aware of the fury of the wind, the sheets of white lightning that split the night sky, the surge of the sea far below the castle.

Jackson was conscious of it, too, when he whispered into her ear, "It isn't just outside. It's in here with you and me. Feel it?"

He was right. They were making their own storm. The raw meeting of two halves that had searched for each other and now were finally melding into a blinding, raging force that consumed them.

BODY AND SOUL.

Secure in his arms afterwards, that's what Meredith wanted to feel. As if she belonged to this man body and soul. It was seductive emotion, even an accurate one, but there were problems with it.

Though Jackson had yet to know it, this was their last night together at Croft Castle. All right, that was not an insurmountable obstacle. They could still see each other when he returned to London. Assuming, that is, he would want an ongoing relationship with her. She couldn't be sure that he did, even though he had sworn how vital she was to him now.

That might be true, but could he overcome his fear of hurting another woman? Of not being all that he would feel she deserved? Or was he not capable of that?

And what about after London? Jackson's life was here in England now, hers back in America where her practice waited for her.

Then, too, there was still the issue of his refusal to believe in the possibility that ghosts existed. True, this particular conflict between them had softened since his ancestor had revealed himself to her. But she knew his doubts lingered, and the subject was too important to Meredith to overlook.

All of it had to be resolved if there was to be a future for them together. A permanent relationship. She could settle for no less. Not with this man. Not after tonight. And if she couldn't have that…well, the alternative was too awful to think about.

Why do you do this to yourself? Why don't you simply savor what you and Jackson just shared, and forget all the rest until—

Her dialogue with herself was terminated by a startling crash from the direction of the bathroom. Meredith's head lifted from Jackson's shoulder where it had been resting. He'd been dozing, and he sat up beside her.

"What in—"

"The window in the bathroom," she said, relaxing as she listened to the steady slamming that followed the initial bang. "I cracked the casement to let out some of the steam after my shower. I fastened the catch again afterwards, but this wind is so savage it must have worked it loose."

She started to get up, but he placed a restraining hand on her arm.

"Stay put. I'll take care of it. I don't want you out of this bed, because I'm not through with you yet."

Meredith had no objection to that. Not when his passage from the bed to the bathroom door offered her a tantalizing view of a naked backside that made her limbs weak.

The bed was cold without him. There was a blanket on a chest at the foot of the four-poster. She was in the process of unfolding it and drawing it over herself when Jackson reappeared.

"I don't feel the wind howling from the bathroom anymore," she said. "You must have got the window closed all right. I hope the glass wasn't—"

She stopped when she caught sight of his face. The expression on it was just short of outright anger.

"What's wrong?"

"Your suitcase," he said.

"Oh." He had obviously noticed it in the alcove on his return from the bathroom.

"You've been packing it, which means you're planning to leave. When?"

"In the morning, after the police talk to us and providing the sea is calm again."

"And just when were you going to tell me? Or weren't you?"

He was a daunting sight towering over like this. And, naked as he was, a highly disturbing one. "Of course, I was going to let you know, but things just, well, got in the way."

"Why are you going?" he demanded. "And it better not have anything to do with us, because I warn you I won't let you—"

"No. I'm being sent away."

"You're *what*?"

"Jackson, this is hard enough. Will you please not stand there glowering at me like that with everything, um, on display."

To her relief, he slid in beside her, pulling the blanket up to his waist. The scowl had left his face when he turned to her. "Now what's this all about?"

"It's true. I've been asked to leave Croft and go back to London." She described for him the scene in the dining room after he and Guy had gone off to the library.

"It's funny," she said when she'd finished her explanation. "All those years I was being angry with my mother for walking out on us, I secretly blamed myself. I used to think if I'd been the daughter I was supposed to be, she would never have left me. But after tonight, hearing her so coldly dismiss me like that, I'm beginning to see just how wrong I was."

Jackson didn't say anything for a long moment. He just looked at her. Then, in a matter-of-fact voice, he asked her, "You ever think of talking to a psychologist?"

She was hurting, and he was being funny?

"Because I have to tell you," he went on, "that, while you're probably a damn good psychologist with other people's problems, you're a lousy one when it comes to applying your science to yourself and your mother."

She stared at him. "What are you trying to tell me?"

"Meredith, *think* about it. Your mother sat there tonight and heard how close you were to death today. She doesn't want you to go because you're of no value to her anymore. She wants you to go because she wants her daughter out of danger, and she's willing to sacrifice the help she desperately needs for Guy and herself to make sure that daughter is safe back in London."

"But she must have realized there would be risks when she asked me to come."

"No." He shook his head. "Not anything like today's."

Could Jackson be right? she wondered. Had her mother's detachment been nothing but a performance? If that was true, then Meredith had permitted her emotions to blind her about Judith's actual motive.

Jackson slid an arm around her waist and drew her close. "Maybe your mother is right. Maybe I should be telling you to go, too." His arm tightened around her protectively. "But, hell, I'm just too selfish to let you go."

There was no longer any uncertainty about it. Meredith knew in that moment she was genuinely, deeply in love with Jackson Hawke. But it was a love that came with an ache, because she also realized something else.

He had told her tonight she had destroyed him when she'd gone into the sea. Had satisfied every woman's ultimate fantasy when he'd knelt in front of her to worship a goddess. Had moved her with his anger because she'd packed her bags and that might mean she was walking out on him. But what he had *not* told her was that he loved her.

Chapter Thirteen

Meredith was still half asleep when, needing to touch him to assure herself of his presence, her hand groped for Jackson. And encountered only the sheet.

Fully awake now, she opened her eyes. The other half of the bed where he had spent the night with her was empty. She sat up against the headboard of the four-poster, her gaze anxiously searching the room, which was gray in the preliminary light of daybreak.

He wasn't here. The room wore the forlorn silence of her solitude. Nor was there so much as a whisper from outside. The wind must have dropped, which meant the storm had passed.

It was silly of her to so poignantly feel Jackson's absence. He couldn't have gone far, probably only back to his own room across the hall. But after last night, even the temporary loss of him was—

Something thumped against her door from out in the hall. Before she could investigate it, there was the sound of a muffled curse. Presumably a result of frustration over the knob that someone was having difficulty turning. The door finally swung inward in a series of jerky movements.

Jackson appeared around its edge, his hip bumping the door open wide enough to admit him with his burden. Both of his hands were busy supporting a loaded tray.

"Good. You're awake."

"Barely," she complained. "What time is it?"

"Early" was all he would admit.

Which meant the sun had yet to tip over the horizon. The man was a sadist. Not only was he up, he was freshly shaved, dressed in his perpetual black, and looking exasperatingly energetic. He was also a riveting sight, stirring memories of last night that made her squirm as he ambled across the room. That he could look so rugged while awkwardly bearing a breakfast tray was a testament to his pure masculinity.

"What are we doing awake at this barbaric hour?"

"Have to be up," he insisted, nudging aside a lamp in order to make room for the tray on the bedside table. "I want us to get down to that doctor's cottage and check on Simon Boynton's condition before the village starts stirring."

And before the police arrive on the island, she thought, eyeing the tray. Jackson might be talented in a lot of areas, including one that threatened her with a blush, but she could see domesticity wasn't one of them.

The milk jug was too full. It had slopped over on its way from the kitchen, dampening a stack of paper napkins. There were grains of sugar scattered on the tray and a plate of split bagels that looked charred around the edges. But Meredith couldn't argue with the stimulating aroma of coffee emanating from an earthen pot that was supposed to be for tea.

"Not much of a selection here," he apologized. "I was afraid I'd have Imogen up and storming into the kitchen if I poked around too much."

"Don't worry," she said, reaching for one of the two coffee mugs on the tray. "I'm not used to being spoiled with breakfast in bed, so this is wonderful." Was the breakfast a lover's offering, she wondered, or was he just being practical in order to hasten their departure from the castle?

Maybe both, she thought when she caught him staring at her breasts with a lascivious gleam in his blue eyes and knew that, with any encouragement at all, he would crawl back into the bed to share more than just breakfast with her.

Much as she longed for a renewal of last night's incredible intimacy, she resisted the lure. Jackson had been right when he said they needed to check on Simon Boynton at the earliest possible opportunity. They could attend to their personal lives later, including where their relationship might be headed. She had some questions for him about that, heartbreaking though the answers might be.

She was pouring out coffee from the pot when she remembered her mother's orders.

"Are you forgetting I've been removed from the case?" she reminded him, handing him the mug.

"I've made an executive decision," he said, accepting the mug and helping himself to one of the bagels. "You are not officially off this case until you board that launch, and by then—"

He bit into the bagel with a determination that implied her departure was not only far from settled, but that he intended to have something to say about it. Were all of the Hawke men this overbearing? she wondered.

TWENTY MINUTES LATER, after returning the tray to the kitchen and asking Imogen to let Lord and Lady Danely know where they had gone, they set out for the village.

The newly risen sun was gilding the tops of the pines when they paused at the bend to look down into the harbor. The waters were so serene it was hard to believe that only hours ago they had been raging with an unleashed fury. The rain had cleansed the air, making the early morning fresh and green. This, and the litter of torn leaves and fallen limbs along the roadside, were the only evidences of last night's storm.

Meredith gazed at the launch berthed against the quay. Her companion sensed the direction of her thoughts.

"She doesn't leave on her morning run for hours yet, Meredith. Plenty of time to make decisions."

He took her hand and squeezed it gently. It was the reassurance she needed, because the thought of boarding that launch, of parting from him… But he was right. They had another priority now.

Except for a tortoiseshell cat washing itself on a doorstep, they saw no life in the street when they passed through the village. Nor did they encounter anyone in the lane that led them to Dr. Merrick's cottage.

"Maybe the old boy isn't up yet," Jackson said as they followed the path to the front door.

"Elderly people are always up early." That is, if he ever went to bed at all, Meredith thought. Curmudgeon or not, Dr. Merrick struck her as the sort of physician who would be attentive to his patient around the clock.

He answered their knock with a spatula in his hand. Both that and the aroma emanating from the rear of the cottage were an indication he'd been preparing breakfast.

"Yes, I thought you'd be here first thing to ask about Boynton. Didn't expect you at this hour, though. Well, come in, come in."

His dog, still somewhere in the back region of the cottage, had started to bark when they rapped on the door. But he was silent now as Dr. Merrick led them to the guest room.

"Boynton survived the night," he said when they entered the room, "but as you can see, he's not good."

No, Meredith thought, gazing compassionately at the small, thin man on the bed across the room, he wasn't. The professor was as still and pale as a corpse.

"Did he ever regain consciousness?" Jackson wanted to know.

The doctor peered at him over the familiar half glasses. "You want to know if he was able to tell me exactly what happened to him. I'm sorry to disappoint you, but he never once opened his eyes."

"That's bad, isn't it?"

"Considering how many hours it's been, yes. The longer he remains in this state, the more critical his condition becomes.

I've already contacted the hospital. They're making arrangements to transport him. I shouldn't think it a problem now that the storm has passed."

"In the meantime," Jackson said, moving close to the bed, "we need to see that the professor is kept safe. Any visitors last night after we left? Anyone that you know of trying to sneak around the cottage?"

Dr. Merrick grunted in scorn, joining Jackson by the bed to check his patient. "If there had been, don't you think my spaniel would have let me know it? No more questions now until I see what these lungs are doing."

There was an old-fashioned stethoscope on the bedside table. Dr. Merrick used it to monitor the professor's breathing. Meredith hung back by the door.

The two men were so absorbed in the patient on the bed that neither of them noticed the shadow that flitted across the wall. But Meredith did. Alarmed, she swung her attention in the direction of the window that had been cracked to admit fresh air.

"There's someone outside," she warned them softly.

Jackson and the doctor turned to look at her and then at the window. There was no face at the glass, no sign of movement now or any sound. Nothing but the hush of a peaceful morning.

"Can't be," the doctor finally said. "If there were, Max would have—"

At that second the spaniel began to bark furiously. Jackson wasted no time in going to the window. Brushing by her, he charged out of the room. By the time Meredith went after him, he was already gone from the cottage, leaving the front door open behind him.

Simon Boynton's attacker? she wondered as she followed Jackson out of the house. Had he somehow learned that the professor was still alive and in the care of Dr. Merrick? And if he had, and he'd turned up here in a desperate effort to permanently silence him—

The dog was still yapping as Meredith rounded the cottage. Jackson was nowhere in sight. Where had he gone? And then she saw him!

There was an old orchard on a slope above the side of the cottage. Jackson was there among the trees. He wasn't alone. There was another figure fleeing from him. Or trying to.

Whoever he was, he was no match for his pursuer's long, powerful legs. When Jackson was within a few feet of his objective, he launched himself with all the ferocity of a linebacker. The impact brought his target to earth.

Arriving on the scene, Meredith found the two men locked in combat on a ground that was strewn with debris from the storm. The air was thick with their curses, their battle such a melee that at first she was unable to recognize Jackson's opponent. It was only when he rolled over on his back and tried to wriggle away that she was able to identify him.

The American photographer! Archie Wallace!

"Oh, no, you don't!" Jackson bellowed, his hand shooting out and capturing Wallace by one skinny leg to prevent his escape.

He was in the process of dragging him back when a steely voice behind Meredith commanded, "That's enough!"

She swung around to discover Detective Chief Inspector Ramsay striding toward them. Close behind him was Detective Sergeant Ware. Meredith looked back over her shoulder. The two men on the ground had stopped struggling, but Jackson continued to grip the photographer's ankle in his determined fist.

Reaching them, the inspector issued another order. "All right, gentlemen, on your feet." They hesitated. "At once, if you please."

Jackson shrugged and released the photographer. "It's your call, Inspector, but you'd better be ready if he tries to make another break for it."

He scrambled to his feet. Archie Wallace followed more slowly, coming reluctantly erect with a bleeding lip and his khaki shorts and matching safari jacket covered with dirt and twigs. There was a sullen expression on his gaunt face.

"Who are you?" Ramsay challenged him.

"Name's Archie Wallace," he answered the inspector defiantly. "I'm an American, and I have rights."

"Got a suggestion for you, Inspector," Jackson said. "Ask him if those rights entitle him to a suspicious activity that just might include murder."

The photographer opened his mouth to howl an objection, but DCI Ramsay silenced him with a stern look on his craggy face. "We'll get to you, Mr. Wallace. But just now I want Mr. Hawke to explain his accusation."

Meredith listened, offering no contribution as Jackson gave the inspector an account of how Archie Wallace had been watching them since their arrival on the island, dogging their movements, and of how he might be connected with the mystery at Croft Castle, as well as Sybil Boynton's death.

"And now this morning," Jackson said, "we caught him outside the room where Simon Boynton is lying unconscious. Like I told you on the phone last night, Inspector, if his attacker learned he was still alive, he'd want to make certain the professor wouldn't talk."

Archie Wallace looked both outraged and scared. "That's bull! I don't know anything about some professor!"

DCI Ramsay gazed at him severely again. "Then why are you here? *Did* you follow Ms. Allen and Mr. Hawke to the cottage?"

"No. I'm a nature photographer, see, and I was up above the orchard scouting for birds to shoot."

"If that's true, where is your camera, and why did you come down to the cottage?"

Wallace was obstinately silent.

"Could it be, Mr. Wallace, that what you happened to spot were not birds but Ms. Allen and Mr. Hawke entering the cottage? That you left your equipment up there and sneaked down to the cottage because you recognized an opportunity to take advantage of a situation?"

"Not to try to hurt somebody! I just wanted to—"

"What, Mr. Wallace? Unless you choose to be taken to Trefarro and charged, you'd better tell us."

The photographer cast a look in Jackson's direction. Meredith was shocked to see the pure hatred that twisted his bony features. "*Him*! He's the reason for it all!"

"*All* being exactly what, Mr. Wallace?"

"Why I came to the island. Why I been watching him. And why I came down to the cottage to listen at the window after I saw him go inside."

"To what purpose?" the inspector demanded.

"Because I knew he was a P.I. on a case here. I didn't know what the case was all about, and I didn't care. All that counted was knowing it was important to him and that it was something real tricky. That meant there was a chance he could fail. And I wanted him to fail," he said viciously. "I *wanted* to be right here on the island watching him get what he deserves."

Jackson, who had been listening to Archie Wallace in what was obviously growing disbelief, could no longer restrain himself. "This is screwy! I don't know how this guy came to learn about me or why he's got it in for me, but I do know this. I never heard of him until he turned up on this island."

Wallace turned on him savagely. "No, you don't know me! But you know Grace Johnson, don't you?"

Meredith could see that the name meant something to Jackson. She watched the first glimmer of understanding register on his face. Wallace saw it, too, and he laughed bitterly.

"Yeah, that's right! I loved Grace, and this bastard's testimony sent her to prison back in the States!"

Jackson gazed at him. "She was responsible for the death of a young man, Archie," he said quietly, and this time there was a note of sympathy in his voice.

"It was an accident! It never would have happened if you hadn't been tailing her everywhere she went!"

"I was hired to follow her, Archie. She'd embezzled funds from her company and it was my job to prove it."

"You were hounding her! She was only trying to get away from you! It wasn't her fault that kid on the motorcycle ran a light! She couldn't keep from hitting him!"

"It was Grace who ran the light, Archie."

"Sure, that's what you told them at her trial, and they listened to you. But they didn't know what I learned afterwards from a guy who knew you." He turned to Meredith and the others with a gloating "The only witness, and he's color-blind! He can't tell red from green, so how would he know who ran the light?"

"Don't be a fool, man. I know when a signal is stop or go from its position on the light. All this came out in court, and you would have known that if you'd been there. So, where were you if Grace Johnson is so important to you?"

"All right, so I was doing time until my lawyer got me cleared. I was railroaded, just like Grace was railroaded."

DCI Ramsay had been listening to their exchange with interest, but now he intervened with an impatient "All this is history that has little, if any, bearing on my investigation. I am curious about one thing though, Mr. Wallace. Did you follow Mr. Hawke to England with revenge as your intention, because if you did—"

"No way! The photography is legit. You can check on that if you don't believe me."

"You can be certain we'll do that. As for now, I'm willing to accept that the two of you being in England at the same time is by chance. But you've already indicated your presence on Croft Island is no accident. Enlighten me, Mr. Wallace."

The photographer hesitated, seemed to decide that the truth wouldn't hurt him, and confessed, "It was on account of the gallery."

"You do plan on being more specific than that, I hope."

"This gallery over on the mainland. I went into the place a couple of days ago. They had a collection of art photos, see. Anyhow," he said, jerking his knobby chin in Jackson's direction, "*he* was in there with this couple looking at paintings."

Jackson's artist friend, Dave, and his wife, Kimberly. Meredith remembered his telling her how they had dragged him around to the art galleries.

"I knew who he was all right," Wallace continued. "I'd seen him on the news after Grace's trial. That's why I hung around with my back to them, pretending to look at the art while I listened to him telling his friends how vital this case was to him over on Croft Island."

"Vital how?" the inspector probed.

"Something about his agency not showing a profit and how he was on trial with the home office back in Chicago and that if he didn't make good on the case they were going to shut him down." The photographer looked at Jackson, a malicious grin on his homely face. "Only you had a little problem over the whole thing, didn't you?"

"All right, Mr. Wallace," the inspector ordered him, "just get on with it."

"Seems they'd saddled him with another investigator. *Her*," Wallace said, nodding toward Meredith. "He was worried about working with her and that she could be trouble and screw up the case for him. And his friends asked him how he was going to handle it. And that's when I overheard him say it."

"What, Mr. Wallace?"

"How, being desperate, he was going to do whatever it took to make her happy. And I guess he did, since she's still here."

Meredith stared at Jackson, waiting for him to deny Archie Wallace's claim. But he said nothing. His face was like stone. It was true, then. Jackson had used her to save his agency. His concern for her, his attentions, his irresistible lovemaking—all of it had been a lie because he'd needed her to be content and cooperative with him. Otherwise, her mother and Guy might have let both of them go before the case was successfully solved.

Secrets. From the beginning, Jackson had kept secrets from her. He'd failed to tell her about his connection with his ancestor, Edward Atheling. Had resisted, until she'd pressed him for it, an explanation for his motive in relocating to England. And now this. That his branch of the Hawke Detective Agency was in jeopardy, that unless he was able to rescue it with this case, he would lose it.

Why, Jackson? Why did you have to go and make me fall in love with you?

Unable to bear looking at him, heartsick at what she could only conclude was calculated treachery, Meredith turned her head away. She listened numbly to DCI Ramsay give brisk instructions to the chunky young woman who was his partner.

"Sergeant Ware, I want you to accompany Mr. Wallace back to the inn after he collects his camera equipment. Check his passport to be sure it's in order and then see to it he packs his belongings. You can take a statement from him in the police boat while I deal with the rest here."

The photographer was indignant. "What is this? Are you arresting me?"

"No, Mr. Wallace, we are merely seeing to it that you cause no more trouble by escorting you off the island. And I would strongly advise you not to try to come back."

"But I got an assignment to photograph sea birds."

"There are birds elsewhere along the Cornish coast." The chief inspector dismissed him by giving his attention to Meredith and Jackson. "I think we'll also go along to the inn where we can be comfortable. I'll want statements from both of you, as well as a full account of what you've learned since I was last here."

Jackson jerked his thumb in the direction of the cottage. "What about Boynton?"

"I already have another officer inside the cottage. He'll remain at the professor's side both here and at the hospital. There are times, Mr. Hawke, when we actually do know what we're doing." DCI Ramsay gestured toward the lane. "Shall we?"

Jackson fell into step beside Meredith as they headed in the direction of the inn. "We have to talk," he said urgently.

Stricken by his unforgivable deception, she merely shook her head.

"Okay, so this isn't the time or the place. But we are going to talk," he insisted.

She didn't argue with him. She was hurting too much for that. They proceeded the rest of the way in silence. And all the way to the inn her mind burned with a cruel refrain.

It's all too clear now why he didn't tell you last night he loves you. Because he doesn't.

Colin Sheppard was on duty behind the front desk when they arrived at the George. The chief inspector excused himself and went to ask the landlord for the use of an area where they could be private.

Left to themselves for a moment in a corner of the lobby, Jackson turned to Meredith. "You owe me the chance to explain things."

"What things would those be, Jackson? Are you going to tell me Archie Wallace was lying? That what he overheard you saying in the gallery isn't true?"

"All right, I said it. But I didn't mean it like that."

"Oh, I know exactly what you meant, and you can feel pleased with yourself that you succeeded. Because if there's one thing you know how to do, Jackson, it's make a woman happy. I learned that all too well last night, didn't I?"

"Damn it, Meredith, why won't you understand that—"

Ramsay interrupted them. "The bar is empty at this early hour. We can use that."

Meredith spoke up with a swift, "Chief Inspector, I would appreciate it if you would talk to me first and separately. I have to get back to the castle and finish packing. I'm scheduled to leave the island on the launch's morning run."

He gazed at her perceptively, as if he knew she had been asked to go, and then nodded. "Yes, Lord Danely rang me up about that. It's not a problem, as long as you make yourself available for possible further interviews."

"I will certainly, but Mr. Hawke will be here for anything that develops."

Not trusting herself to look at Jackson again, she hurried into the bar with the chief inspector at her heels. They seated themselves at a table. As concisely as possible, she gave him her version of the events that had occurred since he had last interviewed them.

Ramsay asked her a few questions, but on the whole it was a painless session. Unlike the last time, she was served no severe warnings about interferring with the investigation. Perhaps he was saving those for Jackson. Or maybe it was because she and Jackson had made progress with the case by finding Simon Boynton, something the inspector must appreciate, albeit reluctantly.

Ramsey released her after instructing her to stop in at police headquarters in Trefarro to sign a statement he would have waiting for her before she left for London.

When Meredith emerged from the bar, DSI Ware and Archie Wallace were coming down the stairs on their way to the police boat. And Jackson was pacing the lobby, obviously not happy with her for having gone into the interview without him. He pounced the instant she appeared.

She forestalled him with a quick "You don't have to worry about anything I told him."

"I don't give a damn about that. I just want you to tell me you'll still be here so we can talk after Ramsay is finished with me."

"He's waiting for you."

"You're not going to stick around, are you?"

"I have to go."

He didn't say anything for a moment. He loomed over her like a sudden storm, looking dark and dangerous. She could tell he was very angry.

"You go then, Meredith. I'm not going to argue with you about it anymore. I'm through arguing. But if you won't talk to me, then the least you can do before you leave the island is to talk to your mother. Or are you going to go on being a stubborn little fool about that, too?"

The chief inspector spoke to him from the doorway of the bar. "Can we get on with this, Mr. Hawke?"

Jackson backed away, his blue eyes pinned on her coldly. Then he turned abruptly and followed Ramsay into the bar, swinging the door shut behind him.

Stung by his last words to her, Meredith was prepared to leave the inn when Gwen Sparrow sailed into the lobby from the street entrance. She lifted a hand in greeting to Colin Sheppard behind the front desk before she spotted Meredith and came over to speak to her.

"A rare treat that storm was last night, wasn't it? All right up at the castle, were you?"

"I think so, yes."

"Storm like that can do damage to an old rubble like Croft, I shouldn't wonder. Our mum once got a sinkhole outside her back door after a blow. Terrible rain, it was."

"I imagine Lord Danely will check for damage when he has the chance."

The redhead seemed to realize Meredith was in no mood to chat. "Well, I'm off to vacuum guest rooms for Colin. His daily is under the weather today."

Gwen departed. Knowing she had to get away, Meredith fled from the inn and hurried toward the lane for the castle.

I can get through this, she promised herself. I *have* to get through it.

But her dull misery sharpened to fresh pangs when she

reached the first of the rhododendrons massed along the road-side near the bottom of the lane. What blossoms hadn't suffered from the storm were beginning to fade and shrivel, their petals falling. Their glory had been brief, and now it was over.

Like Jackson and me, she thought sadly.

Before she could prevent them, the bittersweet images formed in her mind. Jackson in one of his familiar stances, long legs spaced apart, thumbs hooked in the pockets of his jeans. Jackson with a cocky smile on his bold mouth. Jackson hailing her with a brash "Yo."

They were all painful reminders of the man she had lost. But the worst of them, the one that brought scalding tears to her eyes, was the memory of him cocooning her in his arms.

Stop it. Stop it before you're blubbering like an idiot.

Meredith turned resolutely away from the rhododendrons and their connection. She was mopping her eyes with a tissue from her bag when the Land Rover rolled down the lane and drew to a halt beside her. Guy was at the wheel.

"I came along to collect you," he explained from the low-ered window.

How had he known she was on her way back to the castle? "Thank you, but I could have walked."

"Yes, well, it's not that. Jackson rang up from the inn to tell us you were on your way, and would I meet you."

He must have insisted on using the phone in the bar just before his own session with the chief inspector. "Why did he do that?"

Guy got out of the car and came around to open the passenger door for her. "Said he wanted someone with you until you boarded the launch. It's probably a good idea, Meredith. With a killer loose on the island—and he must know you've been after him—you shouldn't be alone."

Jackson is seeing to it that I stay safe, she thought with a sense of wonder as she slid into the vehicle. Guilt? Or did he at least care that much about her welfare?

Be fair about it. He might be unprincipled about what mattered most to you, but his instinct to protect is still genuine.

By the time the Land Rover rolled into the forecourt, Meredith had made up her mind. Whatever Jackson had done, whatever he had said or failed to say, she knew he was right about one thing. She couldn't leave the island without sitting down and talking to her mother. She'd never forgive herself if she didn't seize this last opportunity to try to heal whatever had kept them apart all these years.

Glancing at her watch as she and Guy headed for the front door, she realized she had time to spare before she finished packing and started for the launch.

"I'd like to see my mother," she said when they entered the castle.

"You'll find her in our sitting room," Guy said. "I must get back to the kitchen. A limb came through one of the windows there last night, and if I don't finish covering it before I have a look around outside for other possible damage, I'm afraid Imogen will go on strike. She's deathly afraid of a bird finding its way into her domain."

Guy excused himself and left her. Meredith made her way to Lord and Lady Danely's apartment. The sitting room door was closed. She hesitated a moment, suddenly nervous as she remembered her mother's cool dismissal of her last night. Whatever Jackson's explanation for it, would Judith refuse to see her?

Then, summoning her courage, Meredith squared her shoulders and rapped on the door.

Chapter Fourteen

When Jackson thought about it, which he did as he waited while the chief inspector answered the trilling cell phone clipped to his belt, he was glad that Meredith had walked out on him.

"All right, Owens," Ramsay said, "you stay with him. Any change in his condition?"

Yeah, Jackson decided, it was better this way. With Meredith not wanting to be anywhere near him, she wasn't going to change her mind about leaving the island. And if she was out of here, far away back in London, she would be safe. That's what Jackson needed more than anything right now. To know that Meredith was safe.

"I see," the chief inspector said. "All the same, I want you right there ready to listen if he should say anything."

Not that he was giving up on her, Jackson promised himself. When he was done with the job here, he was going to find her. London, back in the States. Wherever he had to go. And whatever he had to do to convince her she meant more to him than his agency. A *hell* of a lot more.

"I'll see to it that someone relieves you at the hospital later on this afternoon."

If Jackson had to get down on his knees and beg her to forgive him, he would. But that would have to wait. Right now, with his mind relieved that Meredith would be all right, that

Judith and Guy would look out for her until she was on that launch, he could concentrate on this case.

Ramsay closed his cell phone and returned it to his belt. "I apologize for the interruption. Where were we?"

Jackson had pushed back from the table when the phone rang, long legs stretched out in front of him and crossed at the ankle. His response now was equally casual. "I think we've covered just about everything you wanted to know, Inspector. I take it that was the officer you placed in Dr. Merrick's cottage with the professor?"

"They're no longer in the cottage. They're in the emergency vessel with the paramedics on their way to the hospital."

"And Boynton?"

DCI Ramsay shook his head. "He's not responding and remains in a coma."

Not good, Jackson thought. The hope that Simon Boynton would awaken and name his attacker was fading with the professor's vital life signs. "That phone call Meredith and I told you about. The one we overheard between Sybil Boynton and whoever rang her up at her father's cottage. You ever able to learn where it originated from?"

The chief inspector hesitated and then apparently decided it didn't matter whether Jackson knew. "We did, yes. It came from the public phone right here at the George. But since the call occurred at one of the inn's busiest hours, with people coming and going, anyone could have made it."

Another dead end. But Jackson had thought about this investigation while Ramsay questioned him. And he'd determined that he and Meredith had been approaching it from the wrong direction. They'd spent their energy looking for what their mystery man was so desperate to find when they should have been focusing on his identity. If he could learn that, Jackson decided, then the rest stood a good chance of falling into place.

The chief inspector collected the pocket recorder he had

used to tape their interview and scraped back from the table, getting to his feet. "If we're finished here, I need to get back to Trefarro."

There was something else that had planted itself in Jackson's mind. An idea that should have occurred to him long ago. This was his opportunity to act on it.

"You mind, Inspector, if I catch a lift with you in the police boat? I've got some business over on the mainland."

Ramsay agreed, maybe because he thought it would remove Jackson from a scene that was the domain of the police and not a private investigator's. He'd already warned him again about interferring in police matters.

DSI Ware and a surly, silent Archie Wallace were waiting in the cruiser when they arrived at the quay. Jackson ignored the photographer. He was no longer a player in this drama. However, Rob Curzon, the young man who usually piloted the island shuttle, might be. And since Meredith could soon be making the crossing with him, Jackson had to be concerned about that.

He was encouraged, though, by the sight of Fred Griggs fueling the launch that was moored on the other side of the police boat. When Jackson stopped to speak to the old man, he was reassured with a gap-toothed "Aye, I'll be takin' the morning run. Robbie's still off on the mainland somewheres."

Relieved, Jackson boarded the police boat. Seconds later, they were underway. Legs apart to brace himself as the cruiser gathered speed out of the harbor, he stood in the stern and watched the island recede behind them. And he thought about Meredith.

There was no question of it. The woman bothered him on every level. Had been bothering him since they'd first clashed back in the States when she had informed him he had absolutely no professional ethics and he had noticed how luscious her mouth was. He'd also entertained some pretty shameless images of her in his bed.

Those images had caused frustrating problems for him when

they'd been thrown together on the island. They'd also been accompanied by several less lustful discoveries about himself as he and Meredith worked side by side. Things like his respect for her intelligence and courage and his admiration for her not just as a woman but as an equal.

She'd continued to aggravate the hell out of him, though. Refusing to be dominated, not putting up with anything from him, challenging him at every turn. And, worst of all, tunneling into his heart.

That same heart Jackson had refused to risk back home, fleeing when it was threatened. Too late this time. Meredith already owned it. That's when he recognized, with a sense of shock, exactly why she was so vital to him. He was finally able to put a name to it.

He was in love with Meredith Allen! And God help anyone who tried to harm her!

THIS WAS GOING TO hurt, Meredith realized as she entered the sitting room. There was no use in pretending it wouldn't. Not when she saw the look on her mother's face as she rose from the desk where she had been working. It was that same expression Judith had worn last night, her mouth tight, her eyes implacable.

"I was writing you a letter of reference before you go," she said, a note of detachment in her voice, as if Meredith had been no more than a temporary employee whose efforts had satisfied her. "I thought you might appreciate that."

"Thank you, but I'd much rather have something else."

"Oh?" There was a wary look in Judith's eyes now.

Meredith wasn't quite sure how to proceed. No matter what she said, her mother might refuse to communicate with her. She had to try.

"Exactly why am I being asked to leave Croft Castle?"

"I explained all of that to you last night."

"I haven't forgotten what you said, but was that the actual

reason? Or was it an excuse to make certain that I left the is-land?"

"Of course it's the reason. I can't imagine what else you think it could have been."

Judith's voice faltered slightly when she said it. It was enough to convince Meredith that Jackson had been right about her mother's motive in dismissing her. She wanted her daughter safe. The rest couldn't be so difficult. Maybe.

"All right, but I would still like some answers."

The hard expression on Judith's handsome face altered to one of unconcealed concern and caution. "About what?"

"Us. Mother and daughter. I think I'm entitled to that."

Judith hesitated before she nodded slowly. "Yes, I think you are."

She turned her desk chair and sat down again in surrender. There was another straight-backed chair just behind Meredith. She swung it around and perched on it, facing her mother. Only inches separated them physically. But emotionally there was a gulf between them that was the result of long years of resentment and misunderstanding.

Meredith leaned toward her earnestly. "I don't know what went wrong between you and Dad. He would never talk about it. I don't suppose I need an explanation for that, but I do need to understand why you walked out on me and never looked back."

Judith's careful mask had been slipping by degrees. Now it collapsed completely into a face that was stricken by raw re-morse. "But didn't your father tell you? He promised me he would tell you."

"All he said was that my mother still loved me, but I didn't see how that could be true."

Meredith had intended to discuss the issue with all the calm and reason of a psychologist in control. She should have real-ized this wasn't possible. How could she restrain herself after all the pain that had accumulated? She needed to release it. And release it she did, spewing it out in a sudden flow of hot anger.

"I thought Dad was just being kind! I thought he was trying to save me from grief! But I knew better! I knew my mother wouldn't have left me, wouldn't have stopped coming to see me if there hadn't been something wrong! *Me!* I had to be what was wrong! I'd disappointed her somehow! Failed to be the daughter I was supposed to be, and that's why she went away and stayed away!"

"Darling, no! No, *never!*"

Tears streaming down her cheeks, Judith sprang to her feet, leaned down and folded Meredith fiercely into her arms. For a long moment they clung to each other. Meredith could feel her own tears. She wiped them away, drew back and gazed imploringly into her mother's wet eyes.

"Then *why?*"

Judith released her and sank back into her own chair. "I've made a lot of mistakes in my life," she said, "including not insisting long ago that we have this talk. Well, people do make mistakes, don't they? And sometimes they're serious ones. Mine was in ever letting you go, but at the time I was convinced it was for the best. I want you to know that, Meredith. I want you to believe it's the truth."

"I don't understand."

"No, I see that. I—I'll try to explain, but it isn't easy. I know how you idolized your father. I don't want to say anything to spoil your memory of him, because he *was* a wonderful man in so many ways. But where he and I were concerned…"

Leaning forward, she reached for Meredith's hand. Hung on tightly, as though needing a physical connection between them in order to establish an emotional one.

"Is this why we never had this discussion before?"

"Yes."

"It's all right, Mother. You can tell me what you have to about Dad."

Encouraged, Judith continued. "Your father and I had been drifting apart long before you were born, Meredith. His work was everything to him, and I was...well, not important to him anymore. You'll find this hard to believe, but he never wanted children, didn't want anything to distract him from his research. He was livid when I told him I was pregnant."

"Dad?"

"I know, but it's true. Which was why it was so astonishing that he absolutely adored you from the moment he laid eyes on you. I was thrilled. And so young and naive. I believed that our marriage stood a chance now of succeeding. Because, although by then we didn't have much else in common, we did have a child we could share."

And that was never enough by itself to bond two people, Meredith knew.

"I don't want you to ever, *ever* think it was in any way your fault," Judith insisted, squeezing her fingers for emphasis, "when I tell you that your father and I quarreled over you from the start."

"Daddy could be a controlling man sometimes," Meredith admitted.

"There was that. And—something else."

"Go on."

"I was in the way. The two of you were inseparable from the time you were a toddler. Neither of you seemed to need me."

Meredith gazed at her, feeling Judith's anguish. Sharing it. "Oh, Mother, I didn't know. I didn't *know* that's how it was."

"No, you were too young to realize it. But I had to do something. I knew your father would never give you up if we divorced. That it would be cruel to play tug-of-war over you. Even a joint custody would have made both of you miserable."

"Is that why you went back to work?"

"I needed to occupy myself. And since my old job as assistant editor with the same publisher was available again, I took it."

"Dad encouraged you to do that, didn't he?"

"The extra money was welcome, but I realized later it was

an opportunity for him to keep you even more to himself. I'm sure that's why he urged me to accept that associate editorship when the house moved its operation to New York. 'Weekends,' he said. 'You can come home on weekends.'"

Meredith had a dim memory of those weekend visits. She could also vaguely recall the stress that accompanied them. "You used to bring me presents."

"A form of guilt, I suppose, because I wasn't there with you all the time. Or maybe I was just trying to buy your affection. I don't know. I only know it was no good."

"Why?"

"Your father told me that the visits upset you. That your first grade teacher reported you were unable to concentrate on your lessons the first day or so after each of those weekends. You would cry a lot or complain of stomachaches. 'You'd better limit the visits,' he said."

"I'm sorry, Mother. It must have been awful for you."

"Don't blame yourself. You were only a child. You had no way of understanding I was gradually losing you. That even the monthly visits were a failure. I had to face it in the end. Either I could quit my job and stay home, or—"

Judith released Meredith's hand, as though abruptly severing a link, and sat back in her chair. Her face was troubled, her eyes wet again with tears.

"Or you could choose to stay away altogether," Meredith said quietly.

Judith nodded. "I was a stranger to you by then, someone who made you unhappy. I thought I was making a decision that was in your best interests. Your father certainly thought so."

"Was that why you came to England?"

"I had to put distance between us, a great distance in order to eliminate the temptation of having you so close that..." She shook her head in an expression of her helplessness. "The house was opening an overseas branch in London. I could have a senior editorship there. It would mean a great deal of work.

But that was what I needed, something to keep me so busy I wouldn't have time to think about anything else."

"And you met Guy."

"Just after your father and I divorced, yes. Guy has made me very happy, Meredith, but I want you to know there was never a day that went by I didn't think of you and miss you."

"You told me that first morning on the terrace that Dad wrote to you regularly about me."

"Yes, I made him promise to do that, and he was very faithful about it. But it wasn't the same. I phoned you once. Do you remember it? You were in junior high, and I thought by then…"

Judith's voice trailed away. There was no need for her to say more. Meredith *did* recall, and she was ashamed of the memory. Convinced that she'd been heartlessly abandoned, she'd had very little to say to her mother. And what she did have to say must have sounded very cool and unfriendly.

Meredith leaned forward, taking her mother's hand in her own again. A symbolic action intended to renew the link between them. "I think there's a lot I'm going to have to ask you to forgive, Mother."

"No, darling, not nearly as much as I need you to forgive." Her face brightened. "But we don't need to waste time with that, do we? It doesn't really matter now that we've found each other aga—"

The door burst open. Startled, both women turned their heads as Imogen rushed into the room. There was a look of urgency on the cook's face.

"Guy," she said. "You'd better come. He's collapsed on the kitchen floor. Think it's his heart. I've already rung up emergency."

JACKSON COULD HAVE asked one of the officers on the police boat where he could find the local church that served the parish. But he hadn't wanted any of them to question his errand, DCI Ramsay in particular. This was his own quest on behalf of his clients, Lord and Lady Danely, and for now he wanted to keep it that way.

There would be time enough later to share a discovery with the inspector. Providing, that is, he learned anything of value. It was a long shot, but it was all he had.

When they landed in Trefarro, Jackson waited for the others to disembark and clear the area. Then he approached a bearded young fisherman on the quay.

"Can you tell me how to get to the church?"

"Which one would that be, mate?"

"The oldest."

"That'd be St. Bart's. You'll find it at the top o' the town. Up that lane there."

Jackson headed in the direction he pointed, climbing the long, cobbled lane. He came to a lych-gate on his left and paused there for a few seconds to gaze at the building situated in a hollow on the other side of the gate.

St. Bart's must be what most people had in mind when they thought of an English country church, he thought. A squat tower that seemed to lean slightly, a lichen-covered slate roof and mossy stone walls that looked as old as time. And probably were.

There was a house next door. It was built out of the same materials as the church. Jackson figured it was the vicarage.

Passing under the roof of the gate, he followed a flagged path that divided after a few yards. The main branch led to the porch of the church. The other meandered through a garden toward the front door of the house.

There was a woman in a pair of grubby slacks and a floppy straw hat working among the flowers. She straightened when Jackson approached, brushing at a smudge on her face.

"Can you tell me if the vicar is around?" he asked her.

"She is. You've found her."

Jackson was careful to mask his surprise when he introduced himself, but he had the feeling she knew and didn't mind.

"Winifred Lightner," she said, peeling off a glove and shaking his hand. "How can I help you?"

"Came to find out if your parish includes Croft Island."

"It does, yes. Not that its inhabitants manage to get to the services here as often as we'd like. Understandable, of course."

"It's the parish records I'm interested in. They list all the births and deaths, the family connections, that kind of thing, don't they?"

"They do."

"And with a church as old as St. Bart's, they must go back a long way."

"Parish records are among the oldest of their kind to be found in England."

"I thought so."

"Are you trying to trace an ancestor, Mr. Hawke?"

English churches were probably used to such requests from Americans interested in their roots, Jackson thought. "Something like that," he said, fearing she might not accommodate him if he told her the truth.

"Well, you're welcome to search the records, but I have to warn you. If what you're looking for is centuries ago, you will have a problem. Anything that early would be in a script and a language very difficult to read."

Jackson had anticipated this. "I'm no expert, but I'd like to give it a try."

She shook her head. "You'd do much better to ask Timothy Fennel. He was the vicar of St. Bart's before me. He's old and frail now, almost blind, but his knowledge of the families in the parish is amazing."

"How do I find him?"

"Through the burial ground at the back of the church. His little cottage is on the other side."

Jackson thanked her, rounded the church and made his way through the ancient, crooked stones that marked the graves. The cottage on the edge of a lane that bordered the burial ground was thatched and as picturesque as the church. A stout woman, who explained herself as the retired vicar's housekeeper, answered his knock and conducted him out to the garden at the back of the cottage.

Timothy Fennel was dozing in a chair under an apple tree. But he roused himself, welcoming his visitor and ready to serve him with his memory.

Jackson parked himself on a bench and made his request, knowing it was necessary to tell the old man what he hadn't told Winifred Lightner.

"So, what I'd like to know if it's at all possible, Vicar, is whether there's any descendant of Sir Hugh Gwinfryd's still living on Croft Island."

The shriveled old man turned his blind gaze in Jackson's direction. "Now isn't that odd. There was someone else who called on me a few weeks back asking that same question."

Simon Boynton! thought Jackson. This must have been how the professor learned of Sir Hugh's descendant. "And were you able to give him an answer, Vicar?"

"I was."

The old man went on to name Sir Hugh Gwinfryd's successor.

MEREDITH STOOD ON THE terrace, her hand shading her eyes as she anxiously watched the helicopter beat its rapid way toward the mainland. Her prayers went with the man and woman who were on board. For now, it was all she could offer them.

She would have accompanied her mother, been there to comfort and support her if it had been possible. It wasn't. What with the pilot and Judith, the two paramedics, and the gurney bearing Guy, there had been no further room on the craft.

Meredith tried not to think of the way Guy had looked on that gurney as they'd wheeled him out to the helicopter, which had been able to set down in the castle's broad forecourt. His face had been so pale and drawn, his body feeble in its state of

helplessness. Nor did she want to remember the bleak expression on her mother's face hovering close at her husband's side.

*Guy is going to be all right. That's what you have to keep
telling yourself. He's going to be all right.*

It was true that time was on Lord Danely's side, thanks to
Imogen's immediate action. Her call had been responsible for
the emergency helicopter being promptly dispatched to the island, Guy placed on oxygen and the patient airlifted to the hospital where his doctor was waiting to treat him.

*Guy is going to make it. You can't let yourself not believe
that.*

They were the words Meredith had told her shaken mother
before they'd parted in the forecourt. The same litany of reas-
surances she repeated to herself now.

When the helicopter was no more than a speck in the distance, Imogen, who'd been standing silently at Meredith's side,
turned away from the low stone wall.

"Must get back to the kitchen," she said. "There'll be soup
for me to make. Lord D is partial to my split pea."

They both knew it would be some time before Guy would
be able to eat her soup, but it was Imogen's no-nonsense way
of dealing with the situation.

Meredith remained on the terrace after the cook departed.
The launch had left the harbor. She watched it as it crawled toward Trefarro without her. It would be unthinkable of her to
leave the island now. Nor had her mother, in her frantic state,
urged her to do so. She had seemed grateful when Meredith had
promised to stay with Imogen, ready to help with any need
while they waited for her to phone them from the hospital.

But the castle suddenly felt very empty, very lonely. Meredith's thoughts turned to Jackson. She missed him. Longed
for him to be with her, holding her in his arms. Only he wasn't
here. He had walked away from her, left her at her own insistence. She didn't know where he was now, what he might be
doing. Or whether she would ever see him again.

A stubborn little fool.

That's what Jackson had called her. And he was right. She had made a terrible mistake in not giving him a chance to explain things to her. He'd been entitled to that, just as her mother had deserved the same opportunity. And now it might be too late. Jackson might no longer care, and if that were true—

She couldn't stand this! She would go out of her mind if she went on thinking about him. Nor would it help to worry about Guy, either.

Imogen had her cooking to keep her occupied while they waited for word from the hospital. Meredith needed something, too. And then she remembered. Guy had meant to check the exterior of the castle for storm damage after he dealt with the broken window in the kitchen. But his heart attack had prevented that.

Meredith could do it for him. It wasn't much in the way of help, maybe, but it would be one less concern for both Guy and her mother.

There were shallow steps at both ends of the elevated terrace. She chose the ones that descended in the direction away from the forecourt, intending to make a complete circuit of the castle. She would eventually pass the old garderobe tower and the kitchen on the far side of the building before she ended up back at the front. These were areas that were familiar to her, but she hadn't viewed this side of Croft Castle before.

Rounding a corner, she arrived at a small, formal garden. It was a lovely thing, but she took no time to admire it. Working her way along the perimeter of the newer wing, she carefully inspected windows, walls and downspouts. Everything seemed intact. The ground, of course, was strewn with a litter of leaves and twigs, but this was small stuff. No roof tiles among them.

Her survey brought her to the spot where the newer wing had been joined to the old keep with its massive stone walls and small, high windows. Nothing was disturbed here, and probably hadn't been in centuries.

The spot must be rarely visited, Meredith thought, because the terrain was bad. The ground, rough and stony, sloped steeply on its way to the lip of the cliff. She could hear the sea far below as she picked her way carefully through a wilderness of nettles and tufted grass.

It was when she came around an angle of the fortress that she saw it. The first evidence of any significant damage. A tree was down. It must have weathered any number of gales over the years, but last night's storm had toppled it.

Approaching the fallen warrior, Meredith could understand why. The thick trunk of the yew, which had grown so tightly against the wall of the keep it was almost a part of its fabric, was hollow with rot. Split down its weakened middle by the force of the wind, it now lay in raw halves.

The exposed wall behind it was overgrown with ivy. Without the protection of the yew that had been plastered against the tangled mass, tendrils of the ivy had been torn away from the stones to which they'd clung.

The yardman, Fred Griggs, would have have some cleanup here. Otherwise, it was nothing serious. With a last glance at the wall, Meredith was prepared to continue her tour. But something about the shape and pattern of the stones where the ivy had been ripped away stopped her.

She stepped over the fallen yew for a closer look. No, she wasn't imagining it! The stones here formed a corner of an arch.

Her excitement mounting, Meredith grabbed handfuls of the ivy and began to peel it away. The stuff was tough, resisting her efforts, but she persisted. She was right. She could see the whole thing now. It *was* an arch. But what was below it?

Working feverishly, she shredded the ivy from what it must have been guarding for ages. A door almost flush with the wall! A heavy, timeworn oak door had been buried here, unopened and forgotten since it had been locked and abandoned.

How long ago could that have been? Centuries, probably, since the yew that had grown in front of it was ancient. The tree and the ivy weren't here just by chance, she knew. They had to have been planted by design to conceal the door. Why, and by whom?

The gate to hell.

Was it legend or reality? Meredith was determined to know which, and it was possible the answer lay somewhere behind this secret door.

Chapter Fifteen

Jackson was angry with himself.

All the while the bastard was there right under our noses, and we never guessed. But I'm a P.I. I should have considered him as a possibility, even if he was the most unlikely of suspects.

Armed with the startling knowledge of what he was sure now must be the killer's identity, Jackson's long-legged stride carried him away from Timothy Fennel's cottage, past the church and back down the hill in the direction of the harbor.

He caught a glimpse through the trees of what appeared to be the Croft Island launch headed toward the quay. His mind went immediately to Meredith. He couldn't see enough at this distance to tell whether she was on board, but she *must* be. Because if she hadn't gotten safely away from the island—

Damn it, don't do this to yourself. Don't start imagining she could be in any danger, or you'll drive yourself nuts with worry. She's on the launch. She has to be.

But she wouldn't be on board by the time he got down to the quay. Even though he quickened his gait, the harbor was still too far away for him to reach it before Meredith left the launch.

Maybe he could intercept her on her way to the train station. That would probably be her immediate destination. She had no reason to hang around Trefarro. She'd be ready to catch the first train back to London.

But Jackson wanted to give her a reason to stay. Now that he had acknowledged his love for her, he was on fire to have her in his arms again.

He was seized by a sudden fear. What if she wouldn't forgive him? What if he lost her? His gut twisted with the anguish of that possibility.

He was frantic when he finally arrived at the harborfront. The launch was in port, but there was no sign of Meredith. Maybe she'd managed to grab a taxi. Fred Griggs was there, loading what looked like a sack of mail on board the launch. Jackson lost no time in questioning the old man.

"Meredith Allen. She got here all right, didn't she? You know if she's on her way to the train station?"

Griggs tipped his seaman's cap to the back of his grizzled head and regarded him with mild interest. "Young miss weren't on this run."

Jackson felt as if a fist closed around his heart. "Are you telling me she's still on the island?"

"Aye. It would be the excitement up at the castle that kept her there, I'm thinkin'. All the talk down at the inn, it were."

"What excitement?" Jackson demanded.

"Lord D up and had hisself a heart attack, they say. One of them whirly things came and flew him and Lady D off to hospital."

"Leaving Meredith behind?"

"Aye, her and Imogen."

The fist tightened around Jackson's heart. Meredith was at Croft Castle, alone and unprotected except for the cook! Two women on their own, vulnerable to an unpredictable madman. He had to get to Meredith.

"Take me back to the island!" he commanded Griggs.

"Have to wait for goods to arrive."

"You can collect them on your afternoon run. This is an emergency!"

Fred Griggs complied. Within minutes, the launch was underway. Jackson stood in the bow, impatient with the sluggish speed of the craft as they chugged out to sea. His uneasiness mounted with each frustrating throb of the engine.

Scanning the island as it finally loomed in front of them, he fastened his tense gaze on the castle that reared above the headland. Was he imagining it, or were there two figures along the wall of the keep? Yeah, he was almost certain of it, though they were too far away for him to recognize either one. But why were they there?

That fist was now squeezing his heart with all the force of a steel vice.

THE IRON LOCK ON THE door had been made in an age when such hardware was simple but solid. However, it was so old that time and weather had rusted it badly. Meredith could begin to feel it weaken under her repeated blows. A few more whacks should do it.

Whatever lay behind that door, though, no matter how close it was now or how excited she was by the promise of it, would have to wait for another moment or two. Her arms ached under the weight of the sledgehammer, demanding an immediate rest. She lowered it to the ground.

Imogen, stationed reluctantly behind her, used the opportunity to voice a fresh objection. "Shouldn't think this at all wise. What will Lord and Lady D say?"

Imogen was worried by Meredith's determined undertaking. Or as worried, anyway, as a woman of her placid nature could be. Meredith would have left her back in her kitchen, except that common sense dictated someone should be posted here outside the door in case of trouble. And the cook was her only choice.

Pausing to catch her breath, she patiently repeated her explanation. "Imogen, they are paying me to investigate their problem, and the source of that trouble could be on the other side of this door. Stand back, please."

Lifting the sledgehammer again, Meredith swung it at her target with as much force as she could deliver. The lock shattered under the blow. Success at last!

But the door, stiff with long disuse, failed to yield under the pressure of her hand on its ring. It took the weight of her shoulder against the oak planks before the door finally surrendered, creaking slowly inward on rusted hinges.

Both women stood there in wordless awe, gazing at a flight of stone steps that descended into the blackness. Like something out of an old fairy tale, they beckoned Meredith with their mystery.

She was the first to end the silence. Dropping the sledgehammer she'd borrowed from Guy's tools, she turned to Imogen. "Hand me the lantern, please."

"Know your own mind, I suppose, but I should wait for Mr. Hawke."

Jackson had yet to return to the castle. Meredith still had no idea where he was or what he was doing. She had phoned the inn to ask about him when she'd gone inside to collect the hammer and the lantern, but all the landlord could tell her was that he had gone off somewhere with DCI Ramsay.

No, she wouldn't wait. The temptation of the stairs was irresistible. "I'll be careful," she promised Imogen. "Just stay here and listen if I should call for you."

It wasn't as if anything could be lurking down there to harm her. The place had been buried forever, and whoever had sealed it off had long ago carried whatever secret it contained to his grave. The worst threat she could encounter would be structural damage. She intended to be cautious about that, and if she did get into trouble…well, there was Imogen.

Of course, she thought, accepting the battery-powered lantern that Imogen passed to her, there was always the possibility of a ghost. But she wasn't concerned about that either, not when the only ghost that seemed to haunt Croft Castle was a benign one.

Switching on the lantern, Meredith cautiously made her way down into the darkness. She might not have feared an encounter with a ghost, but the cobwebs she met on her descent were very real. She brushed them away from her face, trying not to think about the spiders that had woven them.

A rank smell assaulted her nostrils, the odor of decay and mildew. It was not suprising, since the place was very damp. The walls sweated with dankness, and somewhere off in the distance she could hear the slow drip of water.

When she reached the foot of the stairs, she held the lantern aloft. Its light revealed a cavernous room that stretched away on all sides. A forest of thick pillars bore the weight of the stone vaulting overhead, which in turn supported the keep above them.

The whole thing had been hacked out of the solid rock of the headland. But for what purpose? Venturing forward, she could make out the shape of two enormous fireplaces. The kind whose wide hearths were intended for cooking. It was then she understood.

Guy had been wrong when he'd told her the castle's original kitchen must have been located in a long vanished separate structure. Because this was obviously the first kitchen. But it had been locked up by one of his forebears so long ago that Croft's subsequent owners had been unaware of its existence. The dust alone attested to that.

Why had the vast cellar been abandoned? Meredith intended to learn the answer to that question. If she could.

Returning to the bottom of the stairs, she called up a reassurance to Imogen. "Everything looks solid down here. I'm going to do a bit of exploring."

"Mind you watch your step."

It was good advice. The floor was uneven, almost as rough as the walls beaded with the moisture that oozed through them like a poison.

The steady glow from the swinging lantern flung gaunt,

eerie shadows against those walls with each tread of her careful advance into the depths of the cellar. Once this place would have been illuminated by the ghostly, flickering flames of torches mounted in the great iron brackets ranged at intervals high along the walls. But those fires had been extinguished ages ago.

As the cold light of the lantern pushed back the blackness with her slow progress, Meredith was able to discover that the cellar had served as more than just a kitchen. Along a passage on a slightly lower level was a row of thick doors. Storerooms? Or did the iron grilles in those doors indicate a more sinister purpose? Was this place also a dungeon?

Meredith raised the lantern to the level of the grilles and peered through their bars, half expecting to see instruments of torture in the cells or the skeletons of prisoners shackled to the walls. There was nothing but dust.

At the bottom of the passage were more steps. They ended in a rock fall that blocked further descent. Meredith thought immediately of the cave where she and Jackson had found Professor Boynton. There had been another, similar rock fall in that cave. Were the two of them connected? A deliberate action meant to seal off whatever was between them? Perhaps it was just the smuggler's tunnel that led from the sea up into the castle.

Or a route to something more evil than smuggling.

Meredith thought of the guardian angels that had been erected on the battlements by one of Guy's distant ancestors. And how possibly that same ancestor had barred entrance to the outside door to the cellar, then planted ivy and the yew in front of it to conceal its existence.

All of it meant to bury an intolerable evil?

As Meredith retraced her steps, this time in an effort to find the source of the persistent drip of water on the other side of the kitchen area, she swore she could smell the foul odor of that very evil.

Or are you just imagining it?

The drip grew louder and then suddenly stopped. She had arrived at another passageway. Access to it had once been prevented by a heavy door at its mouth. But that door had rotted away, and what was left of it sagged open on rusted hinges.

Holding the lantern in front of her like a weapon, Meredith entered the passage, traveled its short length, and then came to an abrupt halt. The evil was just ahead of her. She could more than just smell it now. She could sense it with every nerve in her body.

And she could see it in the arch that framed the opening to a small chamber. The entire archway, from top to bottom, had been carved in a series of stone reliefs that were crumbling with age.

Holding the lantern high, Meredith could make out dragons whose mouths breathed fire and whose tails were coiled around human victims, their bodies contorted in an agony of death, their faces grotesque masks of pain. Tumbling over and among them were grinning skulls and openmouthed serpents in the act of devouring other screaming victims.

It was a hideous creation clearly celebrating the macabre. The doorway to—

But Meredith wasn't prepared just yet to put a name to this unspeakable vileness. She needed further evidence. Only in the chamber itself could she possibly find that evidence.

Summoning her courage, she moved through the archway. Immediately she was struck by a cold that seemed to seep into her bones. There was no overt reason for her chilled state. The small chamber was, after all, a very plain, hollow affair.

Except for one thing. There was a circular opening in the floor rimmed by a stone curb a foot or so in height. She went forward and knelt on the ledge. Off to one side, overhanging the shaft, was a platform. It had the look of an altar. A *ghastly* version of an altar, anyway.

You're letting imagination rule your judgment. The platform could have been meant as nothing more than a shelf on which to rest buckets. This is probably just the original well that supplied the castle with its water.

Leaning over, she peered into the depths, but the lantern revealed no gleam of water. Through the years pieces of stone had fallen from the ribbed vaulting overhead. She found a bit of it on the floor and dropped it into the well, listening for a splash below. The stone rattled through the blackness, but no splash echoed back to her. If the shaft had been a well, it had gone dry long ago.

Meredith was prepared to draw back from the edge when she heard them. Or *thought* she heard them. Voices that whispered from the depths of the pit. The mesmerizing whispers of souls in torment calling out to her, begging her to release them.

Unwilling though she was, she was ready now to put a name to this horror to which the invisible drip of water had led her. Sir Hugh Gwinfryd's gate to hell!

Meredith shuddered over her discovery, genuinely frightened for the first time. Whether reality or merely fantasy, she knew she had to get away from this place.

It wasn't until she had fled back into the kitchen portion of the cellar that she was able to breathe again. For a moment she stood there, shivering still but relieved. And that's when she noticed it. The silence.

It's too quiet. Why is it so quiet?

She longed suddenly for the unnerving drip of the water. But it was so still she could hear nothing but the call of those disembodied voices from the pit behind her. At least inside her head she heard them.

Wanting to shut them out, needing to hear Imogen and the faint, comforting sound of the long rollers breaking on the shore below, she moved swiftly toward the pool of daylight from the open door above.

Reaching the bottom of the stairway, she shouted an urgent "Imogen, are you there?"

Silence. An uneasy silence.

"Imogen, please!"

"She'll not be answering you, I'm afraid."

The voice, low and complacent, came from somewhere behind her. Meredith flashed around with a startled gasp.

"I did have to make sure she wouldn't disturb us, you see."

Moving the lantern from side to side, Meredith searched the darkness. But there was no sign of the speaker.

"Here I am," he said, emerging from the back of the pillar behind which he had been lurking.

This was no phantom. He was altogether real. *Frighteningly* real. What's more, she knew that voice. But she couldn't put a face to it yet. He was in too much shadow for that. And something else. There was a strange article strapped to his head that also contributed to the mystery of his identity.

Meredith was unable to recognize it until he stepped forward into the stronger light. A Cornish tin miner's lamp! She had read about them, seen them in pictures. And now she knew the face under that unlighted lamp.

"Yes, madam," he said in that voice that had once sounded so genuine in its amiable servitude but now only mocked it with a note of bitterness, "it's me, right enough."

Colin Sheppard! The landlord of the inn, who had stood behind his bar with a hearty smile on his ruddy face. He was wearing that smile now, but it was false. Behind it was a murderous determination. The realization of that finally penetrated her shock.

Dangerous. He's manically dangerous. He'll kill you as he must have killed Sybil Boynton. As he might have killed Imogen. You have to get away from him. Now, before he comes any closer.

He was a heavy man, and Meredith was light on her feet. She thought, when she whirled and ran, that she stood every chance of escaping up the stairs and fleeing away from him out in the open. But he caught her by the ankle midway on the flight. She went down, losing the lantern that tumbled to the bottom and shattered on the stone floor.

They struggled briefly. Meredith was no match for the burly landlord. He dragged her back into the gloom of the cellar where he jerked her roughly to her feet. Breathing heavily, with his great, meaty hands clamped on her arms, he thrust his face down into hers.

"Being the landlord of an inn does have its merits," he confided. "Sooner or later, it all comes your way. It was like that today. You saying there in the lobby how you'd be leaving the island this morning. Gwen asking about storm damage at the castle. Your Mr. Hawke going off with the police to the mainland. Then word coming down of Lord and Lady D on their way to hospital. You see how it works, madam?"

Meredith did understand. All the while Colin Sheppard had been there in the background, innocuous and unnoticed, but hearing everything. And they had overlooked him. It made her sick to think of the likely consequences of that mistake.

"A rare opportunity, it was. With no one meant to be at the castle but the cook, I could poke around up here a bit by daylight without much chance of discovery. See what the storm might have turned up."

His grip tightened on her cruelly, his voice gloating and triumphant now, the whispered words lashing her as his excited face loomed above hers.

"But you did it for me, didn't you, madam? I watched you go into the chamber back there. I saw your face when you came out. You found it for me, didn't you? It's in there, Sir Hugh's door to the underworld. Everything that should by rights have been my family's all along. But now it will belong to them again. I'll have it after you show it to me, and all that goes with it."

Terrified by the madness in his eyes, Meredith attempted to reason with him. "No, listen to me. It's only an old well gone dry. It can't be the gate to hell. That's not possible. It's pure fiction."

He paid no attention to her desperate argument. She should have known he was beyond logic.

"Your lantern is useless now," he said. "It doesn't matter. I can give us light. The same light I used when I searched the passages in the keep."

One of his hands released her long enough to reach for a switch on the miner's lamp, which must have been converted to battery power. Meredith used the opportunity to try to break away from him. But his other hand was like a steel band on her arm. He twisted her back into the light from the polished reflector that stood above his forehead like the glaring eye of a cyclops.

"You musn't make me angry, madam. I can't be responsible for myself when I'm angry. Come along now."

It was useless to resist, but she was not going willingly into that chamber with him. She dug in her feet so that he had to half pull, half drag her across the kitchen, along the passage and through that horrible arch into the chamber.

His laugh was equally horrible when the miner's lamp revealed the well to him. "I knew it had to be somewhere in or under the castle! And it is! *It is!*"

He drew her to the curb that rimmed the shaft, hanging on to her tightly with one hand while his other hand cupped the back of her head, forcing her to look down.

"See it!" he whispered, indicating the platform. "It's the altar! Sir Hugh used it in his ceremonies! You can still see the blood on it, can't you?"

"No," she said, "it's just water stains."

He turned her head so that she faced him. His face was contorted, lurid in the eerie glow of the lamp.

"Blood," he insisted. "It was necessary for my ancestor to offer sacrifices to the gate below in order to release the power from the other side. Do you understand, madam? I served you down at the inn. Now you must serve me."

Dear God, he meant to sacrifice her, throw her in that deep pit!

Using whatever energy was still available to her, Meredith fought to break his hold on her, her body squirming, her free hand striking out at him, her foot kicking his legs. She was only dimly aware of the pounding of feet along the passage, then a shout of rage as a tall figure raced into the chamber.

With a curse that rose to a howl, the landlord flung her away from him in order to meet the enemy who charged him with all the fury of an enraged demon. Or perhaps it was an avenging angel. Meredith wasn't sure which. The action of Colin Sheppard's sudden release was so violent that she hit the wall and slithered to the floor, stunned by the blow.

Jackson was here. That much she was sure of now, and it was all that mattered.

The beam of light from the miner's lamp swung in a wild arc around the chamber as the two men fought each other, thrashing back and forth, locked in the age-old combat of good versus evil.

Jackson delivered a series of ferocious blows to his opponent, weakening him. Victory was nearly his when the landlord managed to snatch the lamp from his head and shove the light into Jackson's eyes. Blinded, he staggered back, lost his footing, and went sprawling down over the curbing. He hung there on his back above the lethal shaft, momentarily helpless.

Colin Sheppard dropped the lamp, seized one of the stones on the floor that had fallen from the vaulting, and raised it high over his head with a savage "I'll send you to hell!"

The miner's lamp had landed with its beam of light pointed toward the ceiling. And that's when Meredith saw it. One of the stones in a rib of the vaulting was moving, working loose from the others. She could hear the grinding of rock against rock. The stone was directly above Jackson's head!

She cried out a warning as the landlord lunged forward. With lightning speed, Jackson rolled out of the way. The stone, liberated now from the vaulting, plummeted down. And, just as though Colin Sheppard had been its intended target all along, it landed on his shoulder with a thump that made him drop his weapon.

Jackson was on his feet in a flash, driving a fist into the landlord's jaw with such livid force that it rendered him senseless. He collapsed on the floor, unconscious.

Stepping over his body, Jackson came to Meredith. Crouching down where she was huddled on the floor, he pulled her up into his arms.

"Did he hurt you?"

Before she could assure him that, except for what were likely to be a few tender bruises, she was fine, he kissed her urgently.

"Because if he hurt you—"

He paused again to plant another blistering kiss on her mouth.

"—I'll do more than smack the bastard in his jaw!"

There was another searing kiss that left her breathless.

"No one touches my woman and gets away with it!" he promised fiercely.

My woman? For the moment Meredith let that astonishing, wonderful declaration pass. She gently pushed him away with a soft laugh.

"*You're* the one who's going to leave me all swollen and sore if you go on kissing me like this."

He was instantly contrite. "Am I being too rough?"

"Well, maybe you're entitled. A little." She suddenly remembered something. "Imogen!"

"He must have sneaked up behind her and knocked her cold. But I did a fast check on her before I raced down here, and I think she'll be okay."

"I have to go to her. Help me up."

Jackson lifted her to her feet, one arm snugly around her waist to support her. "How do you feel about taking off your pantyhose?"

"I'm going to assume you have some purpose in mind other than a kinky one."

"I wish it was that, but at the moment what I need is something to tie up Sheppard. I don't want him to get away before we have the chance to hand him over to the police."

Meredith glanced at the inert body of the landlord. "From the looks of him, I don't think he's going to try going anywhere for a while."

"Yeah, but it could have been me lying either there or at the bottom of the shaft, if it hadn't been for the luck of that stone dropping when and where it did."

She turned her head, gazing at him solemnly. "No, Jackson, it was nothing like coincidence. I watched it come loose. A deliberate force dislodged it, I'm sure."

"Aw, Meredith, you're not going to tell me—"

"That there was something here in the chamber helping us when we most needed it? Yes, I am telling you just that."

"Come on, you can't really believe—"

At that second the miner's lamp flickered out, plunging the chamber into blackness.

"Hell," Jackson swore. "Now we've got to try to operate in the dark."

"Look!"

In the far corner of the chamber a tiny glow of light appeared. Jackson's arm tightened protectively around her waist.

"What in the—"

The light strengthened, stretching out into a recognizable form as they watched it with awe and fascination. When it had reached its full height, Meredith was able to make out a head of shaggy hair, a tunic and cross-gartered leggings, all on the tall figure of a handsome man.

"Edward Atheling!" she whispered.

The luminous shape hovered there for a few seconds, an aura pulsing around it. Then, in a gesture of both ackowledgment and farewell, it honored Jackson with one of his own two fingered salutes before it dissolved and was gone. The chamber was dark again. They stood there for a few seconds in a wondrous silence.

"Well, I'll be damned," Jackson finally muttered.

"You were saying about ghosts?"

"I don't know what I just saw or what to believe anymore. But there's one thing I'm sure about. From now on, I'm going to have an open mind about your ghosts. And," he pledged earnestly, "a healthy respect for my ancestors."

At that instant the miner's lamp came magically to life again. Or maybe it wasn't magic, Meredith thought. Maybe it was more like a miracle.

The question now was: Would she and Jackson be able to sort out their personal issues and make their own miracle happen?

Chapter Sixteen

"A room with a view and a private bath? Just let me check on the availability of that." Meredith covered the receiver with her hand while she pretended to consult the open register on Judith's desk. She waited for fifteen seconds before she got back to the caller. "Yes, we can accommodate you for that week. Would you like to secure the booking with a credit card?"

Two minutes later, having entered the essentials in the record, she rang off and sat there smiling.

Amazing! This was the second reservation in the space of an hour! Her mother and Guy would be delighted when she told them. After all their troubles, they deserved to hear that it looked like Croft Castle's business was picking up again.

And all this was happening just the day after the mystery was solved. It turned out that the castle had a Web site and that Imogen was in charge of it. She had immediately posted a message on it proclaiming everything was back to normal at Croft Castle. The word had spread rapidly.

It would be some time, of course, before Guy would be able to personally collect his guests from the quay with the Land Rover. But Judith had reported from the hospital that, after undergoing an emergency bypass, he was expected to make a full recovery.

There would be no happy ending for Simon Boynton. He

had died a few hours ago without ever regaining consciousness. That meant Colin Sheppard, who had been removed to Trefarro by DCI Ramsay, would stand trial for two murders. As for the gate to hell he had given his soul to find, Judith had indicated on the phone that she and Guy would have the shaft filled in so it would never again be a temptation to anyone. And since the stonework in the cellar was deteriorating, making it a dangerous place, that would be sealed off once more.

Even Imogen was back in her kitchen after Dr. Merrick from the village had examined her and prescribed aspirin and a cold pack for the bump on the back of her head.

Everything, Meredith thought, her smile fading, but Jackson and me. They had yet to make that miracle for themselves that had troubled her earlier. Perhaps they never would.

The possibility of losing him, if they weren't able to resolve their own problems, was more than she could bear. Frowning now, her pangs deepening to despair, she shifted her gaze to the closed door of the sitting room.

Where are you, Jackson? Where did you disappear to?

He had left the room without explanation after learning the news from the hospital. Was he suddenly reluctant to face her? *My woman.* Did he regret those impulsive words? Was he was one of those men ultimately unable to commit to a permanent relationship?

Meredith couldn't forget how he had fled in guilt from the States because another woman had tried to love him.

This is ridiculous. Stop wallowing in this useless misery. Go and find him. Demand to know just exactly how he feels about the two of you. You deserve that much. And if you don't like what you hear…well, at least it will be settled.

Right.

Getting to her feet, Meredith headed with determination in the direction of the door. And almost suffered a collision with it when it burst open without warning just as she was reaching for the knob.

"Whoa!" Jackson exclaimed in surprise, halting his energetic stride in the opening. "You on your way somewhere?"

"Actually, I was coming to find you."

"I've been making calls on the other line in the library. Had to check in with my answering service back in London."

"I hope they had good news for you."

"The best," he said, grinning with excitement. "Got a new client. I rang him up so he could explain his problem to me. It's another haunting. This time up in Yorkshire."

"So you're off to the North country. I'm glad for you, Jackson. You deserve to succeed."

"Yeah, it looks like the English branch of the agency is going to make it after all. What did you want to see me about?"

Meredith hesitated, then lost her courage. "I just wanted to tell you I was going up to finish my packing. I need to get back to London if I'm going to have any time at all to prepare for those lectures."

"You're leaving?" His eyes widened in disbelief, then narrowed in anger. "You can't!"

"Why?"

"Because I need you in Yorkshire. You didn't think I was going up there without you. Damn it, Meredith, we're good together. Look how we solved this case."

"Are you asking me to be your partner?"

"Well, yeah."

"And what do I do about the lectures?"

"Reschedule them. You can do that, can't you?"

"I could, but I'm not going to." She started to move past him, but he stopped her.

"Don't go."

"Can you give me a reason not to?"

"The hell with the lectures, and the same for Yorkshire! All I care about is us! There! Is that reason enough?"

She gazed up at him solemnly. "What does all that mean?"

"That I want you right beside me wherever we are and whatever we do. Meredith, I'm in love with you. We belong together, and if you can't see that…well, I'm not giving up until you do see it. You'd better understand that right now."

She was ecstatic over his declaration, but dazed. "I'm not sure what I understand."

"It's what Archie Wallace overheard me say in that art gallery that's bothering you, isn't it?" he said anxiously. "About how I planned to make you happy because I needed this case. Okay, that's true, but all I meant was I wanted to keep you from hating me and pulling out. I never intended to seduce you. That just happened, and I'm not going to apologize for it. In fact, I'm going to go on keeping you happy like that for the rest of our lives. If you'll let me."

She didn't say anything. She went on looking at him.

"You've got your head tipped over to one side," he said. "I usually like it when you listen to me like that. Not this time."

"Why?"

"Because you're scaring the hell out of me."

"There's a problem with this whole thing, Jackson."

"Look," he said, wanting to please her, "if you'd rather go on practicing back in the States, I could give up the agency here, go back home and operate there. Anything."

"It's not that. I'd like to be in England, now that my mother and I have found each other again."

"Then what?"

"Joanna and Rand," she said. "How can I live without them?"

"That is a big one. You ever consider a British soap? I hear they're not bad."

"Switch loyalties?"

"I could make it worth your while," he promised, his voice low and raspy as his arms slid around her.

"How?" she challenged him.

He demonstrated by drawing her close and kissing her

deeply, lovingly. "Yes?" he asked when his mouth finally lifted from hers.

"Yes," she whispered.

He breathed a deep sigh of relief. "For the first time in my life," he said, forehead resting against hers, his close gaze probing her eyes, "I mind my color-blindness. I know your eyes are green, but I can't appreciate how beautiful that greenness must be, and I wish I could."

"All you have to see in them, Jackson, is the love I have for you, and that's not going to change."

"Forever, huh? I like the sound of that. There is one thing, though."

"What's that?"

"I owe my ancestor a debt for bringing us together."

"Edward? But how could you possibly repay him?"

"By making sure the family continues. You know, handing the legacy on down."

Meredith searched his face. There was an interesting gleam in his eyes. "That means having babies," she said.

"Right. Please tell me you don't have any objections to that."

"None at all."

"Then we just have one thing left to do."

"What?"

"We've got to find out how you go about getting married in this country."

"Do we do that before or after you kiss me again?"

"Oh, after. Definitely after."

Like a phantom in the night
comes an exciting promotion from

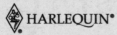
HARLEQUIN®

INTRIGUE®

GOTHIC ROMANCE

Look for a provocative
gothic-themed thriller each month
by your favorite Intrigue authors!
Once you surrender to the classic
blend of chilling suspense and
electrifying romance in these
gripping page-turners, there will
be no turning back....

Available wherever Harlequin books are sold.

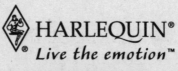
HARLEQUIN®
® *Live the emotion*™

www.eHarlequin.com

HIE3

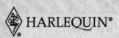

If you enjoyed what you just read,
then we've got an offer you can't resist!

Take 2 bestselling
love stories FREE!
Plus get a FREE surprise gift!

Clip this page and mail it to Harlequin Reader Service®

IN U.S.A.	**IN CANADA**
3010 Walden Ave.	P.O. Box 609
P.O. Box 1867	Fort Erie, Ontario
Buffalo, N.Y. 14240-1867	L2A 5X3

YES! Please send me 2 free Harlequin Intrigue® novels and my free surprise gift. After receiving them, if I don't wish to receive anymore, I can return the shipping statement marked cancel. If I don't cancel, I will receive 4 brand-new novels each month, before they're available in stores! In the U.S.A., bill me at the bargain price of $4.24 plus 25¢ shipping and handling per book and applicable sales tax, if any*. In Canada, bill me at the bargain price of $4.99 plus 25¢ shipping and handling per book and applicable taxes**. That's the complete price and a savings of at least 10% off the cover prices—what a great deal! I understand that accepting the 2 free books and gift places me under no obligation ever to buy any books. I can always return a shipment and cancel at any time. Even if I never buy another book from Harlequin, the 2 free books and gift are mine to keep forever.

181 HDN DZ7N
381 HDN DZ7P

Name	(PLEASE PRINT)	
Address	Apt.#	
City	State/Prov.	Zip/Postal Code

Not valid to current Harlequin Intrigue® subscribers.

Want to try two free books from another series?
Call 1-800-873-8635 or visit www.morefreebooks.com.

* Terms and prices subject to change without notice. Sales tax applicable in N.Y.
** Canadian residents will be charged applicable provincial taxes and GST.
  All orders subject to approval. Offer limited to one per household.
  ® are registered trademarks owned and used by the trademark owner and or its licensee.

INT04R   ©2004 Harlequin Enterprises Limited

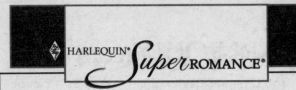

A Family Christmas
by Carrie Alexander

(Harlequin Superromance #1239)

All Rose Robbin ever wanted was a family
Christmas—just like the ones she'd seen on TV—but
being a Robbin (one of those Robbins) pretty much
guaranteed she'd never get one. Especially after
circumstances had her living "down" to
everyone else's expectations.

After a long absence, Rose is back in Alouette,
primarily to help out her impossible-to-please mother,
but also to keep tabs on the child she wasn't allowed
to keep. Working hard, helping her mother and trying
to steal glimpses of her child seem to be all that's in
Wild Rose's future—until the day single father
Evan Grant catches her in the act.

Alouette, Michigan.
Located high on the Upper
Peninsula—home to strong
men, stalwart women and
lots and lots of trees.

NORTH COUNTRY
Stories

Available in November 2004 wherever Harlequin books are sold

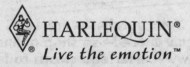

HARLEQUIN®
Live the emotion™

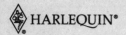
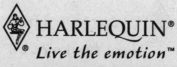